the
PATHLESS
COUNTRY

JAMES HARPUR

LIQUORICE
FISH BOOKS

Published by Liquorice Fish Books
an imprint of Cinnamon Press,
Office 49019, PO Box 92, Cardiff, CF11 1NB
www.cinnamonpress.com

Print Edition ISBN 978-1-911540-11-3

British Library Cataloguing in Publication Data. A CIP record for this book
can be obtained from the British Library.

Designed and typeset by Liquorice Fish Books.

Liquorice Fish Books is represented by Inpress.

ACKNOWLEDGEMENTS

A number of people have given me help and encouragement during the writing of this book, and I'd like to thank in particular Penelope Buckley, Faye Carney, Jules Cashford, Tom MacCarthy, Grace Wells, Ian Wild and Liz Wyse.

I would also like to thank various friends and members of my family for reading the text at different stages and making helpful suggestions, including Alyson, Ania, Francesca, John F., Margaret, Rosemary, Sarah, Ursula, Mel, Pat and Evie.

With some of the historical parts of the story I have been indebted to Mary Lutyens's biography, *Krishnamurti: The Years of Awakening* (Shambhala, 1997); the *Collected Works of Padraic H. Pearse* (Phoenix Publishing, 1924); and *The Joyful Wisdom* by Friedrich Nietzsche, translated by Thomas Common (T.N. Foulis, 1910).

Finally, many thanks to the organisers and judges of the J.G. Farrell Award and the Irish Writers' Centre Novel Fair Award, and to Adam Craig for his literary midwifery; and my profound gratitude to J. Krishnamurti and his writings.

'The country we came from is There, and There is our Father. How, then, shall we return to it? How will we flee? We cannot use our feet, for they will only take us from country to country.'

Plotinus, *Enneads*, I.6.8.

For dearest Gracie, with much love.
May you find your path to pathlessness.

the
PATHLESS
COUNTRY

PROLOGUE

Another cloudless day. We walked through the Luxembourg Gardens to Rue Mouffetard, both of us shrinking from the smell of entrails and cheese filling its narrowness. Mme Bouchet took longer to come to the door. She seemed older but still with smiles and charm. 'You are looking well, and your daughter... she is so beautiful!' Her room was dim, more disorganised, shutters open; curtains drooped like bridal veils. Madame full of fuss and offering refreshments. We acquiesced, then I gave her the typescript. She opened up the cover and flicked through the pages, stopping to read aloud from one of them: 'He feels a terrible strength trying to shift him towards the drop. He can hear the sea hissing and rearing up at him.' A pause, then she said, '*Eh bien*, this is it. This is finally the work, your work.' '*Our* work,' I said. '*Non*! I did little, and what I did was done through me. I am the medium only. What I did was small things.' 'You began the process, and you kept me going; things I had forgotten or had no knowledge of.' 'The spirits need to speak in order to make... a completion. I only write down the dictations they give me. Monsieur Flournoy says it is all in the mind of the medium, in some sort of buried... *niche*. But how would I have the imagination to invent the stories and the thoughts, all the twists and turns, the love, the hate?' As I began to thank her, she shrugged and flicked her hand up, as if batting away a fly. 'And your daughter, I can see, has a glow about her. About her head. *C'est bien*.'

PART ONE

THE CALLING

He is shocked to see St Stephen's Green looking so different. Barricades in the heart of Dublin! People scuttling around holding their heads. Gunshots. He ducks a useless half-second after each bang. Some yards away a uniformed man is going berserk, shouting and pointing at an old man, who has shrunk down and pulled his jacket over his head. He's never heard such shouting, such rage, and wonders why the old man won't do what he's told. *Just do what he says!* He wants to run in the opposite direction, but he's mesmerised by the soldier, who looks as if he might kill the old man just with his shouts. He must do something. He runs over and stands between the old man and the soldier. He thinks he'll scream or burst into laughter at the soldier's contorted face and big moustache and jabbing finger—it's as if Lord Kitchener has jumped out of his recruiting poster. It's strange the way the soldier's finger has turned into metal, as though his hand has been amputated and replaced with steel. The soldier is yelling obscenities, face completely red, comical frowning lines on his forehead, a trace of spittle on his bottom lip. The soldier wants him to do something, but what? His shouting is too disjointed. He either wants him to run away from the old man, or stay rooted to the spot. *He must decide.* Somehow he is too late—he knows this from the sudden noise, loud but distant, like a door banged shut by the wind or something crashing down. The noise thuds into him, knocks him over, shocks a sweet numbness through him. It has the most unusual effect on his brain.

And then he knows what's happening.

He nearly laughs—it is just how he imagined it to be, quite beautiful in its way. The noise is like a key slipping into an infinite number of locks and sliding open drawers of memories. He can feel them flowing precise and luminous in good order. He hears a voice shouting, 'This one's alive, this one is still alive.' He knows the owner of the voice is speaking about him, and knows in a strange omniscient way that if the voice has an Irish accent he will live, because it means he will be taken to hospital. He isn't sure why this should be so, but he knows it to be true. He wants to hear the voice again, to check on the accent, but fears it. Faces are looking down on him, faces of strangers...

HE CAN SEE HIMSELF in a horse and cart with his father, Joe, a bag of clothes and a bag of tools slung in behind them. They are trundling up a boreen in the countryside of south Galway, a morning's drive from the city, and heading for Tulira Castle. The sky is as mottled as the plaster on the city's warehouses, and the grass in the fields has the sheen of lake water.

It's strange seeing his father as a young man. Joe is in his thirties, sitting with the self-conscious hunch of someone tall and rangy, his muscular arms and shoulders befitting his profession; the brown flat cap, pulled tightly down, concealing a thinning widow's peak; skin stretched thin on a face that always did begrudge a smile; his small eyes radiating honesty from the shadows of their sockets.

SUMMER, 1896. A WEEK's work at the castle. He himself is fifteen, already an apprentice woodworker and dexterous with the saw, hand drill, plane, protractor and spirit level. He remembers the thrill of emerging from a green tunnel of trees into a revelation of sunlight, and there it is!—not an actual medieval castle as he had hoped, but a Big House, a grand sprawling edifice with neat turrets, tongue-and-groove battlements, high rectangular windows, a forbidding wooden door framed by a stone arch the shape of a bishop's hat.

He cannot wait to meet the owner of Tulira, Edward Martyn, who, his father has told him, is a writer of theatrical entertainments and known for his disloyalty to Britain: he had refused to sing 'God Save the Queen' at a public occasion. He imagines Edward as a tall man with an unkempt beard and wild staring eyes.

They knock at the back door and wait. The door is flung open to reveal a short, neat, corpulent man in a wine-coloured

14

smoking jacket. He scrutinises them through his spectacles.

Joe says: 'Good day, sir, I am Joseph Bowley, gentleman woodworker and joiner, and this is my son, Patrick. You are expecting us?'

The man's untamed eyebrows spring to life, and a hand as pale as a dove's wing slips from his pocket; he proffers it to both of them in turn while muttering that he is indeed Edward Martyn.

Edward leads them inside and glides them from kitchen to pantry to dining room, pointing out items of work that need to be done. A window frame, extra shelves, precarious table legs, scratches on surfaces. 'A plenitude of little labours,' he says. 'Utilitarian work, but it must be done with the precision of *clipping fingernails.*'

In the library he marvels at the swirling gold and green wallpaper and his heart quickens at all the shelves of beautiful leather-bound books, while Edward addresses Joe: 'In this country we have a distinguished history of creating beautiful things—the Kells gospels, stone crosses, Celtic brooches, and so on. This house, too, is a shrine to our artistic heritage. Woodworkers such as yourself and your son are part of this noble Irish tradition.' He wonders what Joe is thinking behind the nods he offers up to Edward.

They proceed to the Great Hall, where his eyes alight on a painting of two girls. He moves closer and finds himself transfixed by the delicate colours and the human shapes. Ballet dancers off stage in a dressing room. As he stares into the painting he can feel a strange sensation—it's the first time he can remember something like this happening: it is as if the frame of the painting is enlarging and pulling him towards it. He finds himself drawing closer and closer. And then the most extraordinary thing happens—he can feel himself entering the painting, as if climbing into it through a window. There he is, standing in the room with the two girls! He is invisible to them, but actually there, studying their white arms, exposed backs and sheeny blue dresses frilling out from their waists. Their muscles are taut and shapely. One girl is bending over and

15

resting her two forearms on the back of a wooden chair. He walks around, admiring the well-made chair; even more, he wants to admire the girl's smooth, pale skin, but it is cast in shadow. The other girl is adjusting the knot of a great blue ribbon tied behind her back, and her hair has been scraped into a bun, exposing her nape. She is talking to her friend. He can almost hear their secrets.

A tug on his sleeve—he emerges from the painting as if the girls have seen him spying and have shut a door in his face.

He is still half there in the dancers' world when Edward says: 'Like it do you, young man? Acquired it from Monsieur Degas. Ah, yes, when he was at Rue Victor Massé. What was it they said about him?—his studio a thing of beauty, his mind a chamber pot of anti-Jewry. Handsome picture.' Joe again tugs at his arm. 'No—let your son look. This is what art is for: to bewitch and raise our spirits to the ineffable.'

Edward leads them up the stone staircase to the second floor and a dark corridor, where they hear the deep murmuring of male voices in one of the rooms. 'I have visitors, two gentlemen of, shall we say, a bohemian temperament, but they are under strict instructions not to impede you.'

Edward opens a door and shows them into a large bedroom with a high ceiling and a bay window looking out onto the front lawns. The two single beds are nearly as wide as doubles. Paintings hang on the wall, along with a crucifix. Edward leaves the room, closing the door softly behind him.

He follows his father over to the window and they look out at the front lawn, the ancient trees and the driveway disappearing into its leafy tunnel of mottled light; the sun has found an opening in the cloud and has picked out a gardener pushing an empty wheelbarrow; crows are raising mayhem within layers of branches. All he can think about is the painting of the two ballet dancers and how he was able to enter their world. He wants to tell his father what happened, but he knows he can't; it would have been different with his mother.

16

THE FOLLOWING DAY HE's working away in the library with Joe, longing to pause from chiselling and sanding the windows to inspect the books, packed tight like beige, green or gold blocks of wood. When they pause for a break, he takes out a volume of St Chrysostom—it was the name that attracted him—while Joe sits on the windowsill, framed by a vista of full-leafed trees. Bound in greenish calfskin that looks as if it's been French polished, and with pages edged with gold leaf, the book is heavy as a mallet. He balances the tome on his knee, opens it at random and finds the words surprisingly easy to comprehend. He sees a passage about Chrysostom deciding to become a monk and his mother begging him not leave her.

He reads the passage aloud to Joe: 'My son, my only comfort is to see in your face the faithful image of my beloved husband, no longer with us. I ask only one favour from you: do not make me a widow a second time; wait at least till I die. When you have joined my ashes with those of your father, nothing will then prevent you from retiring into monastic life.'

He looks up from the book: 'Wonder if he did his ma that favour?'

'He did.' The reply comes not from Joe but from Edward Martyn, who is standing at the open door.

Joe jumps to his feet as if he's been caught opening a drawer of silver cutlery, and his words rush forth: 'Excuse my son, sir—he's been brought up to read and revere books—you see we are of the Quakers' tradition and we take our literature and spiritual succour from the Word, the Word of God, of course—the Bible is the hearth of our studies—but also George Fox's *Journal*, the *Pilgrim's Progress*, the writings of John Wesley, and many others.' Joe pauses for a moment, but the silence unnerves him and he continues in one breath: 'We're also, I might add, not averse to those authors with a gift of poetry and storytelling, and I often read aloud to my wife and son the more improving works of Mr Dickens, Mr Tennyson, Mr Hardy and Miss Eliot. In short, sir, your bookcase is... a harvest of temptation.'

With a flick of his fingers, as if disentangling them from a spider's web, Edward brushes aside Joe's apologia: 'Refresh yourselves in my books whenever you're not at your labours. And as for Chrysostom—"Golden Mouth"—we could do with his oratory at the moment, couldn't we? Our patriot leaders lack passion and eloquence. True, Mr Parnell did have a splendid golden mouth; but what a shame about his less-than-golden eyes that *lusted* after Mrs O'Shea. If thy eye offends thee, pluck it out, what?'

Edward lets out a heavy sigh and loses his train of thought. His eyes swivel from Joe to the bookcase. 'What was it Chrysostom said—Christ catches people using the bait of their own crafts? A fish to trap a fisherman, a star to trap a magician? How would he catch a woodworker, I wonder? A finely made table? I admire Chrysostom for honouring his mother. Then, with her passing, he pursued his calling with a passion. Ah, the eternal conflict between life and work!' Edward gives another sigh, signifying some mystery that would seemingly take too long to unravel, and walks off.

NEXT MORNING HE IS entering the drawing room to sand the windows. He stops dead when he sees two men sitting there, conversing. They look up at him with glances of irritation; he mutters an apology and turns to leave. One of them tells him to stay a moment. He is wearing glasses and has a mop of hair which he flicks away from his eyes.

'Young man. You're a carpenter and therefore an indisputable arbiter of beauty and good taste. I've written a poem I now regret creating. A youthful affair. My friend disagrees. We should value your estimation.'

'I know nothing of poetry, sir.'

'Do you have ears? A brain?'

He nods.

The other man has a pale narrow face, fair hair and eyes that blink a lot: 'Have you ever been in love with a girl?' His voice has a distinct English accent.

'Arthur! You're embarrassing the lad.'

18

'How will he understand the poem if he hasn't been in love?'

He wants to run away.

'You don't have to *know* love to appreciate a love poem. I cannot make a table but I can appreciate one. Let us see what he thinks.' He lifts up a book and begins reading in a slow chanting voice, looking up from time to time to study the reactions of his two listeners.

'... and now they stood
On the lone border of the lake once more:
Turning, he saw that she had thrust dead leaves
Gathered in silence, dewy as her eyes,
In bosom and hair.
"Ah, do not mourn," he said,
"That we are tired, for other loves await us;
Hate on and love through unrepining hours.
Before us lies eternity; our souls
Are love, and a continual farewell."'

After a polite pause Arthur says: 'A toothless vagrant could declaim that and it would sound like the music of the spheres. The ending is exquisite, a delightful cadence: "Before us lies eternity; our souls are love, and a continual farewell." Perfect pitch.'

The two men turn to look at him, but he has nothing to say. The 'dewy eyes' and 'bosom' and 'hair' make him think of the ballet dancers. And the last line makes him feel momentarily wistful.

Arthur snorts out the approximate sound of a laugh as if to give a full stop to the episode, and changes the subject. Within moments the two men have become too wrapped up in another topic of conversation to notice him creeping out. He makes himself busy in another room while wondering what sort of lives the two men live. How can they just sit there talking about poetry? How do they earn a living? He is tempted to go to the Great Hall and try to enter the painting again.

IT'S THE DAY BEFORE he and Joe are due to leave and he is working outside on a ground-floor window at the front of the house. He stops for a rest and crunches across the drive to the lawn. He sits down with his back to the trees and hears footsteps. It's the man with the floppy hair who read the poem to him.

'Good morning, you must be the woodworker Edward has been swooning over.' The man gives no indication of ever having seen him before.

'That would be my father, sir. I'm Patrick, his son.'

'May I join you? I've been puffing away through the trees and could do with a soft nest of grass to bear my weight for a minute or so. You seem to have picked the only spot on the lawn with a patch of sunshine. Enchanting to see a touch of radiance around your head. A crock of gold, no less.'

He is puzzled by this remark, for the sky is uniformly grey.

The man, probably in his early thirties, lowers himself to the grass.

He wonders what the man's accent is. It's Irish all right, but the manner of his speech is unusual, with sudden pauses followed by a rush of words. His appearance is rare, too; short delicate nose and gold-rimmed glasses that give him the air of a teacher, though his hair seems too dishevelled for that profession. A green tie luminous against his grey double-breasted jacket.

He senses he is expected to say something. 'Splendid house, isn't it, sir?'

The man raises his eyebrows. 'Splendid? Splendidly vulgar, I'd say! What you see is a fantasy, a place of Edward's Gothic dreams. But I'll say this for it—I haven't stopped having dreams since I came here. Powerful as visions, some of them. Have you had any?'

He stares into the sky and is about to mention his experience of entering the painting of the ballet dancers then decides not to. 'I've not had any.'

'Of course you've had them. You just can't remember them. Takes practice. Know what a centaur is?'

He nods.

'I saw one galloping along, night before last, vivid as my seeing you. Wild and beautiful, the colour of snow or swans' feathers. Then I saw a woman, like a goddess, standing on a pedestal, *and she was naked*. She was holding a bow and arrow and she shot an arrow at a star.'

The words paint pictures in his head. The naked woman excites him; the arrow penetrating the night sky makes him think of a shooting star leaving behind a silvery streak. Before he can stop himself, he says: 'I had a dream in the daytime. The painting in Mr Martyn's hall, of the ballet dancers.' He stops, thinking he is about to sound foolish. But the man leans forward with such obvious interest that he gains the confidence to describe how he entered the painting and stood beside the dancers.

'To be honest, sir, it's the strangest thing that's ever happened to me. I fear I may be unwell. I haven't told my father.'

'Nonsense! Nothing wrong with you. In fact there is everything *right* with you by the sound of it. Never fear the imagination. Embrace it. It's a gift for all of us, but few of us use it. If the same thing happens again, surrender to it, be enveloped by it, cherish it.' The man stares at the grass, then turns to him again: 'So you're a carpenter?'

'I'm learning the trade. My father's teaching me.'

'And a fine trade to have. But never listen to fathers too much, Patrick. Everyone has a destiny, and it's governed by the age we live in. And by the stars and where we're born. When did you first see the light of day?'

'1881.'

'And where?'

He wonders how much he should say. But the man's eyes somehow induce deep trust. He blurts out: 'In Cashel. My mother and father were not joined in marriage at the time. She is of the Roman faith. He belongs to the Society of Friends. She had to leave home before the birth.'

He fears a look of disapproval or disgust, but the man says: 'Of course, of course—I understand. These things happen.

Neighbours. Gossip. Scandal. You could be doing without that for the rest of your life.'

'She and my father went to his brother in Cashel, but everything had to be done in secret. Not even the maid was to know. I was born in an outhouse on the farm. They were married just after. A minister of the Friends did it.'

'Fine folk, fine folk. The Quakers are an example to us all. So, Cashel, 1881. And two religious contraries in your blood, Catholic and dissenting Protestantism—hasn't done you any harm by the looks of things. We all have a definite time and place when we enter this world, and this informs our destiny. We are mapped by the stars. Take Charles Stewart Parnell for instance. There he was, wind in his sails, leading us out of British captivity and then... political suicide! Perhaps he was fated to love another man's wife? A fool, yes. But which one of us can say Mrs O'Shea would not have stirred illicit feelings of desire in us?'

At this the man gives a vulpine grin and mops his forehead with a cream handkerchief pincered from his top pocket. He leans forward, as if to share a secret. 'Parnell. What an opportunity lost. But perhaps not? There are cycles of civilisation, one after the other, and the point when one ends and the other begins is when a soul of destiny appears. If Jesus hadn't existed it would have been someone else. The spirit of the age seizes the sensitive soul—it's like being possessed. If you resist it, you become desiccated, like stale bread, crumbling to nothing. If you let it take over your life it can destroy you.'

From the downstairs window Joe shouts at him, and he gets to his feet.

The man raises a hand and says: 'Farewell for the time being, young fella. Follow the arrow to the star.'

THEIR FINAL MORNING AT the castle. They are standing by their horse and cart. Edward emerges from a back door and gives Joe an envelope. 'Thank you kindly for your care and skill. The house is better for it.'

Edward disappears into the house and he and Joe climb into the cart and set off down the driveway, the branches of trees nodding at them as they pass. Before they reach the end, they see a figure walking towards them, gesturing. Joe pulls on the reins. It is the man he spoke to on the grass. 'Aha, you're off. Edward was delighted with your work. Worth your weight in fairy gold. And you, young fella, you've a spiritual face on you. Have faith and the great deities will place you in their arrangement. With due respect to your papa, get out of Galway. Ireland. Don't be ditchwater—be an ocean to yourself.' The man raises his hat and continues his walk, swivelling his head from side to side as if to catch the slightest movement in the trees and bushes.

Joe tugs at the reins and the horse breaks into a trot. He himself sees nothing but the two ballet dancers, dressed like pale blue swans and smiling; they lift their graceful hands to caress the air with sensuous goodbyes.

He is working inside a church: St Nicholas's, Galway city. Sanding and varnishing pews. March 1901, just before his twentieth birthday. It's the first day of his week's work in the church and he feels like a trespasser. He expects someone to jump out at him at any moment yelling, 'Out! Out! You Quaker-Papist mongrel!'

A woman is fussing around the interior, rearranging things that already appear to be neat and tidy; she seems to have limitless time on her hands. She comes over and introduces herself as Mary Coleville. Her cheeks are bulbous and set. Her fine dark brown hair seems to balloon up at the back and wisp away from its myriad pins. She has the look of someone who would take craftsmen for granted, as part of her birthright. She tells him how much she loves the church and insists on showing him around. He says, politely, he has work to be doing, but she waves her hand as if to brush away his hesitations.

She leads him to a stone tomb with a Norman inscription on it. 'Supposed to be a crusader beneath that. Always been a fighting tradition in this church. St Nicholas was patron of the Byzantine army. The Connaught Rangers are honoured here.'

She mentions the Boer War then looks at him as if to gauge whether what she's about to say is worth saying. Her face, made paler by lipstick, has a female delicacy, but her expressions have the mannered forcefulness of a politician. 'War won't stop until women have a voice in the affairs of state.' The fine vertical frown lines between her eyes have deepened. 'War is a man's business, run by men, for men against men. The world would be different if women were treated as equals.' She looks at him, oozing centuries-old Protestant certainty. 'Do you think I'm wrong?'

'I don't know, ma'am.'

'Don't know? Let me put it this way. Should women be allowed to be… carpenters, or is there some law stating they should never be so; that they should never contemplate being anything other than wives and mothers?'

He can feel his thoughts float away like sawdust.

She relents. 'The younger generation must change their thinking about women. Young men like you. As with our neighbours across the water—there's a movement happening in Ireland to change things, and mark my words, women will soon be heard. Even in the provinces. Yes, here in Galway. Things will change. Voting in government elections. Employment. Men won't care for it, but it will happen. My husband doesn't believe it, but my son Singleton's generation will benefit. He's only twelve, and when he's twice that age he'll be living in a world quite unlike the one we know now. Women will be equals, not skivvies.'

They proceed to the chancel and Mary points to the five lancets of the stained-glass window, describing some of the details that he can easily see for himself. As she goes on talking, directing his attention to the different sections of the window, he begins to feel light-headed and distant from himself; it reminds him of the sensation he had at Tulira Castle just before he entered the painting of the ballet dancers. A sunbeam has struck the second lancet, which shows Jesus healing the daughter of Jairus, and is spilling streaks and droplets of colour across the stone floor towards them. The light washes through him, as if he were becoming a rainbow; he is drifting from Mary Coleville's words into the frame of the lancet, into a reverie so sudden and luminous it's as if he's stepped into another world while retaining all his faculties. He feels a moment of panic but then remembers the words the strange man told him at Tulira Castle and which he's never forgotten—surrender to the imagination, or whatever it is that induces states of deep reverie. Although he is still aware of Mary speaking beside him, he allows himself to look around him and it is as if he is standing next to Jesus as he gazes at the sick girl! Jesus is wearing a deep red robe and there's halo, like a full harvest moon, behind his head; he feels he could reach out and touch the pillow of the sick girl and he can hear her shallow breathing. Jesus reaches out and touches the forehead of the girl. There is a great sense of peacefulness…

He is jolted back to the church by the sound of Mary's

voice repeating, 'Are you feeling all right?' He nods, but he is not all right. The vision was as real as the church is now. He wants to sit down; he is bursting to tell her what he has just seen.

His brain tries to readjust his emotions: surely it was just a daydream, an effect of the coloured light? But his heart is not convinced.

Before he can feel more disoriented, she leads him to a wall memorial of a certain Jane Eyre. He mentions Charlotte Brontë. She tuts: 'No, this is another one.'

She directs his eyes to the inscription, which he obediently reads aloud, glad of something to distract him from what has just happened: 'Her piety, prudence and well-disposed bounty to the poor, giving bread to the hungry, and clothing the naked, made her a worthy example to her sex.' Beneath this are the words: 'The sum of £300 is given by the Widow, Jane Eyre, to the Corporation of Galway, for the yearly Sum of £24, to be distributed in Bread to 36 poor Objects, on every Sunday, for ever.'

Mary is smiling at him, as if inviting him to share her pride: 'That's a true hero, *and* a woman. Not Redvers Buller firing his wretched cannons at wretched Boers and everyone else. Nor a Gladstone issuing orders across the empire. A simple woman who was kind and used her money wisely. *And* a Protestant. I will confess we haven't been archangels over the centuries, but not all of us are landlords, soldiers or evangelisers.'

They both gaze at the engraved words, but he is still shaken. *He was standing next to Jesus.*

Mary decides the tour is at an end and bids him goodbye, twitching her mouth in lieu of a smile. She walks off, lunging to tidy a stack of hymn books on a table at the entrance as she leaves.

HE'S BACK HOME, IN the parlour, talking to his parents about his day. He waits until his father is out of the room then tells Bridie about his vision or reverie. She is sitting forward on her chair, her freckly face flushed from the fire, her chin tucked in. She listens and grunts every so often with approval. 'The gift is in your blood, Patsy. Your nan would've been proud of you. She had it too. She'd often be seeing the faces of those passed from this world. And I dare say you'd be able to as well. Second sight can be a curse… and second sight can be a blessing.' He knows what she is going to say next and is thankful his father isn't there to sigh and summon the higher deities with a rolling of his eyes to witness the ramblings of his wife.

Bridie half turns towards the fire; her hair, temporarily combed back into a bun, glows in the light of the flames; her eyelids droop as her brain switches into memory. She puts her mug down and he can smell the aromatic malt. She begins with her usual words, ' 'Tis strange what can happen to folk out of the blue.' She shifts in her chair. 'Your dreaming yourself into that window is what I'd call fairy dreaming. But there's queer things abroad if you know how to look. Who'd've thought anything peculiar would be happening on that evening in Knock?'

He knows her telling of the miracle at Knock almost off by heart, but in the light of his own visionary moment he is glad to hear it yet again.

'August 1879—a little over twenty years ago—and the whole of Mayo under cloud, the rain splattering the earth and turning roads to puddles and mush. Daylight giving up its ghost and cottages leaking lamplight between curtains.' She takes a sup and continues, using her hands and fingers to describe the moment when the two women are stunned to see white ghostly figures standing at the end of the church.

When she has finished the story she smiles like a child who knows she has done something adults will be pleased with. 'A miracle. Those women saw angelic figures sent by Our Lord. 'Tis how the times are at the moment. First there was Lourdes. Then Knock. As if God is trying to *contact us*. Warn us.'

Joe enters the room. 'So this Mary Coleville of yours is for women being equal is she?' Joe winks at him and stands behind Bridie, puts his hands on her shoulders and leans forward to kiss her on the cheek. 'What do you think of that, *Mrs* Joseph Bowley?'

Bridie does not rise to the bait: 'Mrs Coleville's a good soul. I'd know of her. She'd help the sick and the poor, and all the cats and dogs, Catholic and Protestant, no matter what; and there's more of us should be doing that. And it's women like her whose sons are being sent off to South Africa to scrap like lurchers for a scrubby patch of desert.'

Joe gives out a sigh that moves towards her like a slow-moving arrow. In his most kindly, school-masterly manner he says: 'It's not a *desert* but a principle, the British'd be saying. If the Boers have their way, God knows what'll happen next. India? Ireland? You see... the empire's like a huge chair with cross-bars strengthening the legs. Take one away and it weakens the whole thing. That's why they'll fight us on Home Rule. British hearts might agree to us ruling ourselves... but British heads will take away whatever they offer.'

Bridie isn't listening but nods frequently enough to encourage Joe to keep talking. When he eventually stops, she emits a grunt, indicating any number of inexpressible thoughts.

HE IS WALKING TOWARDS St Nicholas's, picking his way through handcarts with their long handles touching the ground and backsides in the air, and women crouching beside pots and pans, trays of trinkets, and baskets and boxes full of vegetables—some of them as earthy and gnarled as their feet. He watches a small boy standing on a mattress on an iron bed pretending to shoot passers-by.

It's his last day at work.

Inside, he is tempted to go over to the lancet window again and try to enter its frame. But something stops him. It feels too soon to have another powerful reverie.

The church is empty apart from a woman sweeping the floor of the south aisle and another woman, or girl, sitting in a pew two along from the one he is working on. After a while she turns round. She is humbly dressed but pretty, dark haired, with a hint of a turned-up nose and sleepy looking eyes. She looks about seventeen.

'Mad for the work are ya?'

'It's my last day,' he says, looking at the girl's lips.

'You don't look the sort that'd be coming to this church.' She speaks with a knowing air.

'You're right on that. And you don't look the sort either.'

'You're right too. I come here to escape the crowd at home. I'm living in Bowling Green. A shout away. And shouting's all I hear in the house. Drives me mad. 'Tis peaceful here. Are you courting?'

He's taken aback by her sudden switch of interest. He shakes his head.

'Have you ever courted?'

Warmth blossoms in his face. 'Are *you* courting?'

She gives a long sigh.

'You don't sound happy.'

'Three fellas I've had a fondness for, and all of them's dead.'

'Sorry for your trouble.' She looks too young.

'My friends call me "Man-killer". A lad I knew died in Africa this year past. 'Twas the fever got him, not the bullet. Bloemfontein. Lovely name for a place of death? So you haven't stepped out with a woman?'

He shakes his head.

'Is it the priesthood you're headed for?'

'Not at all.'

'That's grand altogether—you're a nice looking lad, a good height on you and a bulge in the muscles.'

His cheeks respond.

'I'm Nora.'

'Patrick.'

'I've seen your face around town alright.'

'Do you work?'

'Laundry. Hate it. Hate home. Me mam's always screaming. She threw my da out for drinking. I'm going to run away to Dublin and meet a rich man and sail away to France or Italy.'

He pictures her hanging onto the arm of a top-hatted gentleman, watching the waves of the Mediterranean Sea. He imagines the man taking off her dress. How can he be so jealous after knowing her for five minutes?

'Ye'll be varnishing benches all your life?'

'I'm a… woodworker and joiner.'

'A woodworker then?'

He wants to say no he won't.

'Don't you want to see the world a bit? Have women friends? Do things? Change the world, Pat, before it changes you. I heard someone say that.'

He can tell from her expression that he is oozing melancholy.

'Come here to me. I want to show you something.' She leaps up from the pew and waves at him to follow her. He wonders if she'll show him the Jane Eyre memorial. It's the last thing he wants to see. She walks to a column in the north aisle and leans her back on it, out of view from the rest of the church. He stands in front of her.

'Come here, I want to whisper something.'

As he bends down towards her she reaches up with her two hands and gently pulls his face towards her. The speed of her action catches him unawares. Her lips press against his. He instinctively opens his mouth slightly and to his thrilling joy her tongue slips into it. Blood rushes to all parts of his body. Kissing a girl. Kissing a girl in church. A Church of Ireland church. *He is kissing a girl for the first time, in church.* Nora pulls back and looks into his eyes. ''Twas lovely. And all the better for being in here.' He is desperate to join his lips with her beautiful smiling lips again; he wants to touch her breasts, but he knows from the look on her face that the moment has come and gone. The clop of footsteps on the other side of the church alarms him. Yet as he looks into Nora's pretty face all he can think about is kissing her again.

'I've kissed one or two fellas in my time, and that's as good as any.' She takes his hand and squeezes it. 'Best be off. Wait here a minute.'

'Will I see you again?'

'Sure Galway's small enough.' He can feel her sensing his dismay. 'You're a looker, Pat, a good set of bones in your face. You'll be making plenty of girls turn their heads. And if you don't see me you can remember our kiss. Take care of yourself, Pat.'

He watches, helplessly, as she moves away from him and leaves the church. He returns to work; his heart wants to escape its cage; he is filled with such joy, and such unutterable sadness.

He is trying to recall the years between his encounter with Nora and his leaving home; it's as if all the details of these years, his mid-twenties, have merged into mild grey summers and cold grey winters. He was still living at home, working with his father but also taking on his own work, carpentry and painting, in the city and even occasionally around the county: Athenry, he remembers, with its cows in the fields rubbing their backsides against crumbly medieval ruins; and Clifden, buffed bright by westerly winds and looking out across the Atlantic to America. Those early years after the death of Queen Victoria were full of hope that there might be change in the country. But the British government was as agonisingly stubborn as the Home Rule movement was toothless. The country, like his own life, was a backwater of inaction and dullness, ready to stagnate further into bitterness and anger.

He waits for a solid recollection to break the surface, like a silvery fish wriggling on a hook. Eventually, a ripple, a stirring, and he can feel the atmosphere of a rare hot summer emerging: 1906. Images of faces and places start to form themselves into sequences of memory. One in particular he thought he'd banished forever—but there it is once more, his 'dark secret', rising unadulterated into the light.

HE'S SITTING AT THE front of St Mary's, the church beside Galway's harbour, attending mass with Bridie. His eyes are drifting to the wall to the left of the altar and the niche framing a mosaic picture of Galway Bay in which waves are bucking and curling around a fishing boat. As he gazes at it he can feel himself slowly being drawn through the frame into the heart of the picture—he manages to let himself surrender and enter the scene. In a flash he finds himself standing on the cliffs above the bay and looking down at the vessel as it slices through the water, as smoothly as a fin. He then transfers himself by a flickering of thought to the boat's deck and feels the brisk, briny wind in his face as he skims into a world of light. He revels in the unbounded space and freedom: the horizon, empty and shining, beckons him. He can physically feel all his worldly cares—routines of life, the grey façades of the city, his want of female companionship—dissolving into a beautiful radiance. For a moment he thinks this is what 'God' must be—not an entity like a supernatural person but a state of grace, a feeling of being shorn of one's sense of self and basking in a state of unbounded peacefulness, freedom and love. Surely this is what religion is!

The spell is broken by a stirring of people turning to their neighbours or getting up to leave. Bridie adjusts her headscarf and with a nudge of her elbow indicates she is ready to go. He feels infused by a lightness of being and a joy that makes him nod and smile at everyone around him.

They step outside the church into the fish-smouldering air and join the crowd that's gathered on the quayside for the city's annual Blessing of the Bay ritual. Fishing nets have been spread out on the pier like huge black spiders' webs, ready to be blessed; a small armada of currachs, light hookers and other boats eases up and down on the water. Fishermen stand, sit and kneel in their vessels, some holding oars, others adjusting sails.

He hears a booming voice—like the voice of God!—and sees in one of the boats a white-robed priest, like an alabaster statue, intoning a prayer about multiplying the fishes in the ocean and calling upon Mary, Star of the Sea, for her protection. As the priest utters his blessing, Bridie and others cross themselves in unison—the action is so spontaneous it moves him to do the same. The priest sprinkles holy water on the sea and the fishermen who are standing sink to their knees in supplication; their sudden obedience feels truly humble and gains more force from their being out in the air among the boats and the sea, not inside a church. A hymn sung in melodic unison even seems to pacify the breeze.

The singing, the actions of the fishermen and the simplicity of the prayer make him suddenly grasp why Bridie feels her Catholic faith connects her with the first apostles, those fishermen whose lives were turned upside down by Jesus.

And he appreciates how her love of simple piety brings her close to Joe's own uncomplicated Quaker faith of silence, prayer and holy writ. He can see the ancient orderliness in the Blessing of the Bay, and yet… the peacefulness he's feeling has come from the reverie he's just had in the church. Can grace be conferred by prayers, rituals and services? And if so, the rituals and services of *which* church?

As the hymn draws to a close, a discordant yell—almost a scream—rings out, followed by a splash and a collective cheer. People are standing by the end of the pier, looking down into the sea. A man who looks as if he's throttling his hat is shouting at the water, as if his wits have left him: 'Ye throw folk out of their homes for the want of a penny of rent—well, ye can try throwing the fishes out of their homes!' It's difficult to gauge whether the man has taken leave of his senses or is shouting at someone; then a small figure, apparently flailing and gasping for air, is hauled out of the water to a chorus of boos and jeers. The sodden man is wearing the bottle-green police uniform—now made even darker—of the Royal Irish Constabulary.

A FEW DAYS LATER—or was it weeks?—during the same summer, he's sitting on a bench on a patch of grass near the canal, beside the buildings of the university of Galway, where he's being employed to install oak panelling. The shadows are sharp on the grass and the rushing frothed-up waters of the nearby Corrib are making the air tingle. Studious-looking youths with eyes full of purpose pass him and vanish into the university compound.

He remembers choosing that particular bench because of the attractive young woman sitting on it. He has seen her in the confines of the university a couple of times and has been wondering who she is—the daughter of a professor? A governess? A teacher? She has the poise of a pianist and is wearing a long grey dress with puffed sleeves; she's using her straw hat to waft air across her fine-featured face; strands of her brown hair, tied back in a neat bun, flicker away from a central parting of the smoothest ivory.

He nods at her as he sits down, and remarks on what a fine day it is. He knows that his work clothes and muscular frame will distinguish him from the students, and also that his accent, shaped by the Quaker community, will reassure her of his social class. The woman's tentative but gracious smile encourages him to say a few more words beyond speculative pleasantries, and before he knows it he's talking more about his work than he intended to. He stops and looks down at his dusty boots.

Eventually she says, looking straight ahead: 'I'd say you'd need to know your geometry. The spaces to be filled, the angles. The amount of wood needed.' She half-turns to him: 'We think of woodworkers being brawn and neatness, but they need Pythagoras and Euclid too.'

Her genuine interest takes him by surprise. 'Have you a family member who's a carpenter?'

'No. But I'm interested in mechanical matters. I study engineering here.' She points behind her shoulder to the university buildings.

He laughs. He's never heard of a woman studying engineering. He didn't know women were allowed to study *anything*.

The restrained impatience in her eyes prompts him to apologise. He wants to say something else, but nothing comes to mind.

'You're not the first to laugh, and in mitigation I believe I'm the first of my sex to study here.' She turns to face him fully for the first time. 'I blame Mr Darwin.' She pauses until she's sure of his complete attention. 'We can all agree humans are superior to the ape. But his theory seems to suggest an ordained ladder of intelligence. Someone is always superior to another; and to a man of an uneducated mind it may seem that from the facts of history a man has a greater intellectual capacity than a woman.'

He's grateful that the gentle tone of her voice softens the implication that he himself has an 'uneducated' mind.

His rushed response is full of his wish to make amends. 'In my father's faith—the Society of Friends—women are given equal prominence. There's no ladder. No male priests. No priests at all in fact.'

Her laugh is really a short abrupt noise. 'Some would say the Friends are not a faith at all—just a group of kindly folk, listening for God.'

He wasn't expecting such a summary. 'What's your affiliation, may I ask?'

'Presbyterian.'

She's the first Presbyterian he's ever met and he looks at her as if to pick out distinguishing physical marks. But all he sees is her beautiful slender neck and her moist lips, the slightest tremble of which seeming to indicate the process of her thoughts. 'Presbyterian? Sure, isn't that all hell and damnation?'

'That is the received caricature. Hell and damnation. But also heaven as well. I like the certainty. Suits my temperament. You know exactly where you are. Black and white. We are all predetermined to be saved or damned, and if you carry out the virtues and follow the precepts of the elders, it is certain to be the former. Same with engineering. You don't want a bridge to wobble from *uncertain* principles, do you? You'll appreciate this from your carpentry. You value your spirit level because of the certainty it brings.'

He hasn't come across a young woman, any woman, like her before and feels daunted by her fluent thoughts. He introduces himself more formally and she tells him her name is Alice Perry. He's curious to know her background. She reveals that studying is a family tradition. Her sisters are at universities too, and her father helped to found the Galway Electric Light Company.

She seems so certain of herself. So confident. It makes him want to question her further, and perhaps... even shake her edifice of conviction?

'But can you compare religion to building a bridge? My father is a Quaker, my mother a Catholic, and I've witnessed the mysteries of both faiths—isn't religion more like... love than a scientific practice?' As soon as he says 'love' he knows he's admitting to himself that Alice is more alluring than he has any right to feel.

She closes her eyes to think and he takes the chance to appreciate her face, her unblemished skin. She turns to him: 'Love is the effect of religion, not the reason for its being—isn't that so?'

He's not sure he's understood this and doesn't know how to respond; she seems to sense his awkwardness and relents: 'You're right, faith is more complex than I'd have it. University is a small country, its language is reason, and one can become too used to it. Sometimes theorems seem omnipotent!'

She smiles at her last remark, but it's a smile that's humouring him and has no warmth in it. It makes him want to impress or even unsettle her: 'Indeed. As Mr Thomas Hardy says in his work *Jude the Obscure*: "Be kind to birds and animals, and read all you can." That's one of my rules of life. In fact it might well sum up our Quaker faith.'

She leans back and wafts her face with her hat: 'I'm not sure I would cite the fatalistic Mr Hardy in the cause of Quakerism or any faith. Ah, yes, poor old Jude. I fear that book will have put you off seats of learning.'

'It's made me wonder about the state of marriage.'

'Indeed, I hope not. Marriage is the foundation of life—of providing life. We do God's work by marriage and creating children. Is there anything more important than that? We are God's children, destined to carry out his work.'

Her mouth is held in the shape of a smile, but her eyes do not match it. He wants to alter her expression: 'But to carry out God's work—to be *sure* our work is his—presumably we have to be Presbyterians?'

She considers this point. 'All I can say is that we worship simply, imbibe the scriptures, encourage the pursuit of learning, of education. I'm not sure I'd be studying here if I'd been raised in the Catholic faith.'

'And what about the sacraments?'

'We respect them. But we do not regard them as some *magical entry* into heaven.'

'And I suppose that you, as a Presbyterian, are sure to escape the flames of hell?' His words emerge harsher than he intended.

Her eyes, up to this point so luminous and pretty, have now assumed an unnerving glitter. He waits for her to say something but it's as if she has lost interest in the topic and, more to the point, himself.

He tries to imagine being a Presbyterian. The world divided between the saved and the damned and knowing that you're *on the right side*. He can feel these new thoughts actually changing the way he views Alice physically. While he's considering whether she is still as attractive as before, she sees a dark-haired man wearing a long black academic gown walking on the other side of the road. She calls out to him and raises a hand to catch his eye; then, standing up and murmuring indistinct words, she crosses the road. He watches as they stride across the canal bridge in the direction of the cathedral, as serenely as a couple who know exactly where their destiny lies.

It's LATER THAT SAME day, nightfall, and he's walking home via one of the narrow streets—St Augustine's?—leading away from the harbour; his head is full of Alice Perry, her confidence, her long grey dress, her milky skin. With some effort of imagination he's managed to forget the steeliness in her eyes and is enjoying the thought of gazing into them and kissing her. Even Presbyterians must make love.

As he passes a recessed doorway, a woman's slurred voice asks him for tobacco. He stops to say he doesn't take any form of tobacco. Although it is dusk and she is standing in the shadows, he notices that above her long skirt she's wearing just a blouse—a garment far too flimsy for the chill that's in the night air. When his eyes adjust further, he sees that what he's taken to be a strip of pale beige linen running down the front of her blouse is in fact naked flesh, from her neck to the top of her skirt. He's so taken aback by this revelation that words fail him; yet he doesn't move.

The woman says: 'Liking what ye see, Mister?' He doesn't know how to reply. He knows he should march off, but the unexpected bareness of her body keeps him rooted to the spot.

The woman's long black hair is loose and a strand has fallen over her right eye to her mouth, and she is sucking it, puckering her lips.

She adjusts the tilt in her hips, and as she taps her foot on the ground he can see a bottle next to her ankle boot. 'University lad?'

He doesn't reply.

'Never mind.' She begins to pull her blouse wider apart until he can see her breasts. She looks like a goddess of love. 'Thruppence and ye can touch me. *Here.*' She gives a yawn-sized smile and dips her chin to indicate her breasts. He looks at them in awe. Before he can stop himself he puts his hand in his pocket, finding only a sixpence. He tells himself he is simply going to give it to the woman and walk away, as if she were just a beggar and not offering something so temptingly delectable. He gives her the coin and in doing so finds himself unbearably close to her, almost feeling her body warmth.

He still doesn't walk away, and feels poised, like a Presbyterian, between heaven and damnation.

'A tanner's welcome, but 'tis above the skirt only. Come here and kiss me, like we're sweethearts. Don't want snoopers sticking their noses in.'

Before he can digest her words, she grabs his arm, pulling him up to her. As if possessed by some elemental force, he takes her cheeks in both hands and presses his lips against hers, kissing her with such force that she pulls away with a light laugh. 'Gently!' She puts her arms around his neck and kisses him lightly on the lips with a surprising delicacy and tenderness; he feels the same intense sensation that he had when kissing Nora. This time it's different. He can smell a faint scent of ale on her breath and he's aware of fighting off the idea that God is looking down on him. Condemning him. He has a flash of Alice Perry, and she's condemning him. It was different with Nora. He'd felt an upwelling of deep mutual affection, like a swirl of what he imagined love was.

The woman removes her hands from his neck and pulls his hands onto her breasts. He is tempted to squeeze them hard, just to make sure they're not unreal. Instead he strokes them, feeling their beautiful softness, pressing a finger or two onto the nipples, feeling them pucker and harden. For a moment he shuts his eyes and pretends he's touching Nora. Then Alice.

He feels he could stay in this doorway forever; and he also feels he wants to run away and never come back to Galway.

THE NEXT DAY HE can hardly get out of bed for the shame of it. Hardly look his mother or father in the eyes. The more he tries to erase the image, the more it gains in sumptuous detail. The worst thing is that whenever a thought of Alice Perry comes into his head—her cool, grave manner, her intelligent talk, her elegance, even her disturbing certainty—that same thought inevitably leads to the shadowy doorway and his lust. It becomes his dark secret that only he and God know about.

He is standing on deck with other travellers and migrants, men and women standing beside or sitting on bulging suitcases strapped up with venerable leather belts. They are staring at the massive stone wedge of Ben Bulben, its top sliced off by a cloud as thick as a slab of solid cream. They are on the open sea at last, leaving Sligo and the mainland behind. Summer, 1911.

HE IS THIRTY YEARS of age and at the lowest ebb in his life. He cranes over the railing and watches the ocean seething against the side of the steamer; he thinks about all his failures: not leaving home, not finding sufficient work to make himself independent, not finding a woman to love. His single most decisive action in recent months was to make a bedroom out of the shed in the yard. There, night after night, he shut the door on the lamplit windows of the house, reading by candlelight or staring into futureless space; or having fantastical dreams about being a seaman, or shopkeeper, or undertaker—anyone with companions at work. And of having a wife and family, and his own home. Of being in bed with a woman and making love to her.

All he wants is a conviction that life is more than replacing rotting windows and making bookcases and cupboards. Is he merely to shrug off and forget the strange experiences that seemed to suggest a different way of seeing reality, perhaps one more in tune with the idea of a divine presence in the world? His visionary moment in the church when he entered the lancet window and stood next to Jesus; the painting of the ballet dancers at Tulira Castle; the mosaic picture of the boat on Galway Bay—will he merely come to re-tell those incidents as a fireside entertainment, subject to charitable smiles?

Ben Bulben and its soft crown of cloud are diminishing. Most of the passengers have gone inside. The deck is shiny with spray but the night itself is dry and soft. Liverpool awaits, then London and his aunt, Faith. He wonders how much of a Quaker she will remain after ten years in the London of the

Vices' as Joe calls it. Will she still have the Bowley zeal for spiritual discipline and moral service?

He thinks of his mother Bridie, garrulous Fenian Bridie and her republican heart, and her love of the stories of the distant past before the English invaded Ireland, when the legendary hero Finn MacCool and his warriors were roaming the forests of the country. He pictures his father standing in front of the hearth, always quick to recall that the Bowleys dispensed soup during the great famine; proud of giving coins to beggars, clothes to the homeless, and protesting about factories and the condition of fallen women. He smiles at the teasing he used to get—that Joe enjoyed patrolling Middle Street at night a bit too much, belabouring street-walkers and their male clients. He lets out a groan as a flash of his own succumbing to female temptation comes and goes.

He thinks of Bridie needling Joe about his rectitude, daring herself to test his patience, as if all her deprived senses craved the great rush of his rage. No wonder, too, she began to rely on a bit of drink to relax the grip of his righteous living. Yet he can also see how, below the surface irritations, they could love each other at a deeper level. For Bridie, Joe must have seemed a strong and uncompromising figure, honest, true, and when the stars were aligned, affectionate. For Joe, Bridie was his connection with the world outside, with the streets, the markets, the wider circle of friends and family. Her spontaneous eruptions of emotion or words allowed him to be calm and thoughtful, his most preferred modes of being. Both of them shared an unwavering faith in Christ and God, and both of them were brave to confront their respective families about marrying someone from a different church. He wonders who was the braver.

Twilight is blending the edge of the sky with the edge of the sea. No stars yet. It's the most northerly point in the world he has ever been to. No faint outline of land in any direction. He prays for the guiding hand of God, no longer sure what he feels about God. Religion has engraved him with principles, as if he were a tablet of stone, but offered insufficient solace. His father's own spirituality has shrunk to a regimen of re-reading George Fox and Bunyan. He himself knows these books off by heart. Now he longs to read about other peoples' lives, and their thoughts and spiritual beliefs. Better still, to meet them in person. He has always gone to mass, albeit fitfully, to humour his mother; but lately he sensed that she, as much as he, hadn't cared for the gallop of mumbled prayers and the priest denouncing parishioners for small misdemeanours.

He thinks of Alice Perry and her Presbyterian faith, and wonders why he is not more envious of her certainty. He can imagine a Presbyterian service with neatly dressed families, their shoes as shiny as their virtue. As for the Church of Ireland—a complete mystery to him! Small, gaunt, turreted churches rising from secluded fields and surrounded by dry moats of Protestant gravestones. Yet he is certain he believes in God, or, at least, some divine being or dimension transcending time and place—similar to the atmosphere arising in Friends' prayer meetings when a silence descends like the sudden cessation of a storm, infusing him with calmness and a lightness of body.

The one thing sustaining him most during his darkest days has not been Bunyan or Fox but the distant, yet still luminous, memory of kissing Nora in the church. That intense delicate communion still haunts him ten years on. It wasn't just the physical sensation of his first kiss. It was the way she arranged it, the way she wanted it as much as he did, the fact it was inside a church. And it was also her spirit that had affected him. She had seemed a dreamer, fearless—had she not called him to adventure? *Change the world before it changes you.* And he does want to change the world, or at least his country. The sense of national anger turning to violence seems to increase with every year that passes. He cannot bear to witness the British government dithering about Home Rule; but he abhors the thought of any violence, even of the most justifiable sort. He wants to do something, say something. But to whom? And where? And how?

His thoughts revert to Nora. For several months after their

encounter he took walks around the streets where she lived, but he never saw her. Perhaps she moved to Dublin or the Paris of her dreams. Yet the memory of her kiss, and her spirit—someone who was ready to change her life—had always acted as a counterweight to the wild thought he sometimes had had of walking into the sea, his coat pockets full of heavy stones.

Night has arrived but left its stars behind. He looks out to where he guesses Norway might be. Darkness. Cold salty darkness. England. The empire. It hardly seems possible. He remembers the day Joe insisted on walking with him to Salthill. Almost unheard of for Joe to suggest such a thing; he knew something must be important. They walked in silence until the shifting grey mass of the sea seemed to loosen Joe's tongue, who spoke as if correcting a point someone had already made:

'Patrick. Yes, your home is here, for good. But you need to see another part of the world. You're fading away here.'

The words were like a wave knocking into him; and the shock of Joe's tentative, heavy arm around his shoulders increased the giddiness.

'There's things waiting for us, and it's our job to find them. God helps us, but we have to take the first step. Fox began his life as an outcast, a wretched soul. Who would have predicted that by the end of his days he'd have brought millions of lives into the fold? The Almighty has a plan that's best for us and watches while we wander blindly. But if we cast off into the ocean, trusting Him absolutely, like St Brendan the Voyager, we'll be guided.'

It was Joe at his best, kindly and firm, clear and wise. The sea was beating against the city strand, trying to wash away his fear of the unknown, but at that moment all he sensed was the great vastness waiting for him.

And now here he is out in the ocean, sailing from Ireland and looking into that great vastness. He turns away from the darkness, goes inside and finds a corner to lie down and shut his eyes.

44

LIVERPOOL! SUN BREAKING FROM the clouds and fanning a red glow over warehouses the size of cathedrals and bare-armed dockers, loading and unloading huge cargo ships. *Liverpool.* The name has resided in his head for as long as he can remember; almost a place of legend, like the land of eternal youth, Tír na nÓg. For the first time he realises what an imperial power looks like— the scale of the buildings, the number of people—everywhere he turns his gaze it's as if a football match has just ended and the huge crowd has spilled out onto the streets. He thinks of Galway with its bobbing fishing boats and tiny narrow lanes and feels the size of a child.

HE STEPS ONTO THE train for London and prays that Faith will be there to meet him. The train jolt-starts and soon the carriages click away and rock him into drowsiness and a dreaming back: of the night-dark sea, the jutting silhouette of Ben Bulben, the station at Sligo, the train in Galway waiting to depart, and his parents on the doorstep—all move through him in procession as slowly as a hand waving goodbye.

THE TRAIN IS HISSING him awake. People disembarking. Euston Station teeming, its glass canopy the largest roof he's ever seen.

He is lugging his case over to the ticket barrier and recognises Faith from a photograph. She spots him and gives a restrained wave. She is tall, like himself and his father. She has the recessed Bowley eyes. She shakes his hand and looks up at him. 'The Lord save us, you've put on some height since I saw you last.' It's the sort of remark that is usually accompanied by a smile. He waits for the conversation to develop, but she leads him in silence to the Underground, where they join the flow of people, mostly bowler-hatted men, silent as undertakers, descending into the bowels of the earth.

They reach an ill-lit platform and hear a gathering rumble—a long sleek train bursts out of the darkness like a serpent that's been startled from some hellish place. Doors open: he is shoved in and up against his first Londoners, no one speaking or laughing or singing, as if they're all coming home from a funeral. Coughing and the smell of tobacco, like being in Finnegan's bar. He is expecting Faith to say something, but she is just like his father. Why say anything unless the situation demands it?

At last, Wimbledon. The street leading from the station is broad, its high triple-headed lamps glowing like illuminated shamrocks. Large houses rise against the fading summer light. An electric tram glides past; already he has seen more people in one day than in the whole of his previous life.

Faith leads the way up a hill towards what turns out to be a stretch of parkland—Wimbledon Common. They arrive at a three-storey house with a wrought-iron gate and steps leading up to the front door. 'Don't be getting ideas! It's the top floor alone I have. Two bedrooms. A devil of a squeeze; the rent is not nothing, and your contribution will be a help. There are views to the common; I use it as my garden.'

Inside the flat Faith relaxes more. She shows him his bedroom and brings in a pot of tea and slices of buttered bread. About to leave, she pauses and manages a tired smile: 'You're welcome here, Patrick. I'm used to my solitude and silence, but there are times when the company would be welcome, and I'm sure we'll make the best of things.'

THE MORNING SUN IS beating at his window. He pulls the curtain and looks out onto the common and huge chestnuts, shaggy with leaves. *He is in London.* A woman with a small white dog on a long red lead walks across the road, trailed by their shadows. He can see tall stately houses through the heavy branches of trees. A knock at the door. Faith shouts something.

The kitchen is big by Galway standards and a window looks down onto a walled garden at the back. He is sitting at the table and Faith is putting out cutlery; she is wearing a pale green pleated dress that makes her bony face seem greyer. He asks her about her job in a book publishing company. She is dismissive at first, just as his father would be, but then enthusiasm gets the better of her. She talks a lot about the man for whom she is secretary, Hugh Chaigneau.

'He lives nearby. Went to Oxford. Knows everything. A socialist. Believes women should be allowed to vote. He's interested in philosophy and religions—and I can tell you, Patrick, he's opened my mind to all sorts of things. Indian religions, Buddhism. And theosophy.'

'Theosophy?'

'Theosophy… is about these Masters of wisdom who live in the Himalayas. No one ever sees them, but they teach their wisdom by sending messages to the minds of people who are trained to receive them.' She pauses as if waiting for an objection: 'Jesus and the Buddha were Masters of wisdom.'

He is surprised by this but cannot think of any response.

'Hugh wants me to join the theosophists. I met him at a séance, not far from here; a man called William Stead holds them. Hugh said my face looked Irish and reminded him of his Irish ancestors, and there and then he invited me for an interview. A job as his assistant. It's the first time my face has been of practical value!' Before he can make a courteous remark, she adds: 'He's a widower. One daughter.'

FAITH IS LEADING HIM out into the summer's day. Everything looks glorious: roses climbing around doorways and over high brick walls; the composed movement of people on the streets, some holding parasols, a few pushing perambulators; trams gliding here and there, packed with workers and shoppers. Paintwork gleaming. Strings of small red, white and blue flags, still celebrating the coronation of George V a few weeks back.

As they stroll around the common itself Faith descends into leisurely chatter, and her accent sounds more Irish. 'The English are a shy breed, and some of them never open up to you. But they can be diverting if you persist with their company. There's many who've Irish connections, and some are friendly because they're Catholics and they assume you are, or they feel apologetic about us not having Home Rule. And there's many who are aloof and treat us badly; those who think we're purloining their jobs or are a nation of ungrateful rebels. This district is a good one. Folk are civil, and there's money to be earned. You won't be on your knees begging for work.'

He's standing in an Underground train heading for Oxford Circus and the carriage smells of sweat. It's late June and he's on his way to meet Faith outside Queen's Hall. They're going to a talk by a leading theosophist called Annie Besant. It was Faith's idea, an enthusiastic recommendation from Hugh Chaigneau.

He imagines the Underground as a series of drainage pipes buried deep below the earth and is relieved to join the dimming brightness of the upper air and the crowded pavements; he turns full circle to find his bearings. He asks a newspaper vendor how to get to Langham Place and soon he is seeing Faith in the distance, outside the hall, slowly elevating her gloved hand, almost as if she doesn't want to be noticed. When he reaches her, she looks him up and down in his new charcoal grey suit, a cast-off she obtained from someone at her publishing office. She adjusts his tie: 'Glad to see the suit hangs well. I was worried your muscles might bunch up the material.'

They take their seats in the auditorium, which looks as if it would hold the entire population of Galway city. A few times the audience falls silent, but no one appears on stage. Eventually a master of ceremonies introduces Annie Besant, and she glides into view, her long white gown matching the colour of her short crinkly hair. She stands by the lectern, small of stature, surveying the audience with a serious, mannish face. Murmurings and coughs subside and the auditorium lights dim.

He is so fascinated by this small radiant figure that he begins to concentrate on her words only when she says that a great world teacher will come and make all religions one. 'Many people once talked about a *German Fatherland*… but it was only when the hearts of the Germans were properly receptive that it became a reality through Bismarck the statesman and Moltke the general. Where an idea is burning in the souls of the people, *some great person is born in whom that idea takes shape.*'

He looks over at Faith, whose mouth has eased open. Annie Besant has paused and is staring at her notes; the footlights are making her white dress shine angelically.

She looks up again: 'From pulpit after pulpit we hear the longing for a great teacher who shall draw men's hearts together and make the brotherhood of religions an actuality in the world.'

Again she pauses; again resumes, and challenges the audience to think of the future Christ taking the body of *a coloured man*. At this there is an audible stirring. 'After all, we forget that the Christ was an Eastern man. But those who worship him often despise the Eastern peoples, who are actually nearer to him in blood than they are themselves!'— another stirring, like someone's uneasy shuffling multiplied by a thousand.

'Do not put a check on the love that flows out... If you do not see Him it is *your* eyes that are blinded.' He can feel the effect of her words flowing from his mind to his body, as if his heart has expanded and more blood is flowing beneath his skin.

She ends by saying that those who yearn to see the world teacher will see his beauty when 'he treads the roads of this earth *before very long*'. She looks down at the lectern and walks off to a moment's silence before cascades of applause tumble down from the galleries. People rise to their feet, unable to stop themselves clapping.

OUTSIDE QUEEN'S HALL: FAITH is leading him to a hotel called Langham's, across the street. She is flushed and wants to preserve the immediate memory of the talk.

The hotel is like a palace. He can't believe he can be in such a place. Thick pale-blue carpets are soaking up the sounds of discreet conversations; the icicles of chandeliers shed flakes of light on polished surfaces. Dried flowers intermingle with peacock feathers in huge oriental vases. Somewhere a piano is tinkling away.

While they talk about Annie Besant they feel their second and third sherries warm their insides. Neither of them is used to the effects of alcohol. His thoughts begin to blur and he notices his aunt's cheeks colouring like two roses opening their petals. He feels a sudden contentment, as if he's been swimming in the sea and entered a patch of warm water. At long last he can say he has arrived in London! The Underground holds no fears anymore; he has been to a grand event; he is sitting in the most luxurious hotel he's ever been to; he is sipping sherry like a gentleman. He looks at Faith and admires the way she has made a life for herself; a Quaker girl from Galway sitting there, in the heart of the empire; and he admires the way she is exploring things of the spirit and intellect. His father would sooner have protested outside the hall than gone in to hear Mrs Besant! Faith has his father's reserve and dignity, and a surface primness; but there's something childlike in her sudden enthusiasms, which his father lacks or has lost.

He watches her holding a sherry neatly between thumb and middle finger, her eyes scanning the surroundings. Her expression changes from glazy relaxation to animation: 'Patrick, will you look who's coming in.'

He turns and sees an elderly woman with a black hat and cloak entering with companions. Beneath the cloak is a long white dress.

Annie Besant and her entourage take up several seats adjacent to him and Faith, and he finds himself sitting next to what appear to be two Indian boys. He has never seen Indians in the flesh before. He tries not to stare at their dark brown skin. Hard to guess their ages. One could be a young man. They both look ill at ease. The older one has long black glossy hair, like a girl's, and a dreamy, pretty face. The other is good-looking too, with shorter hair parted in the centre. Both are dressed in black suits and starched white shirts. He wonders whether they are Annie Besant's servants, or sons of servants. Annie herself leans back in her chair between two distinguished-looking ladies, who chat across her. He notices that Faith is agitated. The pink in her face has spread to her neck. She leans across to him: 'Patrick. I'm going to tell her how much I admired her talk.'

Before he can ask her whether this is wise, she gets up and

goes over to Annie and crouches down on her knees like a courtier. He can't hear what's being said but is relieved to see Annie responding with a half-smile. He turns away and sees the younger Indian is looking miserable. His heart goes out to him, partly from the effect of the alcohol. He leans forward to speak.

'Were you attending the talk?'

The boy looks startled. He repeats the question.

'Yes. I enjoyed the talk.'

'Are you servants of Mrs Besant?'

'No, not servants! She is… like a mother to us.'

'You're from India?'

'That is correct.'

'I'm from Ireland. I have just moved to London. I'm finding it big and strange.'

The boy smiles at this. 'We too. So many big buildings everywhere and everyone going somewhere. In India it is busy, but there is nowhere to go.'

'Why are you here? What is your connection with Mrs Besant?'

The boy looks embarrassed and turns to the other boy, presumably his older brother, and repeats the question. The older boy says, 'My name is Jiddu Krishnamurti. This is my brother Nitya Krishnamurti. How do you do.' He is more confident in his bearing and fluent in his English.

'Christian Murphy?'

'No. Krishna-mur-*ti*. Krishna is a Hindu god. "Murti" means "image". So, I am an image of a god!' Jiddu's face is all boyish smiles.

'I'm just Patrick. From Ireland. Irish.'

'Yes, Irish, I know. St Patrick and the snakes! Mrs Besant has Irish ancestors. She has told me about Ireland—she says it's like India, under the rule of the British.'

'That's right.'

'You are the first Irish man I have met.'

'You are the first Indian I have met.'

'That is good!'

'I was asking... Nitya... what brings you here. Do you work for Mrs Besant?'

The two boys look at each other as though they are going to giggle.

At this point Faith returns to her chair and taps him on the arm; her face is eager to tell him something. He disengages with the boys and turns to Faith. 'Patrick. You'll never believe this. Don't look, but... that Indian lad, the one farther away.' He nods. 'You won't guess who he is.' He waits for her triumphant news. 'He's the *world teacher* Annie was talking about.'

At first he thinks she is joking, but he has never seen such a smile on his aunt's face. He's dying to look at Jiddu again. *The world teacher!* A dreamy young Indian? He swivels round; the brothers are staring into space; they look suddenly serene and spiritual beneath their awkwardness, or is he just telling himself that? Jiddu looks up at him and their eyes meet. He finds himself holding his gaze, and Jiddu does the same, and their eyes lock together. It is almost as if he is looking at himself through Jiddu's eyes, and perhaps vice versa. The background murmurings and variations of laughter diminish and he enters a deep silence; for a moment he feels panicky, as if he has had too much drink and is going to faint, but instead the silence breeds calmness; he is still looking at Jiddu and he hears him say something; he thinks it odd because he doesn't see Jiddu's lips move; yet the voice comes again, inside his head, and tells him that he misses India; he is worried about Nitya's health; he is lonely; he needs help; they both need help. The words, or thoughts, are urgent and unmistakable. He doesn't know how to respond. He gives an apologetic wistful smile; Jiddu reacts in kind with a shrug of the shoulders. They break off eye contact at the same time and he turns back to Faith's beaming face. He feels a deep pang for Jiddu's apparent plight, deepened by his own sudden homesickness. Nitya gets up and leaves the room and Jiddu looks at Patrick as if to invite him to sit next to him and talk. He leaves his aunt's side.

'This will sound very odd, but I think I heard you speaking to me just then. I thought I heard your thoughts.'

'That has happened before to me. But it is rare.' Jiddu looks away, as if searching for words.

He wants to ask Jiddu more about this mysterious way of communicating but other thoughts crowd in and he ends up saying: 'My aunt says you're the world teacher. Why have they chosen you as the world teacher?'

Jiddu tucks his hands in beneath his thighs and leans forward. 'Because of Mr Charles Leadbeater. He is a theosophist. One day he saw me on a beach in India. He came over to me and said he could see a bright aura of light all around my body and knew at once I was the world teacher—we call him the Maitreya. He asked my father if he could take me and Nitya to England to educate us as gentlemen and theosophists and teach me how to be the Maitreya. So that is why we are here. If Mr Leadbeater had not seen me on that beach, I would not be sitting in this hotel speaking to you.'

'And what do you have to do as this world teacher?'

'I'm being trained. They are educating me. I will have to give talks to people and make them believe they are more spiritual than they think they are. I must tell them that we are all evolving as human beings, becoming more enlightened. That there is only one God, one religion. We must not be divided into all these different faiths—Hindu, Christian, Muslim, Catholic, Protestant. God cannot be sliced up like a slab of cheese. We are all brothers and sisters, together.'

'If you're the world teacher, does that mean you can heal people, like Jesus did?'

'I think we all can.'

He laughs and Jiddu looks dismayed.

'Please, do not laugh. I know you can. I can see your aura.'

'My aura? What does it look like?'

'Pale gold. It is coming from the top of your skull, like water from a fountain, and is surrounding your head and body. It is like you're standing in a patch of sunlight.'

'It's probably the soft light in the room.' He gestures to a lamp.

'With the greatest of respect, it is not. I have seen auras

many times. I know what they are and what they mean. You are a good person.'

His first instinct is to laugh, but somehow he doesn't. 'It's good to know I've a light around me. I've never healed anyone.'

'Have you tried?'

'I haven't.' He looks at his hand to try to inspect the mysterious glow.

'It's difficult to see your own aura. Easier to see the auras of other people, and that happens only when a person is extremely calm, or extremely passionate. The lighter the aura, the more enlightened the person.'

He gives up looking at his hand and changes the subject. 'We could do with a world teacher, a Maitreya, in Ireland.'

'I know of Ireland only from what Mrs Besant says.'

'There's many Irishmen wanting to govern themselves. Home Rulers they're called. And there's some who are impatient and want to throw the English out by force. But… what does your brother, Nitya, think about you being the Maitreya?'

'He says he's proud of me! Mrs Besant treats him like a son, too. But he is in poor health. I am anxious about him. He also has no job to do and I fear he will be bored just being my companion.'

'And do white people object to the Maitreya being an Indian?'

'Yes. But Mrs Besant tells them the Buddha was an Indian, and Lord Krishna was an Indian, and Jesus Christ was a Jewish man. She asks them: "How many English world teachers have there been?" Nobody replies!'

'Do you *feel* as if you're the Maitreya in your bones, in your soul?'

'I feel I am as I have always been. No different. I take exercise, sleep, eat, learn French verbs, pray to God, sometimes play golf. They have founded an organisation and made me head of it. The Order of the Star. I have a leaflet for what it says.' He fishes in his pocket for a piece of paper and hands it to him. The paper is headed 'Order of the Star in the East' and beneath it is a list of principles.

'How old are you, Jiddu?'

'Sixteen.'

He glances round at Faith to tell her Jiddu's age, but he sees she has gone over to Annie Besant again. Faith catches his eye and waves to him to come over. He murmurs a word of explanation to Jiddu and joins his aunt and Mrs Besant.

He can't quite believe he is looking into the face of the woman who was holding two thousand people spellbound. Her chin is tucked in and her expression sombre, but her eyes have well-grooved smiling lines. 'Ah, here's the Galway man.' She doesn't wait for his response: 'I grudge the blood the English put into my father's veins. But I do celebrate the fact his mother was Irish and that he was born in Galway and attended Trinity College. The Irish tongue has always been music to my ears, and the Irish nature dear to my heart. The people are indomitable.'

He knows he should comment on this and says: 'Perhaps you are right, ma'am, that we're indomitable. But I fear... if a nation is oppressed for long enough, the people will resort to weapons.'

'You need Home Rule, dear boy, there's no gainsaying that. India must have it too. But above that, you need a spiritual doctrine that *unites*, not divides, people. Thackeray visited a Cork church and remarked that the shadows of the Protestant graves were no longer or shorter than those of the Catholics. We are one humanity.'

He repeats the last words to himself, then blurts out: 'I have just understood that Jiddu—Jiddu Krishna... is the new world teacher.' He manages to say this in a straightforward way while gesturing towards Jiddu, who has been rejoined by Nitya.

'Indeed. That's what we believe. You can never be sure which human body the spirit is going to enter. One time it was an Indian prince, who became the Buddha. Then a lowly Palestinian peasant, Jesus of Nazareth.'

She studies his reaction and decides he needs more elucidation. 'My scientific friends tell me thunderstorms occur when the atmosphere is configured in a certain way. It is the same with societies.'

He watches as Annie illustrates with her hands how hot air rises from the ground, cools, and forms thunderclouds. 'All of a sudden—flash, a peal of thunder. That's the atmosphere we have now. We saw it with Germany—the rising hot political air, so to speak, then bang! Bismarck, Moltke—men of destiny.'

He knows nothing of politics in Germany and merely nods to show he understands her point.

'The spirit searches for a body in which to become incarnate. Now is the time again. Can't you feel that change is in the air? Is it an accident that the women of the Western portion of civilisation are *now* beginning to object to their lot as second-class human beings?'

He thinks of Mary Coleville in St Nicholas's Church and Alice Perry on the bench outside Galway university and mumbles his agreement.

'In years to come it will be a mystery why at the start of the twentieth century women were not allowed to vote for candidates of government.'

'In Ireland *none of us* can vote for our own government. Only a British government.'

'And that is something you must change.'

'We've tried! For seven hundred years. Good men have failed. O'Connell, Parnell... Now we rely on the good will of the British. The good will of Mr Asquith and his Liberal Party to be precise.'

'Home Rule is a fine ambition. In the past the Irish Fenians applied a violent solution to what they thought was a political problem. The problem is not political, it's *spiritual*.'

He glances at Faith, who looks vexed, as if she can't quite hear what is being said or is worried one of the interlocutors is going to say something she will disagree with or not understand.

'Perhaps we Irish need Jiddu,' he says, unsure of his tone. Did he sound too frivolous? His brain is muddled by the talk, the sherry, and he's starting to be irritated by Faith, hovering there and not saying anything, but with her skin becoming like an overripe tomato.

'There is a sense in which we can *all* be a Maitreya.' Annie's voice is lower by an octave and the look in her eyes has turned inward. 'You don't have to wait for a Maitreya to come to Ireland. *You can be that person yourself*, and inspire your fellow countrymen. If that happens, you will find the question of self-governance will resolve itself.'

He can feel shivers up the back of his neck and he stares back at her as if she is personally commissioning him to be a world teacher.

As he thinks about this prospect, a smile comes to his face, and the smile starts to turn into an uncontrollable giggle. He tries to disguise it as a cough, thrusting his wrist to his mouth and half turning away, but he is aware of Faith staring at him as if he's a misbehaving child. Annie does not seem to notice, or is too preoccupied in her thoughts. He regains a semblance of composure. He nods at Faith to indicate they should go.

They take their leave of Annie, who, like a priest standing at the door of a church at the end of a service, gives them a parting salutation: 'Blessings on Ireland. The Island of Saints shall once again be the Island of Sages when the wheel turns round.'

As they move towards the door he sees that Jiddu and Nitya are talking to a man in a frock coat, who is gesticulating with his top hat to make a point. He catches Jiddu's eye and raises his hand in what feel likes a sort of rueful salutation. Jiddu spots him and does the same and follows them with his gaze until they disappear from view.

LATER THAT NIGHT HE is stretched out on his bed, his feet extending beyond the end, mind hopping from thought to thought. Jiddu—the Maitreya? Ireland's problems spiritual not political? He sits up and surveys the spines of the myriad books in his bookcase, most of them given to Faith, she had informed him proudly, by Hugh Chaigneau—who increasingly sounds more like a personal tutor than a boss.

His eye rests on a book by William Stead, who he remembers is Faith's neighbour and the organiser of séances. *If Christ Came to Chicago.* Tiredness is growing behind his eyes. He would like to see Jiddu again. He pictures Annie Besant walking onto the stage, regal and pure in her white dress. He takes the book and opens it at the end: 'The new religion has but one formula—Be a Christ! If Christ came to your city, would He find you ready?' It sounds similar to what Mrs Besant said.

He closes the book and wonders whether he *would* be ready. He reaches for a pile of magazines and journals beside his bed; he takes the top one, *The Pall Mall Gazette,* and spots that Stead has a short story in it called 'How the Mail Steamer went down in Mid Atlantic, by a Survivor'. He races through the story: a mail boat collides with another ship and begins to sink. Panic ensues, men barge their way to the too-few lifeboats only to be stopped by sailors at gunpoint. Hundreds of people die, but the hero, Thompson, survives to tell the tale.

He turns out the light and in his gathering somnolence he can see heads bobbing in the water. He switches his memory to the hotel, trying to reconstruct, again, the events of the evening. Sleep is pressing on him. He can faintly hear Jiddu saying, 'God cannot be sliced up like a slab of cheese.' It seems so obvious. So obvious.

He and Faith are walking round the edge of Wimbledon Common past the pond towards Cambridge House, William Stead's home. It's Saturday night, a week after Mrs Besant's talk. They are going to what Faith calls 'a spiritist evening'.

The house rises grandly from a terrace of solid red-brick houses and well-stocked front gardens. They are met at the door by a maid, who shows them into a dining room, where a dozen men and women in suits and sober dresses are standing around a large table. The curtains have been drawn and the overhead electric light is covered in red paper.

A man with kindly eyes tucked in below his high forehead and a chin sprouting a bush of a beard comes over and shakes Faith by the hand, then turns to him and introduces himself as William Stead. 'Welcome to what I call "Julia's Bureau"! This is where the spirits find ingress. If it's your first occasion, do not be anxious. The conduit between the living and the dead is a natural one. We are privileged this evening to be guided by the medium Mrs Etta Wriedt from America. She will conduct proceedings and make contact with the other side. You may hear voices or see phantasms. It may be the voice of a stranger or of a loved one. This is perfectly natural. I myself am hoping for communication with my dear son Willie. In any case, I hope your visit will be fruitful.' He ushers them to two chairs.

The attendees take their seats and wait in silence. A middle-aged woman appears from a door at the back of the room, as if she's been waiting in the wings. Etta Wriedt's greying hair is wiry; her face is pale despite the effect of the red light. She sits at the head of the table and picks up a slender silver trumpet. Faith murmurs to him: 'It's to magnify the whispers of the dead.'

Stead turns off the light. The darkness is total. Etta begins to speak with a distinct American drawl. 'If there's anyone here who has lost someone recently, please concentrate on him or her.' Silence ensues. He cannot see beyond his nose but the presence of other people is palpable. He has a disturbing thought that the company in the room may not be of the living.

A whispering distracts him. At first he thinks it is Faith and is on the point of telling her to be quiet; but the whispering grows louder and he hears a voice—similar to Etta's, but more distant and unearthly—saying the words: 'I have a message for my father.'

Silence.

William Stead says: 'W-Willie, is that you, my son?'

'Yes,' replies the first voice. 'I am whole now, Father. I am happy.'

Stead's grunt tails off into a squeak. Silence ensues before the voice continues to speak, describing what it is like to be on the other side: bodies do not exist; those who have passed over are like angels; they can make contact with the living, if the latter believe in them.

After a pause of a few minutes, there is further inaudible whispering, like the scratching of autumnal leaves; then the voice says, more audibly: 'Father, are you still there?'

'I am Willie, I am.'

'Be careful where you go. Be careful on journeys to far-away places.'

'I shall do that, Willie.'

'I feel your presence beside me. We shall be together again soon.'

'It is my fervent wish, Willie.'

'There is someone else I can see. Someone who is a stranger. I can see him. He is in a large room with lots of other people. His mother has white hair and a white dress. He will reject and be rejected...' The voice reverts to an inaudible whisper.

He pictures Bridie and her mass of red hair and feels suddenly safe, and tender and grateful towards her.

HE AND FAITH ARE walking home after the séance. Light is dawdling in the heavy trees and he is feeling peaceful. He does not know what to make of Etta Wriedt, or the proceedings. It all seems incredible, in one way; and yet... he believes, or does not *not* believe, in ghosts, angels, and even the banshee. Why would contact with the dead be so impossible? William Stead speaking with his son... It felt authentic in the darkness of the room. Why would anyone want to stage a fraudulent spectacle?

Oxford Street, early spring 1912. He and Faith see among the passing lines of shoppers a group of about thirty women uniformly dressed in long black skirts, white blouses and wide-brimmed black hats. They look like a gathering of governesses or superior nannies. Some are holding banners that declare, 'Votes For Women' and, 'Who Are the People?' and, 'Words Not Deeds'.

They approach the women and Faith makes herself known to the one who seems to be in charge. This tall erect woman has impassive eyes and a mouth that looks as if it's been cut into her face; she looks them up and down as if they are itinerants calling at her back door. She tells them they can join the group, but her tone is unwelcoming.

It is exactly what he feared when Faith suggested they join this suffragette protest. She had won him over by saying it was in the great tradition of the Quakers to champion the weak and oppressed, and also, he would make his father proud. He had also remembered Mary Coleville's words about the rights of women as well as the example of Alice Perry: if someone as intelligent as Alice was being prevented from voting in a general election simply through being a woman, then something was seriously wrong. *Change the world, before it changes you.*

The suffragettes start walking around in a tight circle, chanting 'Votes For Women', and he is taken aback to see Faith adding her voice to the chorus. He wants to show his solidarity... and yet he's conscious of the querulous glances of passers-by, some of whom are forced to walk in the road.

The organiser then leads her group across the road to the top of Regent's Street. Two of the women are pushing prams. He and Faith follow at the rear. Farther down the elegant curve of Regent Street he can see a clump of dark-blue figures and wonders if they are policemen.

The suffragettes halt outside the grand façade of Liberty's department store and gather around the prams, reaching in as if to adjust blankets around their babies. Instead they pull out stones and bricks.

He is transfixed. Faith looks at him as if to say: 'Surely not?'
The window glass is huge and pristine, like frozen air—even to
touch it seems a sacrilege. Uttering a war-cry, one of the
women throws a stone that creates only a neat spider's web in
the glass; another hurls a brick at point-blank range and it goes
straight through the window accompanied by an eruption of
cheers. The ice is broken: more missiles turn the glass into a
shock of savage angles; pedestrians run from the scene.

He is aware of shouts farther down the street and sees the
dark-blue blur gaining clarity. The women are too intent on
destruction to heed the police until they are among them,
batons raised. A terrible farmyard shrieking. He sees a
policeman punch a woman in the stomach and feels as if the
breath has been knocked out of his own lungs. He doesn't
know where to look, what to do. He swivels round and right in
front of him another policeman is locking his arm around a
woman's neck with such power it looks as though it must snap
off. Before he can react, he sees Faith dashing over to help her
and beat at the policeman's arm. Another officer tries to
manhandle Faith to the ground, and her scream jerks him into
running at the policeman. He grabs the man's powerful
forearms and with a huge jerk prises them away from Faith,
who tumbles to the ground; as he glances to make sure Faith is
alright he is caught off guard as the policeman turns and
throws a right hook at him; he can still see the fist moving
slowly towards his face. He hears Faith shouting terrible
imprecations. He feels her trying to yank him up from the
pavement; he gets to his feet and the two of them stagger-run
towards Oxford Street. He stops for a moment, looks back and
sees policemen leading handcuffed women away; the sunny
pavement is glittering unnaturally; banners lie crumpled; and
there rises low deep wailing laden with a sadness he hasn't
heard since the keeners back home.

The darkness and anonymity of the Underground with its
labyrinth of tunnels make him feel safe.

They sit in the train, speech boarded up in their mouths.
He takes his handkerchief away from his nostrils and sees there

is no more fresh blood on it; for the entire journey he keeps touching the numb protuberance of his nose to check it is approximately the shape it should be.

BACK IN THE FLAT, Faith is too upset to say anything, and they go to their rooms. He picks up the first book he can find to distract himself and lies down on his bed. His face feels thickened and is throbbing. He opens the book and flicks his gaze at a page and stops when he comes to the words: 'A more manly and warlike age is commencing.' Warlike age! Yes, already started—and on Regent's Street. And who'd think it would be the women of London starting it! He glances at the cover: *The Joyful Wisdom* by Friedrich Nietzsche. He tries to pronounce the name to himself. A bit of 'joyful wisdom' might calm him down. Fragments of screams and jagged glass cut into his concentration. He riffles through the pages and keeps touching his face, almost savouring the swelling. On one page he spots the name of the Buddha, which makes him think of the Maitreya, then Annie Besant sitting in Langham's Hotel— seems like a lifetime ago! He forces himself to read: 'After Buddha was dead, people showed his shadow for centuries afterwards in a cave—an immense frightful shadow'—the image reminds him of looking into the dark cavernous interior of Liberty's. His eyes scamper through the next words: 'God is dead: but perhaps there will be caves for millenniums yet, in which people will show his shadow.' He reads this last sentence again. How can God be dead? God is unkillable. He wonders who this 'Nietzsche' is. Socialist? Russian? German? Perhaps he is right about the warlike age. The Boers! Ireland and India becoming more bellicose. But, *God* dead?

He turns the pages listlessly, finding the mere touch of smooth paper a hypnotic balm; a yawn ambushes him. Flashes of the demonstration become less frequent. He sees the word 'demon' and pauses to read the paragraph: 'What if a demon crept after you into your loneliest loneliness and said: "This life of yours—you must live it again and again, innumerable times;

65

and there will be nothing new in it; every pain, joy, thought and sigh, and all the smallest and greatest things, will come to you again, exactly as before, in the same sequence."' His heart beats faster. He marks the page with a scrap of paper and turns off the light. Life repeated innumerable times.

Cycles of history. Maitreya. Life repeating itself. He is not sure whether he feels enlarged by the idea, or frightened; the thought of repetition induces another huge yawn that stretches his face and makes it throb even more. The same suffragette demonstration would recur. Same prams with bricks in them. Same punch in his face. Himself lying in bed thinking these thoughts again, and then again and again. Arriving in Liverpool. Meeting Jiddu. Kissing Nora again, and again...

He and Faith are again walking to William Stead's home. A mild Wimbledon evening in late May, 1912. The trees of the common are in full leaf and rise like ships' masts from a level green sea.

Faith is dabbing her eyes and he is trying to keep up with her. It's strange seeing her vulnerable. He wonders whether his father would ever have cried in the same meagre way.

He remembers how, a few weeks before, Faith had come home from work and slapped a newspaper on the kitchen table in front of him. He read the headline, 'The *Titanic* Sunk', and thought it must be a newspaper prank: the ship not even God could sink. He'd read the succession of stark phrases: 'Loss feared of over 1,500 lives. Iceberg struck. A wireless call for aid. Liners to the rescue. Ship goes down in four hours. Passengers and crew take to boats.' Faith took the paper from him, turned the pages to the passenger list and pressed her finger on a name: 'Stead, William.' Her face became a tragic mask. 'He was on his way to a peace conference. With the president of America. His son warned him, do you remember? At the séance. His son, Willie, warned him. I want to go back to his house, to a meeting. I want to know where he is.' He then remembered Stead's short story in the *Pall Mall Gazette* about a ship sinking and people drowning. Perhaps he had foreseen his future?

As they approach the front door Faith stops: 'What am I doing? I hardly knew the man. But... dying alone in that cold dark sea. I want to know he is in *a better place*.' He looks at the door as if it is holding back the Atlantic Ocean; he feels the sickening tilt of the ship's gigantic steel frame; the lights going out; silence; isolated shouts. There's darkness and a cold wind and the huge crashing of waves against the hull, as if the vessel were being rammed by whales. He is running to an exit, any exit, to get out.

The front door opens and pours out calm and soft colours.

A maid conducts them to Julia's Bureau, where the curtains are already drawn and an electric light reveals the presence of ten other people around the table. The new convener of the spiritualists, a distinguished gentleman wearing a black suit and matching tie, takes out a silver watch from his top pocket, studies it like a map, then turns to Etta Wriedt, who is again sitting at the head of the table, composed and serious.

The light is turned off. The Lord's Prayer is recited. After minutes of silence, he hears Etta whispering, as if to the spirits of the dead. Suddenly a globe of a light appears over the cabinet and within the light, to his astonishment, there is an image of a face resembling Stead's.

One person says, 'Dear God, it's Stead! Is that you Stead?'

An unbearable tension before a deep gravelly voice replies: 'It's wonderful to be with you all.'

There is a collective murmur in response and the sound of someone blowing their nose. He can't believe it's Stead speaking... and yet. He tries to remember Stead's actual voice; certainly this voice is similar; but is it the same?

No one speaks. The light over the cabinet goes out, the face disappears and they are plunged back into darkness. There is an uneasy silence, then the mysterious 'Stead' voice begins to relate what happened on the *Titanic*: he had a premonition of the disaster while the boat was docked at Cherbourg. Later on in the voyage, when the vessel was actually sinking, he jumped into the sea and soon went under; he passed over into another dimension and saw hundreds of people who had just died, unable to comprehend the next stage of their existence. They were wandering around, begging to be shown the light.

The voice stops talking; more whispers and the sound of objects moving on the table. He is trying to make sense of everything. Is Etta putting on a conjuring trick? He can hear Faith sniffing; he thinks he can smell roses—is that the scent of the afterlife?

Etta announces the séance is about to end. He braces himself for the light. When it comes on he sees Faith's eyes are pink and puffy.

They get up, scatter their goodbyes, and make their way to the door.

Outside they wait for a moment to orientate themselves and breathe in the early summer air. The door opens to let another spiritualist leave. He knows immediately who the man is, but can't remember where he has seen him before. Floppy brown hair, a pince-nez. The man notices him and looks puzzled, as if he were trying to recall him too. Before he can say anything, the man says: 'Tulira. Edward's pile. The carpenter boy. Sitting in a pool of light on the grass. And a boy no longer by the look of you.'

Of course, it is the man he talked to on the lawn all those years ago. 'Patrick Bowley. I was working with my father, Joe. You saw the dream of the centaur.'

'Indeed I did—well remembered! And who is your companion?'

'This is my aunt, Faith Bowley.'

'A Galway girl I'd say, and far too young to be your aunt.'

Faith's face refuses to soften.

The man turns to her directly: 'What did you think of our American cousin, Etta Wriedt?'

'I found the meeting very moving. I knew William Stead a little.'

'Did you? A fine man, fine man. But in a better place, and wasn't it a great thing to hear his voice from the other side? You never know who's going to contact you from the spirit world. The other day I was here and was contacted from the other side by the spirit of a long-dead Arabian poet, Leo Africanus! Some people think it all nonsense... all to do with what Mr Freud would call our subliminal consciousness, whatever that creature may be. But I believe it's authentic. What do you think Patrick?'

'I'm not sure what to believe. I did wonder whether I was hearing Mr Stead.'

'Indeed... is that so?' The tone of the man's reply betrays the fact his mind has been taken over by a thought; he looks over their shoulders as if seeing someone in the distance. 'The world is a lot stranger than we think. There are great forces at work behind our daily lives and we can discern them by the stars or palm reading or a hundred other ways. We live in a divinely ordered pattern. One thing leads to another; there is nothing haphazard.' The man comes out of his momentary reverie, which requires no response, and holds out his hand and shakes theirs in turn. 'It's been a pleasure to meet two fellow souls from our emerald home, and please God, a home that will soon be ruled by ourselves, as long as Asquith holds his nerve. Farewell and I hope our paths cross again.'

THAT NIGHT HE IS lying in bed, trying to stop his brain from tilting from one side to another like a ship's deck; he reaches for the book he is reading, *Buddhism* by T. W. Rhys Davids. After a page his eyes lose the thread and return to inner space. William Stead. Aunt Faith. Asquith. Ireland. A strange sadness creeps up on him. He admits to himself that the suffragette fracas feels like a turning point, as if the punch in the face has affected his spiritual vision. His eyes that saw only good things in London have been refocused: loutish commuters spitting on trains, child prostitutes gathering with their handlers around stations, slummy houses, drunks and beggars, and the inherited disdain in the faces of the noble-born and wealthy. He has been daydreaming more about Galway and the great sweep of its bay, the reek of salt in the air, the fishing boats in the Claddagh. More about his father and mother. He wants to talk to Jiddu Krishnamurti again. His enquiries through Faith via Hugh have been in vain. Jiddu always seems to be on the road in different parts of the country and abroad. Stead's death and the séance are adding another layer of confusion. A person embarks on a ship to go to a peace conference and the vessel hits an iceberg. What's God's purpose in that? What is the nature of the afterlife? Can the communication between the dead and living be as straightforward as séances make it seem? He turns back to *Buddhism*. He reads how everyone has been shaped by previous lives; foolish to hanker after heavenly bliss; just being alive brings sufficient pain, brought on by craving things, whether riches or the desire for life after death. He is consoled by this. It's not just the poor who suffer.

He reads on into the night, absorbing little; yet he keeps going because every time he stops he can hear the muffled screams of people drowning in the Atlantic.

The Northern Line Underground train is almost empty because it is Sunday. While Faith reads over scribbled directions to the house of a certain Mr William Rothenstein, he himself stares into the window opposite and watches his dark twin. He thinks of the Buddha sitting under the Bo Tree about to enter nirvana. What is the opposite of nirvana?—probably a poetry reading by a famous Indian poet. It was all Faith's doing. Hugh Chaigneau had persuaded her that it would be a unique occasion, educational, uplifting.

All he can think about is a room of highly bred and over-educated Englishmen. He leans back and notices that the curve of his mouth is the exact opposite of the Buddha's serene smile.

HAMPSTEAD TURNS OUT TO be as grand as Wimbledon, but more compact. Tall houses and high-walled front gardens with pale climbing roses peeping over the top.

It is late afternoon by the time they reach the house, but the deep-grey sky englows the world and makes it seem more like an evening engagement.

They enter a large hallway flecked with chandelier light and proceed to a reception room humming with the murmur of thirty or so guests. A tall man with a face whose features look squashed up between the weight of his thick greying hair and the size of his jutting chin waves at Faith and joins them. The man is wearing a maroon bow tie with white polka dots and Faith introduces him: it is none other than Hugh himself. As they shake hands he notices how Hugh's eyes pass over him discreetly. What conclusion has he come to? Suit not quite dark enough? Shoes a little scuffed? He draws himself up to his full height and is comforted that his eye level is measurably above Hugh's.

'Well,' Hugh says, as if about to summarise a meeting, 'it's a pleasure to meet the nephew of my wonderful secretary. I can see they breed fine men in Galway.'

Faith blushes at Hugh's throwaway pleasantries. He himself sets a facial expression to show he is unaffected by charm. Hugh continues: 'I hope you'll find this evening to your liking. Rabindranath Tagore is rather unusual I'm told. A poet of the soul, of God, of love—the Indians are rather good at that sort of thing. Do you take an interest in poetry, Patrick?'

Caught on the hop, and without knowing why, he blurts out the end of the poem that was read to him at Tulira Castle: 'Our souls are love and a continual farewell.' Hugh looks at him with barely concealed surprise, perhaps even respect? Then, feeling a tug on his sleeve, Hugh turns round and reveals a young woman standing behind him. 'Oh, there you are Agnes. Faith you know, of course, and this handsome young chap is Patrick, her nephew. Patrick, this is my daughter. I am not sure whether an Indian poet will be a young lady's *tasse de thé*, but we shall see.'

He dislikes Hugh's tone of voice. Thinking of Alice Perry, he says: 'I do not know what a tass de tay is, but I'm sure a young lady has as much chance of appreciating Indian poetry as the likes of myself, or indeed yourself.'

'Touché! Well spoken, sir. Serves me right, serves me right.' Hugh scrunches his face into a mock-embarrassed smile and turns to Faith, leaving him to engage Agnes in conversation.

Agnes is blushing at his petty gallantry and he is struck by how pretty she is. Her clothes are so different from his aunt's. Her body is slender and shapely, draped in a long pale blue cotton dress with a loosely tied turquoise scarf hanging down from her neck. Hazel-green eyes full of confidence; a delicate smear of eye-shadow. She must be in her early twenties. She, in turn, he tries to reassure himself, is looking at him as if she is half-believing her father's compliment about him.

'Thank you for your faith in my powers of literary appreciation.'

'I'd say they'd be greater than mine. The only poems I know are ones my father used to read out to us—Tennyson, Kipling and an Irish fella called Thomas Moore: "'Tis the last rose of summer, left blooming alone; all her lovely companions are faded and gone".'

'That's a sad poem!'

'We're a race of sad people. In love with the melancholy.'

'Well, it's better than being in love with power and conquering the world.'

'Don't let your father hear you say that!'

'He's the *first* to say it. Theosophists are against empire, wars, fighting, power.'

'We need a few of them in Ireland, I'd say.'

He continues the conversation, asking Agnes about herself, and she responds uninhibitedly about living in Wimbledon; how her mother died from illness when she herself was ten years of age; how her life now revolves around learning French and playing the cello. As she speaks, he stares at the way her lips form each word. He wonders what it would be like to kiss those lips and finds he hasn't listened to the last thing she has said. At first he thinks she hasn't noticed, but then she smiles. Her eyes dilate, as if to say 'a penny for your thoughts', and he says he was just thinking how pretty her scarf is.

'And how, may I ask, do you earn your living?'

The moment he's been dreading. He tells her he's a joiner and cabinetmaker, hoping that sounds more sophisticated than a woodworker or carpenter. She probes him—what sorts of things does he make. He tells her the truth: 'I make doors and windows, bookcases, wardrobes. Sometimes I paint walls and ceilings. At the moment I'm making a coffin for a woman in Southfields. She wants it to fit her exactly. She wants the lid to have her initials inlaid. She intends to display it at dinner engagements before she dies. She will festoon it, she says, with books and plants and all the things she plans to take to the other world.'

'How *old* is this woman?'

'About thirty.'

Agnes sounds as if she's swallowed her drink the wrong way. She places her hand quickly and lightly on his arm. 'You're very amusing.'

This small moment of intimacy is cut short by a spoon being tapped insistently against a crystal glass. The talking drains away and at the end of the room a man whom he assumes to be William Rothenstein raises his hands with his curved palms facing his guests; his large tanned shiny forehead is framed on either side by neat patches of hair clinging to his temples like brown moss; two lines of dark eyebrows give definition to the delicate rims of his round glasses. His soft voice informs the room what an honour it is to have Rabindranath Tagore in his home and that his poems will be read in English by an Irish friend of the poet's—at the mention of which there are knowing chuckles in the audience.

Tagore steps forward. His beard, tied-back hair and robe are all the more white for being set against his skin. He speaks in English, declaring what a privilege it is to be among friends and writers. He thanks, in particular, William Butler Yeats, for helping him with the translation of his poems and for agreeing to read them. More applause. A figure dressed in a white linen suit steps out from among the guests. He has dark floppy hair and a pince-nez. Faith turns round, catches his eyes and whispers from the side of her mouth, 'Isn't that the man we met at Stead's, after the séance?' He nods. He is amazed to see the man again so soon. Amazed that he is the poet, William Butler Yeats. Now it all makes sense—Tulira Castle, reading the poem to him, talking about poetic things—the dream of the centaur and the naked woman.

All eyes are fixed on Yeats, who waits until there is absolute silence, staring in the direction of anyone who has the temerity to whisper or cough or laugh. 'These poems, which I am honoured to read this evening, will not lie in small handsome books only to be referred to at idle moments, or be carried by university students only to be forgotten when they join the world beyond the academy. Travellers will hum them on the highway. Men will sing them while rowing upon rivers! Lovers will murmur them! These poems are full of images of the heart turning to God.' Sweeping back his hair with a flourish of his hand, Yeats begins to read from a small dark book.

He remembers the way he recited the poem at Tulira—a

cross between speaking and chanting—and his foot taps to the rhythm. He looks at Faith, who is rapt. Agnes is shifting beguilingly from foot to foot. He fights off his desire for Agnes and listens to the words as carefully as he can. One poem has the lines: 'Whom do you worship in this lonely temple with all the doors shut? Open your eyes and see your God is nowhere to be seen.' He finds this shocking—the idea that God is not to be discovered in a temple. What is the point of a sacred building if not for getting closer to God? His thoughts flicker briefly to the idea of God being dead, then turn back to Agnes, who has folded her arms and is tilting her head to one side so that her short-cut wiry brown hair almost touches her right shoulder. He remembers where he has seen that style of hair before: at the suffragette demonstration. Agnes is probably one of them. He imagines her shouting in the street, full of anger. He imagines her casting a brick into a window and her face lighting up with passion. 'God is where the ploughman is ploughing the stony ground and where the path maker is breaking up stones. He is with them in sun and rain, and his clothes are covered in dust. Take off your holy gown and join him on the dusty soil.' Yeats pauses to let the words take maximum effect, then declaims: 'Seeking her I have come to your door, my Lord... Dip my empty life into that ocean... let me feel the sweet touch I lost.'

The rhythmic chanting of the verse and the lofty sentiments flow through him, and this time they lift him into another sphere of consciousness: nothing seems to matter anymore; London, Galway, his parents—all his worries evaporate and leave a residue of happiness. He looks over at Agnes who, as if sensing his gaze, turns to meet his eyes. He bathes in her glance. He is in love with her.

The evening ends abruptly. Yeats stops his recitation to sharp, intense clapping. He and Tagore interlink arms and bow together and Rothenstein shakes their hands.

Guests drift away. Hugh and Agnes come over to say goodbye and Faith takes the opportunity to invite Agnes to visit her home. He suspects that she would prefer to ask Hugh himself to pay a visit but for her fear that it might seem too presumptuous and inappropriate.

On the way home in the Underground, his euphoria is already being replaced by a desperate longing. He thinks of the Buddha's idea of suffering being caused by desire, and he curses it, and the Buddha.

He is at home in Faith's flat, listening to every soft footstep on the stairs. The kitchen door opens and Agnes enters, willowy in a plain white cotton dress; she is followed by the greyer presence of Faith.

He gets up and bows his head in a way he hopes is correct and pulls out a chair for her. It is the second time Agnes has visited at the invitation of Faith, partly encouraged by himself. The first brief occasion he was hardly able to look at her face; all he saw was her bonnet being undone, her gleaming hair springing up. He was aware of laughing too readily at her slightest light remark, while she was so composed, so un-Irish, yet full of frank opinions and ready to reveal her feelings; for example that her life was full of duties and expectations, and that her father was urging her to become a governess. He'd laughed at this—perhaps because he had imagined her playing the cello in orchestras in Paris and Berlin rather than scolding spoilt children.

She sits down and he finds himself staring at her chin. He is still unready to engage her eyes. He is scared that by looking into them he might divine her true thoughts, or she might divine his.

The conversation turns from another re-living of the Tagore poetry event to William Yeats, then to Ireland.

Agnes says: 'My father's family came from Cork. The Chaigneaux were wine merchants. Huguenots, I believe. Quite a few of them in Cork, my father says.'

'Cork? I never knew that,' says Faith. 'Hugh's mentioned his Irish ancestry alright, but not Cork.'

'He has a deep sympathy with the Irish people—he thinks John Redmond is the new Parnell and hopes the Home Rule party will spread a spirit of moderation throughout the country.' Agnes pauses, as if she has one more thing to say on the matter. 'I would love to go Ireland.'

'You'd be in for a shock,' he says. 'Let's say you'd be walking a long way in Galway before you'd find a cello teacher... or gardens with roses.'

'There are other things in life apart from the cello.' Her

words have a neutral tone, but he takes them as mild rebuke, as if she were refuting an accusation that she would be happy only in a world of high culture. He takes the opportunity to move the conversation on: 'Does your father know the theosophists' new world teacher?' He cannot resist a smile as he matches the words 'world teacher' with his memory of shy, polite Jiddu.

'The Maitreya? Young Jiddu Krishnamurti? Of course he does. He is going to take me to one of Jiddu's talks. Father thinks he is going to change the world.' Her enthusiasm for this induces an unexpected pang of jealousy.

'We've actually met him,' he says, becoming aware it sounds like a boast. 'Just for a few minutes. In a hotel after Mrs Besant's talk at the Queen's Hall. I'd like to meet him again.'

'I'm sure that would be possible,' says Agnes. 'My father sees him all the time. Perhaps we could all go to a talk together.' She looks at him and Faith as she says this, but he is sure, the way her eyes linger on his for a fraction more than they need to, that she has just him in mind.

He wants to ask her personal questions, but the presence of his aunt deters him. Faith is at her politest, generations of Quaker modesty and decorum in every twitch of her lips and movement of her fingers as she sips her tea soundlessly. He listens patiently while Agnes tells them how her father works too hard and ought to remarry. He sees Faith blushing at this sentiment and hopes Agnes hasn't noticed. She also describes her father as St Jude, the 'patron saint of lost causes'—India, Ireland, and perhaps the suffragettes. Faith interrupts her and starts describing the protest in Regent's Street—the bricks, the police, the mayhem.

Without saying anything in response, Agnes mysteriously opens her handbag. As she bends her head to look inside it, he takes the chance to admire the way her hair keeps its springiness. She pulls out a piece of paper and gives to him to look at. It's a petition in support of Gladys Evans and Mary Leigh. He half-remembers those names—English suffragettes protesting in Ireland a few weeks' ago? Agnes explains how they had been arrested and sentenced to five years of penal servitude. He looks at the signatories and sees 'Agnes Chaigneau'; he savours each spiky letter before taking a pen and adding his name below hers, pretending it is a marriage certificate. He passes the petition to Faith and looks up and sees Agnes gazing at him; he can almost read her thoughts.

He says: 'They were brave, those suffragettes in Regent Street. I confess I was shaky for a good while after it.'

'You were there, too?' Agnes looks at him, then Faith.

'I was.'

'You were *there*, supporting those women?'

'Well, I did little enough, and I had a policeman punching me in the face for my trouble.' He expects either Agnes or Faith to give a little laugh. But he sees Agnes staring at him as if she's seen a fire flare up in a grate.

'I can't think of any man among my family or acquaintances who would have done that—who would have stood with those women.'

'Maybe we Irish have a fondness for the oppressed.'

'Perhaps you do. But even my father wouldn't have gone that far. I admire you Patrick Bowley. You must be brave; and kind-hearted.' Her face looks hot and there's moisture on her slightly parted lips. He doesn't disabuse her of his minimal participation in the demonstration, and Faith says nothing.

THIS TIME, WHEN AGNES makes a move to leave, she accepts his offer to escort her home. He hopes that being released from Faith's presence their conversation will spring into a new intimacy; especially now that she is impressed by his support for the suffragettes. But their coordinated footsteps across the common elicit exchanges that remain on the surface. He wants to tell her things that have been lodged in his soul for years, but he is oppressed by the thought she'll find him dull or below her dignity. Yet she seems fascinated by the strangest things: the lay-out of his parents' home, what Irish women wear, whether he has heard the banshee. Is she being polite? Or is he just some link between her and her Irish ancestors?

They arrive outside her parental home, a four-storeyed terraced house that extends below pavement level. Two white columns guard the steps leading to a black door with a golden knocker and letter box. He shakes her hand and in their farewell mutterings they agree to see each other again. She has climbed two steps and turned round, and their eyes are at the same level; he wants to pull her towards him and kiss her. He is mesmerised by an unexpected dart of her dimples as she smiles without parting her lips. A kiss would be such an easy and simple action, so eminently possible, yet impossible.

AGNES'S NEXT VISIT IS following the same pattern as the previous ones; tea in the kitchen, Faith talking endlessly about publishing, Hugh, theosophy and books she has read, while he tries to find deeper connections with Agnes. He tests the water by mentioning Bunyan being his father's favourite book, and she says, 'One day a book will be written with a woman as the pilgrim.' He and Faith laugh, and he watches the colour rising in Agnes's cheeks, not from embarrassment but anger; it is curious seeing her familiar face becoming another person's. 'We're not put on this earth simply to give birth to children and mop our husbands' brows.' He hastily concurs and she looks down at her hands. He notices her musician's slender fingers encased in white leather gloves; and her neck, exposed by her suffragette's hair, reminds him of the ballerinas in the Tulira painting. He is aware he is giving off profound desire; but he isn't experienced enough to know whether she feels the same. He looks for signs beneath her politeness; the plain fact of her accepting invitations to visit seems evidence enough of her liking him; but perhaps the draw is the company of Faith, and being in a milieu more easeful than the formality of her own home.

Again he escorts her home. Before they reach the citadel of her house, they stop and sit on a bench. From an easy relaxed silence the conversation begins to flow. They talk about God, the séances at Stead's house, and theosophy. He becomes confident enough to reveal how he communicated with Jiddu by thought. She accepts this as if he's been talking about how to make a tongue-and-groove joint.

An hour goes past and the sun is at the level of chimney pots. They keep on talking and the subject of love comes up; she shocks him by saying she thinks love and marriage bear no relation to each other; one is an unpredictable gift, the other something you do to rear children or have steady companionship. If both happen to coincide then so much the better. He senses that she senses the dismay in his reticence; she touches his arm and says: 'You're the first man I've been able to say things like this to. In fact the first person. I don't know whether it is because you're Irish, or a Quaker, or what it is. But I find it a strange and liberating feeling. It also scares me. You listen to me and respond to what I have to say. Nobody has done that before. Nor do you seem to judge people on manners and accent, or whether they are a man or a woman. It makes me appreciate how confined my world is.'

'Confined? You can play the cello, speak French, you can go to theosophical meetings... you can meet strange young men from Ireland.'

'But only with the blessing, permission, caveats, of my father! You've travelled here, by yourself, from Ireland; you can work anywhere in London, anywhere where there's work. You can earn money and deposit it in a bank. You can go out to the theatre by yourself. You can take an Underground train with impunity. My lot is to be reliant on the goodwill of men, whether I like them or not. Crossing Wimbledon Common by myself is about the limit of my adventure. Being a suffragette is not just a political affair. It's a way of life. A cry for freedom. Your support for those Regent Street women means... more to me than you can imagine.'

Their parting at her house seems more drawn out than before, each of them reluctant to let the other go.

The street lamps are taking on a deeper glow; it's still mild enough for him and Agnes to sit on a bench on the common. Her latest visit has gone well, again—except this time, during the walk home, she has been quiet, in a terse sort of way.

She is looking across the common in the direction of the trees and the lit windows of the houses.

To lift the silence, he says: ' "Our souls are love and a continual farewell." ' Mr Yeats wrote that.'

She doesn't respond, and the sweet melancholy of the verse and the yellowing trees around them deepens his introspection. He wants to turn the conversation to their feelings about each other, but doesn't know how to. He wants to say, 'I adore you'. But this might accelerate a process better left to its own slow, tortuous course. He assumes he has to take the lead in courtship, though she seems more mature in its ways. And if he does declare love... How could she countenance being with an Irish carpenter? Her father, for all his liberal opinions and Irish ancestry, will surely object. Or will he? He can sense that Agnes has a fascination for him. He is not sure why. A symbol of the freedom she lacks? Irishness? Perhaps just his workman's muscles? His attention is caught by someone drawing the curtains in a bay window opposite their bench. When he turns to look at Agnes she is pressing her temples with her fingers, as if she has a headache.

She meets his gaze, and her eyes are those of a stranger.

What has he said? What has he done? He wants to put his arms around her and ask her what the matter is. She looks as if she is going to cry. It breaks his resistance; he leans towards her and... kisses her on the cheek. He closes his eyes in horror. He opens them, fearing a look of disdain. But instead, her gloved hand touches his. He takes this as a sign of acceptance and kisses her again, this time on the lips; she does not respond in kind, but her smile is so fulsome it breaks into dimples and she does not move her face away. Now he is too far gone; he kisses her again on the lips, gently caressing them with his tongue and feeling them succumb. A delicate and unstoppable emotion moves from the tip of his tongue to his entire body. She has tears in her eyes. She says she wants to go home. It is clearly too much for her; his happiness is almost too much for him.

They walk across the common in silence. She has slipped her arm into his. The barrier has been broken. The practicalities will take care of themselves.

As they approach her house, Agnes stops and says: 'I'm sorry Patrick.' She looks down at the pavement. Her mouth barely moves: 'I've had the best afternoon imaginable; so lovely I couldn't say to you what I'd intended to say. It's very frightening for me to say it. I'm saying it now.' He waits for her to say, 'I love you'.

'I can't see you again.'

He lets out a loud laugh, as if she has uttered the punch line of a joke. He watches her face, waiting for her dimples to appear; but the frightful look in her eyes makes his blood run cold. He babbles words at her, anything to fill the gap.

She interrupts: 'It's precisely because I'm growing fond of you. More than fond, much much more, and that's the problem. You're different to any man I've ever met. I feel... I can be myself with you—not an actress, not a hostess, not a daughter, or... prospective wife, governess, or... mistress. I can't explain here and now. It's all too complicated. There are some things beyond our control. I'll write to you.'

She begins to walk, her body and her neck rigid with purpose, and he keeps in step, pestering her with questions.

They stop just before her house and he guides her into a shadowy spot beneath a tree; each waits for the other to say or do something. He leans forward and kisses her again on the lips. To his relief she doesn't jerk her head back. He puts his arms around her waist and repeats the kiss and this time their lips linger and savour the other's softness. He smells her hair and her skin. He is sure the kiss has rectified her grotesque words; has somehow healed the pain she is in. She looks at him as if she were going to say something wonderful; but she breaks away and walks up the steps to the door.

Her back is like a hand shoved in his face.

He watches her disappear into the house and knows they are in love with each other, and love can conquer all. He cannot wait to receive her letter.

Faith is standing by the statue of Eros in Piccadilly, a stiff hand raised only as high as her shoulder, as if she's conducting the traffic. He crosses the road and she appraises his appearance, his well-worn suit and shoes, which he has polished up. She gives no indication as to whether he is smart enough, but he is encouraged by her lack of tutting.

They make their way to Soho, Rupert Street, and the tall grimy offices of a publishing house. A woman directs them to a first-floor room, from where a hubbub of voices bubbles down the stairs they are mounting. He braces himself for his first publishing party.

He knows Faith's insistence that he should come along is simply a ploy to disperse the gloom he's introduced into their flat. He knows she suspects it is all to do with Agnes, but he can't tell her anything more, because he doesn't know himself. It feels like months since he saw her, but it's only weeks, and no letter has arrived from her.

Faith told him Hugh would be at the party, and Agnes was invited too. He couldn't get the date out of his head. The days inched towards it, and the nights; again and again he would imagine entering a crowded room and seeing Agnes turn her head instinctively towards him; she is wearing a narrow black layered dress and looking embarrassed but pleased to see him. He takes his time to get to her side. He touches her hand and asks her how she is. She's hesitant at first. She says how much she's missed coming to visit him. She says she's been thinking about the kiss. They talk to each other for the duration of the party. Before he leaves, he beckons her outside the room and they find a quiet corner. They kiss again and this time she says, 'I don't know why I said what I said. I've fallen in love with you.' That's where the fantasy would usually end.

They enter the reception room and a young woman holding a tray of drinks comes over. He takes a glass with fruit in it, letting Faith advance into the room. It tastes so delicious he drinks it in one gulp, only at the end realising it is alcoholic. An oozy warmth percolates his veins. He surveys the room and sees Hugh standing there, sporting a dark-blue bow tie and an easy smile. He is whispering something into Faith's ear and she is permitting herself a restrained laugh. He glances around for Agnes. The room is full and he can't see her. Perhaps she hasn't come yet. The woman with the tray of drinks walks past and he swoops to pluck another glass. Again he drinks this in one go and reaches over to snatch his third before the waitress disappears; his inhibitions are ebbing.

Faith comes over. 'I'll introduce you to a few people.' He sees that Hugh is now standing with a younger man, clean cut and handsome in a grey suit, a red carnation sprouting from his lapel. Faith says his name is Dominic, an editor and Hugh's protégé. He looks across at the patrician Dominic and at the patrician Hugh, and his courage dribbles away. *Where's Agnes?* Faith pulls him by the sleeve and they join Hugh and Dominic, who shake hands and murmur pleasantries that make them sound as if they are softly gargling.

Hugh says, 'Patrick, I gather from your aunt that you've met the Maitreya? I expect that was a… bit of a surprise for you?'

He tries to stretch his lips into something approaching a smile while wondering whether he should ask Hugh where Agnes is. 'I liked Jiddu. He seemed a gentle soul, and wise; but young to be a world teacher.'

'He does seem young, doesn't he?' Hugh says. 'But I trust Mrs Besant. She's a good egg and knows her oats—if you'll excuse the mixed metaphor.' Dominic heaves his shoulders at his mentor's light remark.

He suddenly finds he cannot bear to look at Dominic full in the face and tries to focus on his dark hair with its sharp side-parting sliced through it. He continues the conversation: 'Jiddu seemed a little lost to me. Lonely.'

'Yes, must be hard for him. And his brother. Still, what would their lives be like in India?' Dominic nods his head, as if he knows exactly what Hugh is talking about. 'The Order of the Star hasn't been going long. An interesting set-up. You could come along to a meeting.' Hugh nods vigorously at his own amiable gesture.

'I'd be interested to hear Jiddu speak, alright.' What he is really thinking is, 'I'd love to go to see Jiddu *with Agnes*'. He looks at Hugh's face and sees Agnes's expression in the eyebrows, which curve down towards the bridge of the nose, giving the slightest air of mischief.

Hugh responds with an eye-creasing smile: 'That should be possible. For a world teacher he really is very accessible.' Dominic smirks at this remark for no apparent reason. There is a pause before Hugh turns to Faith: 'A shame Agnes couldn't come this evening. I *did* tell her that you and Patrick would be here.'

The quiet words are heavy blows to his stomach.

'I'm afraid I'm a pretty poor stand-in,' says Dominic, 'for the prettiest young woman in London.'

'You flatterer,' says Hugh. 'But I suppose you should be excused.'

He and Faith wait for Hugh to enlarge upon his comment.

'Dominic's in top form at the moment. Just got engaged.'

'Congratulations,' he hears Faith say. 'Who's the fortunate lady?'

Dominic's face turns to joy: 'Agnes.'

He looks over Dominic's shoulder and sees a blur of what should be faces. A wave of something washes up from his stomach and replaces the heavy mechanism of his thoughts with a strange lightness. It must be what people feel before they faint. Someone asks him something, then Faith murmurs: 'You all right Patrick?' He hears himself say something like, 'Bit hot. Might stand by the door.' He walks away and wants to shout or cry his eyes out. His Agnes with that Englishman. Weeks of self-pity roll into his loneliness and homesickness and form a lump in his throat. He stands at the open door and grabs another passing drink. He wants to go home. He wants to be sick.

'Patrick are you all right?' He turns and sees Faith. 'It's Agnes isn't it? Her and Dominic. I didn't know you were *that* gone on her. Whatever did you expect?'

'I should go home and leave you to it.'

'Don't be ridiculous. We'll talk about this later. I know what thwarted love feels like.' She sounds angry, and for a second he looks at his aunt in a new light. 'There's an Irish writer over there—Hugh's just introduced me to him. Says he has Galway roots and perked up when I said you were here. Come and meet him.' He shakes his head. He thinks he's doing well just standing upright. 'You've got to get back on that horse. The only thing. It'll distract you.' He doesn't move. 'Come on, this man seems shy. He needs cheering up.'

Faith tugs at his arm and his resistance crumples. His feet are reluctant to obey his will, but she leads him like a schoolboy to the Irishman, who is standing in a small group. Faith taps him on the arm. He is neat, almost wiry, with a beaky nose and glasses and trimmed moustache. His hair is flat, gleaming, combed back. 'Ah, the Galwegian I was promised,' the writer says without smiling and fidgeting with his glass.

He mumbles 'how do you do' and pushes down the surge of misery.

The writer looks at him like a kestrel about to land on some small creature, eyes narrowing as if he's trying to think his way into his mind. Then he swivels his head between Faith and himself and says: 'My kin are from Galway, and I was schooled in the Pale, but my joy—and evidently yours—is to leave the old country behind and rejoice!'

'Do you live here?' He manages not to slur his words.

'London? No, no. Not a bit of it. And not in Hibernia either. We're off to Trieste, from joy to tristesse perhaps, but we'll take our chances. Better to write in exile than twiddle one's thumbs in the cesspit of home.'

The man stares at his glass as if something has dropped in it. After a pause, Faith says: 'What sort of writing do you write?'

'If only I knew what sort!' A wry smile evaporates beneath his moustache. 'Then I wouldn't be perplexing good publication houses such as this one. Mr Boon has declined my volume of short stories; and who would blame him? Didn't like the reference to King Edward. But if you bow and scrape to royals where does it all end? By the bye, Home Rule won't make a jot of difference to our countrymen. There will be scrapers and bowers till the end of time. What sort of writing do I produce? You could say I write about the way people are. How we are all alone with our thoughts, and being aware of them, and *only* them, no matter how much the trivia of the world outside us impinges on our senses. Does that make sense? Or even a sentence? Loss, love. People living in Dublin, mostly. A man walking a dog on a beach, wondering whether a shell contains creation. A soul swooning as it hears the snow falling through the universe... like the descent of the end of time upon all the living and the dead.' The writer looks wistful then returns to his vigil, looking at his glass.

He says nothing in reply. The alcohol is simultaneously drying up his powers of speech and stoking up his sense of anger. He wants to punch the writer's beaky nose very hard and stuff a napkin in his mouth.

'Do you have family?' asks Faith.

'I have only one member here, and a fine one, nay, a fair one, at that.' The man turns to the woman next to him, who is talking to someone else, and prods her elbow.

As she turns around, he looks at her and sees a ghost.

Hairs rise on his nape as he hears the man say, 'This is my wife, Nora, from Galway city.'

She has hardly changed from when they kissed in the church. He stares at her, and she looks through him as if she has never seen him before. Her expression is made worse than blank by a slight downward curl of her lips. Faith launches into a chat with her, finding out where she lived, went to school, and quickly establishing people they know in common. He looks at Nora's feline, impervious face and wants to shout out, *You kissed me in the church*; instead, in one movement he turns and sways past a group of guests on his way to the door.

Faith finds him sitting on the top of the stairs. She touches his shoulder and makes two clucking sounds with her tongue. His convulsions relent and he wants to tell her about Nora; instead he tells her he is going home. Faith doesn't know how to respond, and he is down the stairs before she can protest. At the bottom he shouts up that he'll be fine, then he hits the autumn night.

Outside the offices he sinks to his knees. Drunkenness has numbed his body but is amplifying his desolation. He needs a lavatory. He walks off uncertainly, looking for somewhere to piss. A pub or alleyway. Everywhere is too bright or has too many people. The street he's on leads to another one, narrower, and there's an arched doorway with a dim red light; a big strapping woman standing at the entrance, sucking on a cigarette. He looks at her and says he wants a lavatory and she pulls him by the hand up the stairs. He is repeating that he wants a lavatory and she is saying, 'Of course you do, love, of course you do,' and is pulling him into a small room with curtains with black marks on them, as if people have stubbed their cigarettes on them. The woman turns round and, shockingly, starts kissing him, but in a revolting way, her tongue all over his face, like a puppy grown too old; she starts pulling off his clothes. He pushes her away, but she is strong and his limbs feel limp and drunkenly disconnected; when he slaps her fingers away from his shirt buttons they move to his trousers, and she is coughing all the time, saying 'Deary me, deary me, we'll soon make a man of you,' and then she has pushed him back on the bed—he's feeling faint and nauseous and is not sure whether she really is stronger than him or he's too drunk to resist or whether he's enjoying her animal strength and determination; in any case she is now on top of him, pressing her breasts into his chest and into his face, he feels something soft touch his genitals and her fingers stroking him, he shuts his eyes and pictures a naked woman touching him and arousing him; he pictures Agnes—he can see her hair springing up and down in a rocking movement—she didn't go to the party; she waited for him to leave and followed him to this place; he is now fully aroused and is calling out to her and hears in response the sound of quick breathing; he opens his eyes and sees the woman grimacing at him; she shifts her weight and there's a pain in his genitals; he wants to picture

91

Agnes again, but it feels like a sin in this smoky rancid attic; he is on the verge of letting go of something; he shuts his eyes and Agnes appears to him, an ecstasy on her face; a creeping sensation of pleasure and agitation works its way up, he is either going to piss or ejaculate and he doesn't know which; he opens his eyes and tries to push the woman off, but she keeps rocking on him faster and faster, her stale breath flowing over him; a sensation catches inside him and moves up agonisingly to his neck, then brain, then everything collapses inside and he lets out a cry; the woman eases herself off with a cackle, then she shouts, 'You dirty fuckin' pig, you've pissed on me fuckin' bed, you pig'. She drags him onto the floor and he is dimly aware of her going through his clothes before throwing them on top of him. Water hits his face and he sits up. 'You can fuckin' get out of here or I'll set the boys on you.'

He puts on his shirt, pulls up trousers, grabs his coat and hat and staggers down the stairs into the street. He puts his hand in his trouser pocket and touches his door key but realises his wallet has been taken. He knows he is going to vomit. He needs water. He looks around. A golden window-glow of a pub opposite. He walks over, leans against the pub door and lets his weight carry him in. The bar is half full. He sees a door at the end with a sign that says 'Gentlemen'. He makes his way through clumps of men in coats and hats holding glasses of beer and cigarettes. He reaches the lavatory, opens the door of a cubicle, kneels on the floor and vomits. He wipes his mouth and re-enters the noise and yellow light of the bar. As he moves towards the door he hears a voice from behind the bar shout out, 'If you want a piss you can bloody well buy a pint first.' He turns towards the voice and sees the barman looking at him. Other pairs of eyes, not friendly, are sizing him up. He raises his fist at the barman—if he were sober and back in Galway he would have said something like, 'What kind of pub is it that you can't have a piss without buying a drink?' But his mind is befuddled and all he can shout out is: 'Ye can go to the devil!'

He leaves the pub and feels the reviving air wash around his face. He stands against the wall, trying to work out where the

Underground station is. He is barely aware of the pub door opening and two men standing either side of him. 'Leave yer manners on the boat, did ya Mick?' He sees a thick-set man taking off his hat to reveal an almost bald head. 'I reckon we should teach this chappy a few manners. Maybe he's one of them Irish rebels who thinks our king ain't good enough for him.' He looks at the man's companion, who is large, wearing a mackintosh, his face in shadow. 'Definitely,' the companion says: before he can react, a fist flies into his right eye. He slumps to the pavement, his hand covering his eye socket. The two men take it in turn to kick him, aiming for his face and genitals. He tries to roll over but the blows keep jabbing him, shocking him. Eventually they stop, but the pain has spread throughout his body. He can hear them getting back their breath. A warm liquid splashes on his face accompanied by a filthy chuckle. The smell of piss makes him want to retch again. His mind wants to get up, but his body refuses to budge. He hears footsteps go past him. He thanks God that all the drink he's taken is numbing the pain.

The sound of more footsteps. Someone has stopped beside him. Someone is looking at him. 'Good Lord. What happened to you?'

He wants to turn over and look up in the direction of the voice but can't. Every slightest movement feels like a punch. Hands are gently tugging at him. He sees a face against the sky.

'My God. You're Faith's nephew. What the hell happened?'

Hands are lifting up his torso and placing him against the wall. The man is crouching down next to him, his face too silhouetted to be recognised.

'It's Dominic. We met at the party. I'm the one who works for Hugh. I'm getting you a taxi cab. If it takes you home, can you get yourself into your house?' He grunts enough of a yes.

Eventually a taxi cab chugs its way up the street and Dominic steps out into the middle of the road; he opens the passenger door, and helps him in. He briefs the driver and gives him money.

HE MANAGES TO OPEN the door of the flat and get to the kitchen. Faith enters and looks at his face and makes a sound as if she's trodden on a nail.

She bathes his wounds with iodine and picks details out of him like pieces of glass. He is too pummelled to hold anything back; he expects sympathy, but after he tells her about the woman, as delicately as is possible in his beaten, drunken state, she tuts, sighs and leaves the room.

He thinks of Bridie, with her long hair and grubby fingernails and wishes she were putting her arm around his shoulders. He thinks of her watching the hearth fire while his father is out the back, sawing a plank with savage energy and whistling a tuneless tune. He wants to go home.

Euston Station. The concourse is crawling with men in dark overcoats; piles of bags are ready to be loaded onto trains. Faith is there with him, seeing him off.

Things were never the same between them after that evening; but there's still the warmth of familiarity, shared experiences and family ties beneath the formality. They embrace each other lightly, utter their last farewells, then Faith heads off to the Underground while he boards the train. His carriage is full. A couple of men and women, a child, an elderly man. He looks at them surreptitiously and feels a flow of tenderness. Now that he is leaving England there is a new-born sadness in him. He looks at their English faces and expressions and thinks about all the people he worked for. Decent folk. Even members of the governing class seem more appealing now that he is off to Liverpool. Rothenstein, Stead, Hugh.

The train jolts and shifts and picks up speed through rows of houses showing their grimy backs to him; he daydreams about his year in London. Wimbledon in the summer, the subterranean city of the Underground, Annie Besant's talk and Jiddu and Nitya, the séances, the poetry evening with Tagore, the books he read from Faith's miniature library. He thinks briefly of Nora, but his heart has at last given her up. He thinks of Agnes and pictures her at the altar with Dominic. He stops the thought there. All these people have moved away into their own lives and are forgetting him, even as he will surely forget them. He shuts his eyes and dozes.

LIVERPOOL IS LIKE AN old friend. The accent of the ticket collector reminds him of visits to Dublin, as do the great warehouses and docks. He boards the ship and stands on deck as it manoeuvres its way out of port and heads into the Irish Sea.

He goes inside and sits among families lit up with the prospect of returning home. After a few hours an almighty cheer erupts outside. He joins the passengers streaming onto deck to join those pointing at land. A man begins to sing:

'Oh Mary this London's a wonderful sight
With people here workin' by day and by night
They don't sow potatoes, nor barley, nor wheat
But there's gangs of them diggin' for gold in the street—
At least when I asked them that's what I was told
So I just took a hand at this diggin' for gold
But for all that I found there I might as well be
Where the Mountains of Mourne sweep down to the sea.'

HE SQUEEZES THROUGH TO the railings and sees Ireland heading towards him. He realises how attached he is to his country. London, huge great London, is becoming nothing more than a phantasm.

PART TWO

THE WORK

The countryside is stretching away beyond the train window. With the stillness of a horse at grass, he stares at lone farms and outhouses and green fields penned into oblongs and squares by low stone walls; at the desolation, and beauty, of open space.

At Galway station he circumnavigates the porters and piles of bags and lugs his case homeward.

'WOULD YA LOOK AT him! The London lad!' Bridie's ruddy features are upturned as if gravity has been reversed. She flings her arms around him and he remembers her familiar smell. Joe is standing behind her, waiting his turn for the handshake.

They sit beside the hearth, Bridie firing questions at him, too excited to hear the answers. He tells them only the things he knows they will want to hear, and realises how much he is having to leave out.

A MID-DECEMBER DAY. He is walking around the smoky streets, still reacquainting himself to the sight of corner boys, old women sitting on the ground next to puddles, and men with red bristly faces, pressing their backs into walls as if to hold them up. Everything looks sad; he can feel his recently infused spirit of change ebbing.

He reaches Salthill and finds relief in the limitless grey waves and sky, a colour that has long since leached into the city's crumbling buildings. Wimbledon feels like a mythic place; the house, the kitchen, Faith returning from work, his room with all the books in it; even the Underground seems cosy, people squashed together, each minding his own business, each with a destination.

CHRISTMAS DAY. BRIDIE IS opening a bottle of Jameson's and pouring out two glasses. It is the first alcohol he has tasted since the publishing party. He drinks his in one gulp, savouring the delicate fumes as they slip up his nostrils, and the tang and burn in his throat.

He wonders what Faith is doing. Perhaps invited to Hugh's house, sitting next to Agnes on a sofa in front of a fire and talking about him. He lets the thought go. Then it returns. He thinks of the Soho party and Dominic's clean-cut face and its permanent half-smile. Nora standing there like an apparition. He closes his eyes… and, too late, remembers the prostitute and the beating he received outside the pub; he involuntarily grimaces and lets out a groan.

HE IS IN HIS bedroom shed, kneeling on the ground and praying to God for help. His hopes that the first weeks of 1913 would bring some sort of optimism or spiritual direction in him have not materialised. Work remains thin on the ground. Joe prowls around the house giving out about the weather and anything else he can think of. Bridie goes out as much as she can, visiting her parents across the harbour in the Claddagh, going to markets, and singing and knitting through the dark evenings. He stays inside his freezing shed, spending most of the days lying in bed, drifting from thought to thought and listening to the incessant rain flung like a recrimination at his window. A depression, which for months has never been far away, is now upon him, and in him, like the seamless clouds that never shift from the sky. Little intense moments of anger have been flaring up about being marooned in Galway, which seems the smallest, grubbiest town on the island. Then anger subsides to self-pity and hours of blankness.

FOR DAYS, THEN WEEKS, the downward spiral has continued. He can hardly be bothered to go into the house to eat. He hates the thought that Joe and Bridie will be pretending not to appraise his mood. He needs to get out, go away, but lethargy overwhelms him. He feels like George Fox, with a heavy sack of sinfulness weighing him down. He tries to recall Annie

Besant telling him that Ireland needs a Maitreya, and he fantasises about Jiddu coming to speak in Galway. He needs someone to tell him what to do with his life. That is why he prays nightly, beside his bed, to God. He makes up different prayers, addressing God and Jesus, the Buddha, St Francis, and anyone else he can think of, as if they were in the room. He weeps in their presence; and as he does so, he sometimes feels a release, an easing of the sack-weight.

A COLD FEBRUARY NIGHT. He thinks he has awoken from sleep. His eyes are half open and he senses the presence of a glowing light, as if the moon were full and imitating the first light of dawn through the curtain. It is as if he is in the middle of a dream that has materialised around him. The air is freezing. He wants to go back to sleep but the light is insistent. He raises his head to look at it, to see where it is coming from. He sees it is emanating from his body. It's like wearing a pale luminous rainbow coat that starts at the bottom with a deep red all around his body, then rises into the other colours, ending with an ivory glow. His eyes become used to the light and he marvels at how the colours seep into each other seamlessly and change hue at the same time; the light is filling the room; he breathes gently, and with every breath he imbibes the light into his body and feels it changing him inside, as if his bones, vital organs and skin are becoming light. It moves up his spine, vertebra by vertebra, and blossoms in his head like a radiant many-petalled flower. He has a momentary panic, the thought he might be dying, but he keeps telling himself he is in his shed, in Galway, in Ireland, in February; the panic subsides and his thoughts evaporate one by one until he becomes senseless of time and space; he is aware only of his awareness that he is aware.

He feels a shift, as if he is back in his sleep and dreaming, but still full of the light. In the glowing darkness he sees an image emerge—it looks like a station platform, and a figure standing there, waiting for a train. It might be Galway or Euston. He knows immediately who it is, even though his face is in shadow. 'Jiddu, are you here? Have you arrived in Galway?' He can see Jiddu's slender form and his long shiny hair and well-tailored suit; there's mist or steam around him and people are moving past behind him. He doesn't want Jiddu to go away, and concentrates on his face. Jiddu says something, or, perhaps, thinks it: 'Patrick, you must leave your home and be utterly alone. If you can do that, you will be ready.' 'Ready for what?' 'That you must listen for. Only you will know what your path is.' 'But how will I know? And where are you now?' The Jiddu figure steps away, revealing a station name board behind him; it is blank. Jiddu walks off into the steam of the platform until he's a dark shape, then a pale grey shape folding into the air.

He wakes, properly, and sees his breath materialising in the cold. He can recall the visionary dream in all its visual detail, and more than that, he can feel something has changed inside him, but he isn't sure what it is. It's as if there is a joy in his heart, almost a physical sensation—as if his body has been filled with a glorious liquid.

It's not long after dawn. He gets up and goes for a walk. The weather is still cold and grey but he feels a connection with everything he encounters; the crows clustering around soot-smeared chimney pots, loosening their dirty cackles into the sky; the shine of the cobblestones from a slantwise blast of rain; a man who twitches his head by way of a greeting as they pass each other in St Augustine Street; the smell of rotting seaweed on the sands at Salthill. It is as if there is no self interfering between his perception of what he can see and the things themselves. No thoughts to bother him, to raise questions, to quibble. Just himself and the outside world, in its purity. And everything, he realises, is a manifestation of divine creation: the glittering particles of sand, the gathering and rupture of waves on the beach, the subtle layers of cloud almost allowing light to fall on distant Inishmore; a stray dog nosing around puddles in the road; the beggars outside the church—he feels a compassion for them that makes him want to cry for their condition. He empties his pockets of coins and hands them to deliriously surprised children.

He is stepping into an open boat, thirty feet long, in Ballinskelligs, Kerry. He is the only passenger. It's the spring of 1913 and the far west of Ireland is blessed with a pale windless day.

One of the ten oarsmen casts the rope away like ejecting a writhing snake. The peacefulness that infused him during his visionary dream has been diminishing for several weeks, and now he is anxious about the coming seven days. He believed the dream figure of Jiddu was right: he had to go to a remote barren place, as the Desert Fathers did, to test himself and try to find some sense of meaning or vocation in the great silence of nature. Where better than Skellig Michael—a great spiky pyramid of rock rearing up from the ocean? If the Irish monks who lived there a thousand years ago survived on next to nothing, he will surely manage seven days. He will listen to the silence and hear what it has to say to him.

THE BOATMEN, SLEEVES ROLLED up, caps pulled down, strike up a rhythm with their oars and overcome the resistance of the sea. They pass Bolus Head and collide with the Atlantic swell. The waves that now materialise are shrinking the boat; he feels sick, mainly from the see-saw motion, but also because there is no going back. *It's just for seven days.* He steadies himself, focusing on Skellig's needle-like summit.

The boat is manoeuvred to a jetty on the northeast side and the skipper shakes him by the hand. 'We'll be back the eighth day from today, this time of the morning. Weather permitting and God willing. And don't be disturbing the lighthouse keeper. He lives on Valentia Island, but he comes here to make sure all's in working order and we don't want him prating when his business is to save lives. Skellig has two peaks, and between them there's a lump of flat ground, like a saddle. The northern peak would be the lower one, where the monks lived. That's where you want to go. The southern peak's sharper, higher. Best leave it alone. Follow this track to the middle of the island then head up the stone steps and turn northeast. You'll see the ruins. There's treachery everywhere, but remember a storm passes as quickly as it comes. Good luck t'ya. I don't want to be picking yer body off the rocks.'

He heaves his bags of food, water and other necessities onto Skellig and begins walking along the pathway that skirts the base of the island. After a hundred yards he stops and faces the sea. The drop is already substantial, and in the distance the cliffs of Kerry are dark and featureless, a planet away.

He begins the climb in earnest, step by step, and soon reaches the saddle between the two peaks. He heads for the northern one and sees lines of crumbling walls and stone monastic cells clinging onto the slope like huge barnacles.

He enters the old medieval enclosure. The domes of six small beehive cells are huddled together as if for warmth, their dark entrances pointing to the ocean. He stoops inside one, reassured by the thickness of the curved wall and the fact it seems dry and windproof.

He squats at the entrance and looks out. Little Skellig, a smaller version of Skellig Michael, lies directly ahead, guiding his eye like a sight-line to the Kerry coast and hills. The breeze is light and a glancing blow of sunlight warms his face. His loudest shout would be heard only by the thousands of white birds that cover parts of the rock like snow drifts.

The horizon is drawing down the sun, and he walks to the top of the northern peak to watch it shed its last skin of gold onto the sea. He doesn't feel ready to return to his cell for the rest of the night, but there's no alternative. There, he eats a carefully measured ration of bread, cheese and water.

NIGHT IS CLOSING IN. He takes out a candle, jar and box of matches. He lights the candle and places it just inside the entrance of his cell and arranges his bed; the ground is his mattress, the bag his pillow, and he has brought a light blanket. The sea sounds and the occasional rush of a breeze, flapping like an invisible bird at the entrance of the cell, lull and distract him. He is giddy from the boat ride and the ascent; he imagines he's adrift at sea, gliding towards an empty horizon… he eases seamlessly towards sleep; the ground feels solid, the darkness unthreatening.

HE IS WAKING UP next day and wondering where on earth he is. The briny freshness and the cries of birds—almost like a mass chuckling—jog him into a split second's disbelief.

He paces around the compound of the ruins; already the unruly spirits in his soul are frightened they will be exorcised by silence. There is nothing for it but to begin his intended regime of prayers and meditation. He prays for people he knows; for Ireland and its people; for personal protection; and, most of all, for guidance. When he closes his eyes he can sense the slope plunging towards the sea and the shock of giddiness makes him move a few yards back to his cell and press his back into the stonework.

After an hour's meditation, he sets off to explore the island. It's a relief descending to the flatness of the saddle, and he has to brace himself to climb up again towards the granite spire of the southern peak. His path is soon blocked by a huge rock that's gashed by a long vertical crack. He can just about squeeze through it, like threading himself through the eye of a needle; but on the other side the path takes a sudden upward turn and the drop becomes so sheer he stops in his tracks. He retraces his steps to his cell.

For the rest of the day he reads, prays and walks ritualistically around the stony remains of the old monastery. By the evening he feels unexpectedly lethargic and low in spirits. He withdraws inside his cell and listens to the birds wailing and crying like the souls of the dead.

Daylight is dimming, and he alternates between drowsiness and a confusion of images: his father reading beside the fire, tilting his book towards the light; his mother singing to herself in the parlour; Jiddu sitting next to Nitya in the hotel, their eyes full of wonder and anxiety. He remembers

Jiddu in his visionary dream, urging him to test himself in a desert place. At least he can tell Jiddu he tried.

WHEN HE WAKES NEXT day he knows exactly where he is. It is hard to say how early it is because the sky has cast a grey net over the world. He steps out and feels fine wet particles on his face. Down towards the sea the mizzle is thicker, swirling and shifting; as he retreats inside his cell, he imagines the whole of Ireland, from Donegal to Waterford, suffocated in mist. It makes him think of Home Rule and the three main politicians who hold the country's destiny in their hands, stumbling around in a mist of indecision: stolid, diligent, uninspiring John Redmond, leading the Home Rule party; Edward Carson, hair slicked back, stoking up the Protestants of Ulster to remain loyal to the crown; and the pleasure-loving, silver-haired and timid English prime minister, Asquith, like a boxing referee. All of them waiting for something to happen, or someone to do something. Yet he understands the causes of inertia. If Home Rule is passed, the northern Protestants will go berserk. If it is scrapped, the Fenian patriots in the south, nursing ancient wounds of resentment, will take up arms. Either way could mean a bloodbath.

Meanwhile Britain is preoccupied with anything but Ireland. He knows this to be the case from his time in London. Apart from a few sympathetic souls such as Faith, Hugh and Mrs Besant, nobody had much of an opinion on Ireland, except for a general sense that the Irish desire for Home Rule was an incomprehensible act of disloyalty.

He stares up at the dark curve of the cell and recites phrases he has memorised. 'Be a Christ' is one of them, but it makes him think of William Stead drowning in the Atlantic, the same ocean that is slathering on the rocks all around him like a pack of fox-hungry hounds.

THE REST OF THE day is tinged with melancholy. As the sea fret finally darkens, he prepares himself for sleep. He hears a soft voice reassuring him. One step at a time. Don't look ahead and don't look down: fear comes from seeing too far. Do the practical things and everything else will follow. Trust in God. He's not going to let you fall off the rock or go mad. Nothing can hurt you except yourself.

ON THE MORNING OF the fourth day the fret is still draped over the islet. He hates being penned up in his cell, but he has only one change of shirt. He shivers and stares into the unholy mass of grey air. A voice starts up in his head: What possessed you to come to this godforsaken place? You should be back in Galway, plying your trade, saving your money, helping your parents, looking for a woman to marry and to settle down with. What has put all these notions in your head? The truth you seek is not to be found in books and vigils in the desert but in everyday decency. Remember Jane Eyre of Galway and her piety, prudence and well-disposed-of money?

He feeds on a crumb of self-pity for as long as he can, then eats his food portion. The temptation to consume all his food at once terrifies him. He has to hang on. *It will be the making of me.*

He lies in his cell and can hardly be bothered to pray or meditate or read or reflect. He gazes at his corbelled ceiling and is reminded of home and retreating into his shed to lie on his bed and stare at the roof. Memories feed on his hunger: St Nicholas's Church—standing behind the column with Nora. He can sense the heat of her body, as if she were lying next to him in his cell. He looks into her moist brown eyes, penetrating his soul. The scene switches to London. He is with Agnes and they are sitting in a park, probably Wimbledon Common. The trees are different shades of yellow and brown. She is cold and pressing her head into his shoulder. He puts his arm around her and she blurts out to him that she is distressed about her engagement to Dominic. They sit in silence, the weight of her head a thing of comfort. She lifts her face and gives him a peck on the cheek; it is less of a kiss than an indication of what she wants him to do. He bends his head down and kisses her on the lips, a short gentle kiss. When he pulls away there are tears in her eyes. He admires her pale eyelids as she looks down. She turns towards him and says, 'I love you', though her lips do not move. He holds her hand and they stare into the park, which now seems like an autumnal Eden.

THE SIXTH MORNING. HE wakes and blinks at the glow of light framed by the doorway.

Outside his cell, a sense of the vastness of raw creation overwhelms him. He will miss it! It's as if he has grown into the rocky fabric of Skellig Michael, and the wind and the sea and anything changeable can do nothing to shake him from it.

The thought provokes a burst of joy; then he remembers the Buddhist equation: the depth of joy is equal to the depth of sorrow.

He sets off for a walk and follows the path that leads to the huge outcrop with the eye of a needle and squeezes himself through it to the upward path. The last time, he turned back. Now he advances, one slow step after another, refusing to look down to his left. After fifteen paces he stops. His courage has improved, but not enough to proceed farther.

As he returns towards his cell he stops halfway along the saddle at a spot that seems to be roughly at the centre of the island; the sun's position is discernible by a faint patch of brightness in the cloud. A grand place for a look-out. He lies down and a semblance of a warmth penetrates him. The ground is solid and reassuring. He closes his eyes and the dark behind them seems bright. His thoughts flitter like gnats, then begin to subside. His body relaxes completely. The island feels like a giant boat sweeping him away to some mysterious future. After a while a sharp wash of cold wind makes him open his eyes. He hears a noise and, turning around, he sees a man, sitting on a rock a few yards above him, silhouetted against the brightness of the day. The lighthouse keeper! It's almost a relief he's encountered him at last. He gets up and walks over to the man, who is elderly and wearing a brown cloth cap. Strands of hair stick out of it like silver ferns.

He sits down on a nearby rock and introduces himself, but the keeper doesn't seem interested. The man gazes out to sea and says: 'Jerusalem—'twould be over there.' He points a gnarled finger behind him. 'And Croagh Patrick, 'twould be over there.' He moves his finger in the other direction. 'We're in the middle of the compass. Safest place to be. Can see everything.' The man hardly looks at him but he feels obliged to spill out why he has come to Skellig.

For a while they sit in silence watching the sky and the bright specks of birds.

'There'll be war,' the keeper says out of the blue.

'Why would you say that?'

'I'm here to give warnings. That's my life. I know the sea, I know the weather, and I can tell if a ship is taking on water from a long way out. My eye is like the light of the lighthouse; it never stops. I can feel there's the weather for war.'

'In this country?'

The man looks as if he is going to elaborate, but he doesn't. Instead he turns and points behind him. 'Jerusalem. 'Twould be over there.' He frowns as though he is trying to remember something, but the thought never comes and his face relaxes. He pushes himself up off the rock, takes his stick and looks around as if he's lost something or is about to call a dog to heel; he walks off, quickly vanishing from view.

Night time. He lies on his side and feels his wakefulness turning into sleepiness and the descent of a dream. He becomes aware of a silhouetted woman crouching over him in the half-light. He lifts his blanket and she draws her bare body into his contours, putting her arm around his waist. He realises it is Agnes, beautiful Agnes! He moves his lips towards her, anticipating the warmth of her mouth. She says, 'You're lonely. You've always been lonely for the want of a woman. That's why I've come to you.' Her hand caresses his cheek. She moves her head as if to kiss him. She whispers: 'We'd be happy together. House in Galway, four children. My father would help us with the money. A new life for both of us.' She shifts her position and lies back. 'Lie on top of me,' she says. 'We will become one person.' Her eyes suck into his soul. He is desperate to lie on her and penetrate her. She smiles and opens her lips and pulls him close to her. Her smell is a familiar one... but then he realises it doesn't belong to Agnes. Too stale—a mixture of perfume and something else. He tries to move away but the woman grips him and says, 'Enter me, and you can have everything'—he senses danger and rears up, shouting, and in one movement makes the sign of the cross on her forehead with his finger. When he looks at her face again he sees she's wearing lipstick, smeared, and blotchy eye shadow. She opens her mouth and he sees stumps of jagged, yellow teeth. She hisses at him, 'You fuckin' pig,' and he yells and pushes her away; he roars and wakes up in morning light.

THE SKY IS OVERCAST but no rain is in the offing. He looks across at the Kerry mainland. Tomorrow he will be back in Kerry, sitting in a bar in Ballinskelligs. A bird cries out a rhythmic wave of screeching, as if conveying a message from God which he's perpetually on the verge of deciphering. He watches the sea erupt into tufts of white foam, like sudden blossomings of blackthorn, and the haze of distant land for the rest of the morning. His thoughts wander and he does not pursue them. The wind blows about his face and he finds his awareness of himself extraordinarily fluid, as if he can shift from feeling the wind to actually being the wind; it reminds him of strolling around early-morning Galway after his dream-vision. He shuts his eyes and when he hears the cry of a bird he becomes that bird, flying above the ocean, his eyes alert, floating without any sense of weight. And with this loosening of his fixed sense of self comes what he can only describe as joy, a power that dissolves all his worries and against which, he believes just then, no care can survive.

HIS FINAL NIGHT. HE is falling asleep and dreaming of the boat trip back to the mainland. The dream changes. He hears a voice outside the cell, a whispering that reminds him of the séance and Etta Wriedt, and he knows he's being summoned. He gets up and sees a figure waiting for him outside in the moonlight. The figure is male, but he cannot see his features in the gloaming. Perhaps it's the lighthouse keeper. The man says, 'I hear you're leaving us.' He replies, 'Yes, I'm leaving tomorrow.' 'That's a pity,' the man says. 'I want to show you something before you go. I shall miss you. We shall all miss you. Come,' he says, 'follow me. The stars are beautiful, and it's your last night here.'

The man is walking away and he is following him. Soon they reach the rock with the eye of the needle. The man turns round: 'It's easier for a camel to pass through a needle... isn't that right?' Without waiting for an answer the man squeezes through the crevice and he follows suit. They're on the path he's previously been unable to follow. He senses the terrible drop to his left. The man reads his thoughts: 'Don't be afraid, I'll guide you. You're safe in my hands. Keep your eyes on my back.'

The man sets off again. There are rocks to clamber over and narrow goat tracks and hummocks of grass to negotiate, and all the time they are rising higher and higher. He realises they must be heading for the southern peak itself. He wants to stop. It'd be like standing on top of a cathedral spire! Again the man senses his thoughts: 'Don't worry, Patrick, I'm looking after you. Concentrate on the path.'

Eventually he sees the man scrambling up a ridge. He does the same and reels back: they've reached the highest point on Skellig and he is looking into the abyss. 'We're on top of the world, aren't we, Patrick!' They stand side by side, listening to the wash of primeval sea. The man turns to him: 'Nobody comes here, but I like this spot. I like to bring people of an unusual spirit here. I'm informed you will do great things in your life. People will be moved by your words. That would be quite an accomplishment, Patrick, believe me. There's one deed, though, you have to do before you can really be one of God's chosen; a final test that will prove you have the faith to do *anything*. Jump off this rock. God will save you.'

He dares himself to look down. The sea is restless and expectant, beating itself into foam against the rocks. He wants to lie down and grip the earth. 'Don't be afraid, Patrick. You've come this far. You've been brave. This is the last test. Just think how proud you'll be. Sailing back to the mainland tomorrow you'll be able to recall the moment when you jumped into the darkness knowing that you'd be saved.'

He looks down at the swirl of water, all of a sudden so calm and silent, and peaceful. 'Go on Patrick. You've been blessed by God. Why would he let anything harm you? It's a wonderful thing to become like a bird. Your mother, Bridie, would be proud of you.'

At the mention of his mother, he says: 'How do you know my mother's name? Who are you?' The man doesn't answer his question, but says: 'God will save you.' The man's tone betrays a trace of impatience.

He replies to him: 'We must not test God.'

The man laughs at this: 'Don't be stupid! You're simply testing *yourself*.'

'No, I'd be testing God. I'd be testing whether he would save my life when I didn't have to.'

The man says: 'Don't be *bloody stupid*. You're on the verge of being someone special to God. All you have to do is jump.'

He is taken aback by his own rising anger: 'Do you believe in God?'

'*Believe?* What kind of a stupid bloody question is that? Remember, if you don't jump you will still have to return to your cell and I might not be able to help you get back there. Listen to me: I can see it's more difficult for you than I thought. Let me help you.'

The man comes towards him, his arms outstretched. He backs away.

'What's the matter? We can jump together if you like? Don't you recognise me?'

112

He sees the man's face head-on in the moonlight.

It is his own face.

Before he can move, his 'double' throws his arms around him. He feels a terrible strength trying to shift him towards the drop. He can hear the sea hissing and rearing up at him. He sinks all his weight into the ground and braces every sinew and muscle to resist his adversary; he can feel his feet rooting down into the earth and knows if he can concentrate on them he won't be shifted; at the same time he hears someone whispering to him, *Find your voice, you must find your voice.* He feels he's going to be sick but, instead of vomiting, he hears a roar and the words *Be a Christ!* projected into the air and across the sky…

He feels the pressure of his assailant subside. The figure steps away and is no longer bearing his own face. He recognises the long black hair: it is Jiddu, still dressed in the suit he was wearing at the station in the dream-vision. He has his hands together, as if in prayer, and says: 'Patrick, war flares up in our souls and ends up burning cities and bodies. Someone has to go out into the world—into the towns and countryside of Ireland and tell the people, with urgency, that violence starts in ourselves and we are the only ones who can overcome it. Not politicians, not priests. This country is your destiny.'

A bird's diminishing cry is curling off the curved ceiling of his cell as he is waking up. Dawn has fully broken, but daylight does nothing to disperse the dream. He feels worn out by it, but extraordinarily peaceful. What would have happened if he had 'jumped'? He was close to some sort of death, of that he has no doubt. But he has survived. Surely nothing in a psychical way will test him as much again? He repeats the words in the dream: *war flares up in our souls and ends up burning cities and bodies.*

He is ready to return to the mainland and start his life again.

HE IS STARING OUT in the general direction of Ballinskelligs, trying to see the boat. He shuts his eyes and meditates, then opens them to scan the sea. Still nothing. He has become used to gauging the time of day by the sun, and it is about one o'clock before he sees a speck out on the waves. He makes his way to the saddle for the last time, climbs down the rough stone steps and walks along the track that leads to the jetty.

HE SITS AT THE back of the boat and watches Skellig Michael and Little Skellig recede through the spray of the waves. He pictures himself sitting outside his old stone cell, watching the boat heading back to Kerry. He thinks of the birds and the little stone crosses; and the dreams he has had. At this moment he cannot find the words, or even the thoughts, to articulate his joy and relief that he knows what he must do with his life.

The same skipper who had brought him over to Skellig is sitting opposite him.

They exchange words, and he says: 'I met the lighthouse keeper, yesterday, sitting outside, on a rock. Queer fella, alright. Looked a bit unsteady for the work with his walking stick and that.'

The skipper gives a snort. 'Not sure who you saw, but 'twasn't the keeper! The keeper was on Valentia Island yesterday. He's a young man, good head of thick black hair. No one on Skellig the past week except you.'

They look at each other.

'Well, they say a man can go silly in the head with being on his own too much, hearing voices and things. Or maybe you've the gift. If 'twas a ghost you're after seeing, I hope it was a cheerful one.'

'He predicted war.'

'Sure, doesn't need a ghost to do that.'

He is sitting at the front of Galway's town hall, high summer of 1913, facing the stage, not daring to turn around. He is about to speak to hundreds of women. He has arrived early and the place is still filling up. He can't quite believe what he is about to do.

It was all because he'd gone back to St Nicholas's to inspect his old handiwork and lay to rest the ghost of Nora: he'd met a more venerable version of Mary Coleville, the woman who had once shown him around the church, and, in the course of their conversation he'd described the suffragette demonstration in Regent's Street. It was as if he had sent an invisible dart into her head. Her face frowned and he could see energy gathering in her bulbous cheeks: 'The Galway Women's Franchise League! We have Beatrice O'Donovan, a fine and brilliant young woman, giving an address at the city hall. It would be something of a catch *to have a man* talking in our favour. A witness to our struggle and the crude methods of the constabulary. You needn't speak for long. Just give an idea of what it was like for those wretched London women.' Fearing the hesitations of his thoughts, and remembering the urgings of the dream figure of Jiddu on Skellig, he had said immediately: 'I'll do it, so.' Perhaps this would be the start of a new life.

Now that his talk is about to begin, his heart is beating so hard he can hardly hear Mary's words introducing him. He rises to measured applause. He has no notes. He's just going to tell his story. A tremble transfers itself from his heart to his hands, which he banishes behind his back. Hundreds of women in front of him. He wonders whether Alice Perry might be among them. That would give her a surprise.

He hears Mary Coleville whispering: 'Tell them you were in London.'

'I was in London. Not long ago. Staying with my aunt. Together we went to a protest by London suffragettes. In Regent Street.' He gains confidence. He mentions but does not dwell on the smashing of the window, preferring to describe the fracas and the arrests. He finishes the story and bows his head to warm applause.

He's about to return to his seat when something keeps him standing. 'I just want to say that the treatment of women in this country leaves a lot to be desired.' He pauses because he isn't sure what he's going to say next. The delay invites more applause, which gives him time to formulate a thought. 'Women are considered lesser human beings by men; and the sole cause for this is the bicep. Men are stronger than women, and they've always made brute force count. But force, violence, never wins. It might gain immediate ends, but it will always corrupt those who carry it out. *Victory gained by force is a self-inflicted defeat.* We call ourselves a Christian country. Did Jesus treat women as second-class citizens?' A murmur of approval. 'On the other hand, did Jesus throw bricks through windows?' A voice shouts out, 'Sure, he would've done if he'd been a woman!' Laughter.

There is a commotion at the back. Four or five men are pushing themselves through the door. As heads turn towards them they start singing a song with slurred flat voices:

> 'Put me on an island where the girls are few.
> Put me among the most ferocious lions in the zoo.
> You can put me on a treadmill, and I'll never, never fret.
> But for pity's sake, don't put me near a suff-ra-gette!'

They end their chorus with unbalanced jeers. A woman stands up and shakes her fist: 'Ye should be ashamed of yourselves. Ye can get out and swill yer beer in the pub and leave us in peace.' The men stand their ground. One of them shouts out at him: 'Hey there young fella, you should be at home minding your wife, or maybe it's you're the wife!' The man's companions collapse into something between laughter and coughing.

He leaves the front of the auditorium and walks along the central aisle towards the men. He doesn't know what he is going to say or do, but it is too late to turn back.

The audience falls silent. His footsteps sound far too loud.

'Coming to throw us out, are ya? Why not get some of your

women friends to help.'

The man who speaks is unshaven and red-faced from drink; above his belt there is a button missing and a patch of his sagging belly peeps through.

He looks the man in the face and somehow he knows what to do. He focuses on one eye, then the other. He pours his concentration into each one, and so intense is his stare that the man's bravado begins to melt. The wide sneer that has dented his porcine face loses its shape and his arms drop by his side. His companions don't move. The men look at him uneasily, as if he has a gun or a knife. He continues to fix the man with his eyes and can see the man's courage emptying out, almost physically; he then begins to recite quietly and steadily verses from *St Patrick's Breastplate*: 'I summon today all these powers between me and those evils, against every cruel and merciless power that may oppose my body and soul...' He isn't sure whether the man can hear the words, but as he speaks, the rhythm seems to have an effect. The man's face twitches, and he licks his lips, as if they are too dry and hot. He keeps repeating the words and the man, rooted to the spot, starts trembling. He gulps and gulps then vomits—a great arc of sick exits his mouth, some of it landing on his shoes. The man's companions are jerked from inaction and they pull him from the hall. The sound of the slammed door fades; he walks back to his chair while clusters of women rise from theirs.

The meeting has ended. He didn't hear a word of Beatrice O'Donovan's talk because of the thoughts racing around his head.

Mary Coleville is shaking his hand, reluctant to let it go: 'You spoke powerfully. And how you dealt with those men... It was a triumph. Thank you. It has given me a notion. I'd like to invite you to preach a sermon in our church on Sunday. The rector has guest preachers from time to time. He won't refuse me. You may talk about the suffragettes again. Your voice is worth ten women's voices, much as it pains me to say it. You heard those louts at the back with their mockery. That's what we face. The more that men are seen to be supporting us the better. Do come.'

As soon as she has spoken, he is thinking: *Church of Ireland.* Far more daunting than Galway suffragettes. The latter are members of an oppressed group. He is instinctively on their side. But Church of Ireland? The church of the Protestant governing class; the church of privilege, wealth and power. He nods his assent, but his heart is heavy; she shakes his hand again, her appreciation translating into an infectious smile.

HE IS BACK HOME, telling his parents what happened. 'You'll be getting a name,' Bridie says. 'Won't do you much good being linked with suffragettes and... socialists and communists.'

'I'm none of those things.'

'Then what are you?'

'I'm not anything. That's the point.'

He knows, then, what he'll say in Mary Coleville's church.

IT IS THE THURSDAY before his sermon in St Nicholas's and he is walking by the seafront past the Eglinton Hotel; the seaweed-reeking gusts are filling his lungs and battering his face, but they cannot distract him from his thoughts of the coming ordeal. If someone had told him that one day he'd be addressing an Anglican congregation on a Sunday morning... He walks faster, hoping to outpace the doubting voices. He reminds himself how nervous he'd been before the suffragette talk and how well that had turned out. There's every reason this will be the same. He'll tell the truth and the truth will prevail. What's the worst thing that can happen—a few yawns, a few scowling faces? At least Protestants are well behaved— centuries of decorum drilled into them. He recalls how the suffragette meeting made him feel like a hero—women shaking him by the hand, or blessing him, and even a couple of curtsies. After his initial nervousness, the sense of holding an audience in the palm of his hand had thrilled him; the special look in their eyes—was it a mild form of adoration? And, after all, when he speaks to the Anglicans, it won't be as if he's speaking as a dyed-in-the-wool Catholic. He is half Quaker, from a respectable family. Everybody admires the Quakers! Look what they did during the famine. They will accept him; they will listen to him.

He stops and absorbs the swelling sea, as grey as the sky that makes a gliding seagull as white as snow.

SUNDAY MORNING. HE IS walking to St Nicholas's. Mary Coleville is waiting outside the south door with the diminutive silvery rector, who is courteous and solicitous, guiding him—with the ghostliest of touches on his elbow—into the church and in the direction of the front pews.

The church is filling up, He dares to look over his shoulder and it strikes him how he does not know these people. Although they lack the wealth and imperial bearing of some of those he met in London, in terms of their position in Galway society they are more powerful and influential. They look the part, too, with their ties and waistcoats, and dresses and pretty hats; the children well fed and scrupulously washed; and they all have a look that distinguishes them from Quakers, Presbyterians and Catholics. It's hard to put a finger on what it is—not quite disdain or pride, or reserve in a confident way, but a mixture of these qualities.

THE RECTOR MAKES A few announcements, including that the guest preacher is 'an... informative young man named Patrick Bowley'. He can sense the discreet straining of necks in his direction.

The service begins. He is half hearted during the prayers, knowing he has to ascend the pulpit after the third hymn. He thinks of Jiddu and takes solace. If an Indian teenager can speak to English audiences about theosophy...

His moment arrives. As the words, 'Speak through the earthquake, wind, and fire, O still, small voice of calm,' ring out

119

above the chords of the organ, he leaves the pew, takes his position in the pulpit and faces the congregation. He lets the shufflings diminish and repeats to himself, 'O still, small voice of calm.'

He looks around and sees Mary in the front row, willing him on, just as she had done at the city hall.

'Good morning. I'd like to thank the rector for the opportunity of saying a few words to you. I was brought up under two faiths. The Society of Friends and the Catholic Church. My father and mother buried their religious differences and decided to have me.'

His light remark does nothing to soften their mouths into smiles.

'In my short span of years I have come to believe that God does not permit divisions.'

Mary is looking quizzical. She wants him to speak about the suffragettes, but somehow he's been drawn into another train of thought.

'That is to say, the idea of there being one faith divided into two, or three, or fifty variations is a contradiction. God cannot be sliced up like a slab of cheese. There's only one faith, and that is an individual's faith in God. But we've created divisions between ourselves by constructing walls: Protestant walls and Catholic ones; Church of Ireland walls, and Presbyterian, Methodist, Baptist, and, yes, Quaker walls, and all the rest of them. We can all receive the holy spirit, but not by clinging on to our own special creeds and hymns. We approve of our own prayers but not those of other people. We follow this ritual or that ritual, and we believe we are damned if we follow those of another sect. Does God want to us to despise Catholics? Or hate Protestants?'

He pauses, and it is long enough for a voice to ring out from the back. 'What the devil would you know? You're just Joe Bowley's lad, the carpenter.'

Heads turn round to locate the heckler. All eyes return to him; an unexpected rage wells up in him, accompanied by a deep calmness. The result is a voice that's controlled and icy.

'What the devil would I know? That's what this gentleman at the back has asked me. Because, as he says, I'm just a carpenter. He means that I am no one. Look at me. What you see is *a nobody*. And what he means is this: how can I possibly speak of spiritual things when I'm not a priest, bishop or monk; when I'm not a doctor or lawyer and didn't study in the hallowed halls of Trinity College? Is that what we mean by faith? At the gates of heaven will God ask us what theological degree we gained at university?'

A man and a woman at the end of one of the middle pews get up and walk out; as they are exiting the door, the man stops and calls out: 'You may sneer at a degree from Trinity, but it will reveal more about God than being a miserable Quaker or Catholic peasant.' Clapping breaks out in different places.

The rector stands up and raises his hands. 'My friends, we have invited a guest to speak to us. You may not share his views. But it is an outrage, an absolute *outrage* to show bad manners. If anyone here finds himself unable to control his tongue, let him leave now.'

Half a dozen people get up from different places and walk out. He watches the rector, who waits for them to go, glaring in their general direction. The rector turns and nods at him. His train of thought has been broken; he waits for words to come, but he is too full of anger. He surveys the surly audience, hoping some detail might spark off something. He is edging towards panic and sitting down when he sees a candle flame and blurts out: 'God is like a flame. He cannot be parted by human hands or… shaped by human thoughts.' *Now what?* His thoughts are moving at an extraordinary speed and they settle on words of Tagore: 'Whom do you worship in this lonely temple with all the doors shut? Open your eyes and see your God is nowhere to be seen.' As soon as he utters these words he knows they are exactly the wrong ones to say.

He ends his address, walks back to the pew and the rector announces the next hymn. The organ starts up, but the singing is lacklustre. He looks across and sees Mary's face has a strange expression. He realises he hasn't said a word about the

121

suffragettes. The rest of the service is a blur.

The remaining prayers and blessings are given and received, and the congregation files out through the west door, where the rector has positioned himself. He stays sitting, letting the crowd disperse.

Mary comes up to him, her eyes scanning every particle of his face. 'This lonely temple with all the doors shut is *our life*. Do you have any idea what it is to be part of this church, any church? Do you think we sit around all day reciting our Church of Ireland *creeds*? Do you know what time the rector rises in the morning to set off on his bicycle to comfort a widow or give bread to the poor? We invited you as a guest to our church. It has been a place of worship for centuries and centuries. It has seen weddings and funerals, and christenings; it honours the dead. And you *dare* to call it a "lonely temple".'

He watches her lower her head, her fingers trying to press her tears back. The rector has said goodbye to the last of the congregation and has come over. He touches Mary's arm and leads her away.

He leaves by the south door, hoping his flush of shame will disperse in the overcast August day. Three men, wearing brown felt hats and looking as if they are trying to spot someone, turn their attention to him and walk over. One of them, thin-faced with a pale yellow complexion and a soft voice, says: 'Listen here you Unitarian, papist shite. If we see you hanging around this church or anywhere else in this city you'll get a beating you'll never forget. We know you and your sort. You were at the suffragette meeting, stoking up servant girls who should know better. I'm not having my wife bleating on about bloody rights for bloody women. I don't care if you're Gaelic League, Sinn Féin or God knows what else—just remember this: you're a lazy, ignorant piece of cowardly shite who uses a thumbprint to spell his name.'

The man spits the last words with such venom that he almost ducks to avoid them. He sees right down into the soul of his verbal assailant and it's like looking at a snake rearing up and flicking out its tongue. He stares at the man, automatically doing what he did to the drunken intruder at the town hall—focusing on each of his eyes alternately. But this time the desired effect doesn't work because the man has turned and walked off with his two companions.

He stands there in a pool of self-disgust. He was invited by Mary in good faith and he abused that trust. Not that he hasn't come to suspect that churches might well be lonely temples. Surely God is not confined to any particular space? But he offended people who had received him as their guest. He allowed anger to master him. He knows he can't stay in Galway.

D elia's Bar in Quay Street is noisy and sawdust has been scuffed into small piles by an evening's worth of drinkers. He is adjusting to the fact that he is placing on the table two pints of porter for himself *and* his father, who has not only agreed to come to a pub with him, but, out of solidarity or nervousness or temptation, has decided to have a drink.

He thinks how stooped and vulnerable Joe looks, and how the smear of disapproval on his lips is mixed with apprehension, as if the pub were a law court and he was about to be sentenced for being a temperance fanatic.

Joe looks at him as if to ask why he insisted on him coming down to the pub. He addresses his father's puzzlement with a question: 'Which town in Ireland would you least like to live in?'

'Easy one. Limerick.'

'Why?'

'The feel of the place. The castle. All the barracks. Soldiers. The way the houses are crammed up against one side of the river. The river's too wide for it. Bridges are supposed to pin two sides of a town together. In Limerick the Shannon wedges them apart. And the Friends' community is a small one— crowded out by Catholics and Anglicans.'

With alcohol loosening his tongue, he tells Joe he will leave home for Limerick. He explains he wants to be somewhere where people don't know him and where he will make a difference; he wants to help the country somehow; to speak out against violence, inequality, but not in a directly political way.

'*Do* you now?' says Joe. 'If you speak about inequality you'll be speaking of the disgrace that is the Dublin Lock-out, and then ye'll have to be political. What will you say about employers locking out their workers for wanting to form a union?' Joe's next sip reveals a portcullis of teeth, steeling themselves for his son's answer.

'I'm for treating people with respect and justice.'

'So what would you say to the Dublin coppers who gave the protesters—working men, and women—a battering? Not

124

much respect there.'

He doesn't know about the protest his father's referring to and stares into his dark glass. Joe lets out a tortuous sigh, then takes a deep breath, as if it's the first he's taken all day and it has to last him till the morrow. 'All very well gallivanting around giving talks and sermons and stirring things up, but someone's got to stay at home and read about the world and make sure it isn't collapsing around our ears. Big Jim Larkin, day before yesterday, rallying the workers, whipping them up as only he can do, and then of course the Met police start diving in. Riots break out—Sackville Street, Ringsend, Eden Quay—and the Met cracking heads and asking questions afterwards. Cracked a head too far's what's happened. A fella called Nolan's to be buried. Larkin arrested in the Imperial Hotel. About to address the crowd, he was, but they got him first. More riots.' He can feel his father's passion wafting over him in waves. Joe takes a sup then continues: 'If you go to Limerick you can tell them that your father thinks the Lock-out is a disgrace. And while we're on politics—there's talk of Jim Connolly forming a citizen army to balance the one in Ulster. Soon we'll be looking at a Catholic army down south, a Protestant one up north, and the British Army piggy in the middle. Enough to make you weep.'

Joe looks as if he really *is* going to weep. He himself drinks his porter to the dregs and gets up and orders two more pints and brings them back to the table.

Joe's eyes are lit up, and he takes his pint glass carefully with both hands, guiding it gently onto the table as if it were a new-born baby; his skin is rosy below the cheekbones, which lose their hard edges as he mutters 'thanks'.

Before he can ask Joe other questions in this rare moment of intimacy, they are distracted by the presence of a man swaying towards them. He's dressed like a fisherman, with a shapeless hat pulled down, almost to his eyes, and his chin and jaw softened by a brown beard. 'I know you two,' he shouts. 'Ye're Joe Bowley. And that's your lad, and y'ave no business getting gerrls to be bold to their menfolk.'

The talk in the bar slows to a stop. Everyone looks round at the drunk and then to him and Joe. Tom, the barman, is leaning forward, his two hands flat on the bar. 'Settle down Mick, you've a bucket of drink in ya—don't be bothering these good people.'

'Good people, my arse! Damned communists. God-hating communists. Black Protestants. Bastard Proddy... *bastards*.'

'Ah, come on Mick. Leave them alone.' Tom turns to him and Joe and shrugs.

Then another voice says: 'He has a point.' The owner of the voice slides off his stool and stands to face him and Joe. He's broad-shouldered like a labourer but dressed smarter, with a jacket and waistcoat. 'Me missus told me I could bloody well make my own dinner the other day. Well, didn't I have to give her a little smack to make her see the error of her ways? It's fellas like these,' he continues, looking around the pub, 'that's making trouble when there's none before. There'll be fighting in this country and we'll be needing men proper for the struggle, not altar boys hanging onto the skirts of women.'

The man walks towards them, his eyes squinting, as if he's short-sighted; his fingers have folded into fists.

As the man glares at them, he touches Joe on the shoulder and gets up to confront the aggressor. His fear has been diminished by the porter. He remembers how he faced up to the hecklers in the city hall. But this man looks powerful and in control of his senses.

Joe tells him to sit down, and for a moment he is tempted.

The man says: 'So you'd be the one talking to the women and the Prods?'

'That'd be me,' he says, not liking the man's slow, measured tone. He can hear Joe getting to his feet and he turns round and gestures him to stay still.

' 'Tis you, is it? Then I'd say you best go on home to your women friends. This is a man's pub.' The man raises his right fist. He knows he should clench his own fist and be ready to punch, but—and he doesn't know why—he picks up his pint glass and lifts it chin high as if to toast the man, who looks momentarily puzzled.

The silence in the room is at saturation point.

He thinks he'll play for time by drinking the porter—he swigs it back in four big gulps... then almost immediately lets out a huge unexpected belch—his action is so swift and the belch so loud that two men in the corner burst into chuckles; they try to control their splutterings, but these are not to be suppressed and their wheezy guffaws are so contagious the entire pub descends into a chorus of untempered swirling laughter. The man's eyes have switched from icy menace to shifty embarrassment. He looks around at the contorted faces and walks out of the pub, drawing uncontrollable laughter after him.

The red-brick terraced houses by Limerick station are glowing like embers in the early morning sunshine. It's a few months after his preaching debacle in Galway. September, 1913. He is walking past beggars and loiterers hovering around the entrance of the Station Hotel and making his way to the centre of town.

George Street is much grander than anything in Galway, and he is surprised to see crowds of people gazing upwards. The sky is blue with clumps of white cloud: there are no rainbows or signs of an approaching storm. He walks past clerks who have deserted their posts at the Munster and Leinster Bank to stand by the entrance of the George Hotel, where bell-boys, like miniature Napoleonic officers, are staring skywards like everyone else.

Then he hears it; a faint roaring from the sky.

He looks up and sees four objects moving high above the buildings. Aeroplanes. He's never seen one before; nor have the folk of Limerick, judging by the shouts and fingers pointing upwards. Nor has he seen so many binoculars in one place. The four aircraft circle and dive and crisscross. Each plane has two pairs of wings, one raised above the other, and he can see one of the pilots waving at them, a gesture reciprocated by a roar from the crowd. He imagines himself in one of those planes, like a giant bird watching the tops of buildings and scatterings of tiny people, and he is borne back to Skellig—the wind in his face, the distant sea below, and freedom.

A man standing next to him says aloud to no-one in particular: ' 'Tis the future we're looking at.' The four planes loop and straighten out and intertwine, as if inscribing lines on a vast invisible Book of Kells. Then without ceremony they are gone, their throaty engines diminishing to a hum. People return their heads to a horizontal position and gabble about the miracle.

He's knocking on the door of a two-storey terraced house in St Harry's Mall in which he is renting a room. An old Quaker acquaintance of his father—Douglas Newsome— whom Joe described as a single gentleman, middle-aged, of decent ancestry and adequate private means.

The door opens and his new landlord is much as he imagined: on the short side, neatly dressed with a tweed waistcoat, chubby cheeks, and the bareness of his tanned head balanced by auburn mutton-chop sideboards, the ends of which he strokes as he absorbs his visitor through his spectacles.

He introduces himself, shakes hands and enters into a waft of cooked meats and cabbage.

Douglas shows him round, chattering away as he does so. 'Always woodwork to be done. You can do some in lieu of rent if that suits you. Rain's destroying the windows, and the door needs replacing and God knows what else. This climate's heaven for carpenters. Everyone's looking for one. Won't be short of work here. Not a bad old city. Bit rough around the edges, maybe. Too many soldiers in the streets. We have Castle Barracks, Ordnance Barracks, Strand Barracks, New Barracks, and now there's aeroplanes. The Royal Flying Corps. Icarus, my lad, Icarus!... There's no intoxicating beverages in this household and I like to keep it crisp and neat. But you're Joe Bowley's son—you'll know what's neat and what's not.'

He's reminded of his arrival at Faith's flat in Wimbledon. The same sense of estrangement and excitement.

HE'S MAKING HIS WAY downstairs from his bedroom, sleepy and already beginning to dread the morning conversation with Douglas, who rises early and maintains a cheery demeanour throughout the day, even when his words are grumpy. He suddenly remembers he is due to speak in the Quaker Meeting House in the evening, an invitation issued by Douglas after the two of them had exchanged views about spirituality and the state of the country. They had talked into the small hours of the night—until Douglas wilted before his tales of London, theosophy, Skellig Michael and giving a talk to the women of Galway. When he had mentioned the talk, Douglas revived and asked him if he would address the local Friends: 'We have guest speakers from time to time—a short homily or a choice little speech on something topical and encouraging would be just the thing. We are a small group, but what we lack in numbers we make up for in attentiveness!' He had agreed.

As soon as he enters the parlour, Douglas is talking at him: 'Good morning young man. All set for tonight? Hope you'll be talking more sense than this piece of verse the *Times* has served up for its readers. Seems to be a patriotic piece alright—mentions all the Fenian heroes—John O'Leary, Robert Emmet, Wolf Tone and friends—but its meaning eludes me! Listen to this:

> ' "What need you, being come to sense,
> But fumble in a greasy till
> And add the halfpence to the pence
> And prayer to shivering prayer, until
> You have dried the marrow from the bone?
> For men were born to pray and save:
> Romantic Ireland's dead and gone,
> It's with O'Leary in the grave."

'What d'you make of that? I don't know what these new poets are playing at. When I was young, poetry was a thing of beauty—"On either side the river lie long fields of barley and of rye, that clothe the wold and meet the sky; and through the field the road runs by to many-towered Camelot". That's poetry. None of this fumbling in a greasy till. That's vulgar. If "Romantic Ireland's dead and gone" then it's folk like this fella that's killed it.

'Who wrote it?'

'A certain Mr Yeats.'

'Mr Yeats? He's a good man.' He explains how he met him in London.

'Well next time you see him you can tell him he can keep his greasy tills and his marrow bones under his hat.' Douglas folds the paper, shaking his head. Patrick sits down, reaches for the paper and opens it. He reads the poem while Douglas watches him for expressions of disdain or bafflement.

'I like this bit.' He ignores his landlord's petulant expression and reads aloud:

> ' "Was it for this the wild geese spread
> The grey wing upon every tide;
> For this that all that blood was shed,
> For this Edward Fitzgerald died,
> And Robert Emmet and Wolfe Tone,
> All that delirium of the brave?
> Romantic Ireland's dead and gone,
> It's with O'Leary in the grave." '

'I like the geese spreading their grey wings on the sea. I can picture that. And he makes a fair point. Wouldn't Emmet and Tone be wondering why they bothered if they saw what's happening in the country?'

Douglas is unwilling to concede. 'He's exalting a nation of martyrs! It's not dying in a blaze of glory that mans the soup kitchens. It's good honest folk going about their daily business, saving money and giving to the poor—that's what's going to help this country.' His instinct is to protest. Emmet and Tone have been his heroes since childhood. The very name, Wolfe Tone, had seized him from an early age—he could see Tone in his uniform, leading the 1798 rebels into the fray and stirring up a crowd with his words, 'Our independence must be had at all hazards!' And Robert Emmet, another young rebel, caught and sentenced to death, but not before he had pronounced from the dock, 'When my country takes her place among the nations of the earth, *then and not till then*, let my epitaph be written'.

But a thought tells him that Douglas might be right. Martyrs cannot man soup kitchens. He says nothing.

Seven o'clock in the evening. He is making his way to the Meeting House in Cecil Street. The venue turns out to be a

131

high, narrow terraced house.

He is led inside by an administrator named Ernest and conducted to a ground-floor room; its two windows look out onto the street. About thirty chairs face the end of the room. He guesses there will be an overspill area in the hallway, where more chairs can be put out. He stands around as Ernest and his daughter Emily, a shy young woman in her early twenties, put leaflets on chairs and fill up glasses with water. Ernest has neat centrally-parted silvery hair, which matches the cufflinks on his stiff white cuffs and the watch-chain tucked into his waistcoat pocket. His daughter is fair-haired and pale in a slightly sickly way; her small pointed features are set, but her eyes are full of minute, careful observations.

He hears the grandfather clock by the front door chime twice for seven-thirty, the time his talk is due to begin. He is beginning to wonder whether people have been told the correct time of day, when there's a knock at the front door. Emily goes to open it and Douglas strides in, breaking into a meaty smile when he sees him. After fifteen minutes of small talk Ernest says: 'We may as well make a start. I was expecting a few more interested souls, and some may yet come along. But where two or three are gathered together, as the good Lord informs us. We certainly have a quorum for that.'

He nods, walks to the front and faces Ernest, Douglas and Emily. He closes his eyes to set in train his half-prepared thoughts and words, but all he can see is blue sky and biplanes moving into it, circling, dipping and diving, looping the loop, as if they are the material representation of his thoughts. He waits for words to emerge but still the planes dominate. He can't just stand there and say nothing! He opens his eyes and sees the trio all have theirs shut. The panic subsides—of course, they are used to silence! It's like any old Friends' meeting for them. He shuts his eyes and again the planes circle the sky inside his head. He loses track of time. It might be a few minutes or a quarter of an hour. He drifts from thought to thought; the silence and the sky and planes lead him back to Skellig, sitting high up on the rock watching the birds; he floats up into the air

132

and finds himself sitting in a biplane looking down on Limerick, the Shannon flowing through it and the land either side pinned together by bridges. He sees the street pattern of the city, the long roads sweeping down parallel with the river and the grid of streets connecting them with roads farther inland. He sees the top of St John's Castle in the north of the town, soldiers on the parade ground; and there's the canal and the railway station, with its metal tracks leading off to the east; he sees the park where he has been going to sit in his leisure hours and can even see himself sitting on a bench looking up at himself; he is waving; then a cough brings him back to earth.

He opens his eyes and sees that Ernest, Emily and Douglas are looking at him with expressions that betray neither impatience nor expectation nor excitement.

'I'm sorry. I've brought you here for nothing.'

'Not at all, not at all, dear boy. It was an authentic silence. It was moving.' Ernest shifts in his seat, as if he's been sitting for some time.

The meeting fizzles out. He helps to stack the chairs and, when that's done, Ernest says: 'We must do this again, Patrick, with more people next time. We didn't do you justice, I fear. We didn't spread the word. There aren't many of us Friends left in Limerick, but still and all…'

He leaves by himself. It is too early to return home. He cuts through to the riverside and sees the lights of the boat club. It's golden inside, packed with people, drinking, arms on shoulders, and some of the windows are steaming up.

The river sweeps past, dark and too choppy to reflect the stars. As he watches it he remembers words of someone he has read—he can't remember whether it's the Buddha or Thomas Kempis or St Francis: 'As long as you live, you are subject to change… now studious, now careless; now sad, now cheerful.' At this moment he is sad.

Cruises's Hotel: he's painting a corridor on the second storey, helping to spruce up the interior for the imminent arrival of a VIP. Rumours say it might be Augustine Birrell, the government's chief secretary, or even the viceroy himself, the Earl of Aberdeen.

His relief at getting some work has eased his loneliness. He hasn't met a woman in Limerick beyond an employer's wife or servant or shop assistant. On Skellig he had the company of birds and the imagined presence of the monks; but Limerick, teeming with potential companions, has a strange atmosphere. His father was right: a barracks town; streets long, narrow and gun-barrel straight; soldiers everywhere, on parade grounds, or marching in formation up the main roads, or swaggering, off duty, in arm with local women. He can sense the bitterness between oppressor and oppressed more keenly than in Galway.

He hears a commotion downstairs and puts his paintbrush down. From a vantage point he can see people pushing through the main doors into the lobby: hotel officials, newspaper reporters, two RIC constables and men in mackintoshes are bustling around a man whom he recognises straightaway: John Redmond—Leader of the Irish Parliamentary Party, the Home Rule party! There he is not ten yards away, the great hope of peaceful nationalists.

Dapper in his tail coat and bow-tie, Redmond distributes smiles to all and sundry—then his expression switches rather alarmingly to one of seriousness, or even sadness. He is shorter and more portly than his photographs suggest. His head is squarish, his features concentrated beneath a high expansive forehead topped by a negligible layer of flat whitish hair. Below his beaky nose and strip of grey moustache his small chin is made weaker by a bulge of soft flesh below it. Yet the eyes, slightly protruding, are stern and full of purpose. The hotel manager is fawning over him and leading him away to a reception room.

He and hundreds of others are making their way from the centre of Limerick to Market Fields in dry October weather to hear Redmond speak.

He can see the posts of Garryowen Rugby Club standing like thick white knitting needles above an already sizeable crowd. At the far end of the pitch a stage has been constructed.

He glides through crevices between spectators and finds a place at the front. Redmond is sitting at the centre of the platform beside a gloomy-looking man with a grey-streaked beard pouring from his chin like a dismal waterfall. It can only be John Dillon, Redmond's right-hand man. There they are!— the two men who would remove British rule by appealing to the British government's better nature rather than by force of arms.

Among the officials and policemen on the platform is a woman who seems to be Redmond's wife, her overcoat a splash of green, and her wide-brimmed hat a dash of blue. He is distracted from Mrs Redmond by people jostling beside him. Two middle-aged women, refined-looking in their belted overcoats and matching hats, are bumping their way to the front of the crowd and the edge of the platform; one of them shouts up at the seated figures. He doesn't hear what she says, but sees the speakers looking anxious or irritated. Redmond's wife comes down and speaks to the woman and leads her up to the platform, where she proceeds to talk to Redmond and Dillon. Two men, presumably bodyguards, suddenly take hold of the woman by the arms and force her off the platform. She is shouting something inaudible above the chorus of cheers and jeers that break out. He guesses she's a suffragette and his heart goes out to her.

The incident provokes the start of the meeting. John Dillon speaks first, extolling the merits of Home Rule and a united Ireland.

After a while, with the crowd now eager for stronger fare, Dillon comes to an end and lets Redmond take centre stage. He waves his bowler hat to indicate silence and begins to project his voice across the field, swivelling his head as if trying to pick out someone in the crowd.

'The battle is over. The arguments against Home Rule are dead. The violent language, the demonstrations and threats have done their worst and they have lost.' Cheers from the front of the crowd ripple backwards, eliciting more shouts of encouragement.

Redmond pauses, then jabs a finger at the crowd: 'We can never assent to the mutilation of our nation. Our country is a unit and must remain so. *A country divided into two is an abomination and a blasphemy.*'

Another cascade of cheers and a couple of bowler hats are thrown into the air. 'We do not reject Ulster. By no means. The Catholics of Ulster and, yes, the Protestants as well, have been responsible for many glorious episodes in our struggle for nationhood.'

He pauses, as if waiting for a cheer, but none comes. Nor is there enthusiasm when he declares: 'I am as proud of *Derry* as of Limerick.'

He carries on, by turns rousing and soothing the crowd, eventually ending with a flourish. 'To accept self-government without the inclusion of our cousins in the north would create for all times a sharp, eternal dividing line between Irish Catholics, a measure which would for all time mean the partition and disintegration of our nation. *To that we as Irish nationalists can never submit.*'

Cheers erupt, hats are thrown high and even the lugubrious John Dillon manages to curve his lips into a smile while throwing his bony fingers together in a clapping motion. Mrs Redmond stands up and presses her cheek against her husband's and the meeting comes to an end.

HE IS HAVING BREAKFAST and Douglas is gripping a newspaper. 'That woman you saw. The one ejected from Redmond's monster meeting. Mrs Sheehy-Skeffington. Says so here.' He waits for Douglas to read the article aloud.

'Mrs Sheehy-Skeffington, the well-known suffragette, was

allowed on to the platform on condition of good behaviour. She declined to give that guarantee and was led away from the platform and escorted from the Field, where a crowd greeted her exit with a mainly hostile reaction.'

Douglas puts the paper down. 'Takes brass neck to do what she did, I'll say that for her. Brave lot, those ladies. Mrs Pankhurst rotting in a British jail, and the Davis woman throwing herself in front of the king's horse. But angry deeds cause angry deeds, isn't that so, Pat? Turn the other cheek, that's what we Friends say. Those women should become Quakers. We've always given women respect and equal rights.'

He tells Douglas about the suffragette demonstration in London, and this elicits heavy sighs from his landlord. 'What's the world coming to, Pat. Women breaking windows and being roughed up by Peelers. Is that what we've sunk to?'

HE'S SITTING WITH DOUGLAS by the fire in the parlour. An evening in late November, the east wind beating rain onto the windows and making the chimney echo. He is reading a huge heavy Bible that belonged to Thomas Newsome, Douglas's grandfather. He turns the pages as if they might disintegrate from anything but the lightest of touches. Now and again, at Douglas's behest, he reads out a passage.

Douglas, meanwhile, is absorbed by a letter. 'Listen to this, Pat. It's from my brother Benjamin in Dublin. There's a new mob on the streets: they're calling themselves the *Irish Volunteers* and being led by a certain Eoin MacNeill. Benjamin was curious enough to attend their first meeting.'

Douglas squints at the letter as if it's written in a foreign language.

'This is what Mr Eoin MacNeill said: "We invite the able-bodied men of Ireland to form themselves into a united and disciplined body of freemen, prepared to secure and maintain the rights and liberties common to all the people." What do you think of that, Pat? Do you want your rights and liberties maintained by these *Volunteers*? But you'll like this bit, my boy:

"There will be *no distinction of religion* in the membership of the Irish Volunteers." '

Douglas looks at him, waiting for a response, then prompts him: 'You're always saying how you'd abolish all the churches and that God can't be sliced up—so you must at least applaud their tolerance. Catholics and Protestants drilling together— that's one better than the Ulster Volunteers, with their Protestant sashes and bowler hats. This new lot will have guns that respect no church!' Douglas puts down the letter. 'Cheer me up Pat. What are you reading?'

' "And it shall come to pass in the last days, saith God, I will pour out of my Spirit upon all flesh: and your sons and your daughters shall prophesy, and your young men shall see visions, and your old men shall dream dreams… And I will show wonders in heaven above, and signs in the earth beneath; blood, and fire, and vapour of smoke." '

Douglas's eyes bulge with epiphany: 'Good God, "wonders in heaven above"—it's those aeroplanes. And "vapours of smoke"—the motor car! The last days are upon us, Pat.'

When he goes to bed, he finds himself thinking about the new Irish Volunteers. Apart from the strife caused by the Dublin Lock-out, with employers and workers at each other's throats, the country is in the grip of a mad military escalation. Organisations breeding new and opposing organisations. He used to smile at Douglas's claim that he got himself to sleep at night by counting up the country's factions: the United Irish League, the Gaelic League, the Gaelic Athletic Association, Sinn Féin, the Wolfe Tone Club, Ulster Volunteers, the Orange Order, Irish Women's Franchise League, the Ancient Order of Hibernians. He can add the Irish Volunteers to the list.

CHRISTMAS DAY, 1913. HE and Douglas are walking along the river. Clouds, like huge snowdrifts, are dimming the low sun, intensifying the colour of brick walls and slate roofs; churchgoers stream in and out of grey churches.

They return home. Lamps darken the world beyond the window. Douglas resumes cooking the pot of stew; two bottles of porter and two crystal glasses wait on the linen tablecloth. They exchange presents before dinner. Douglas gives him a pair of socks, and he reciprocates with an ivory comb that Douglas greets with unfeigned delight. After a silent prayer, the two men begin their dinner. It reminds him of his first Christmas with Faith in Wimbledon. Just the two of them thinking of home.

As he eats his lamb and sips his porter he feels content but unaccountably sad. He and Douglas have become attached to each other, and his life in Limerick is comfortable and safe. He has sufficient work to pay his way and to distract him from larger concerns. He meets agreeable people from time to time, not least Ernest and other members of the Quaker community. Compared with the strikers in Dublin or the poor anywhere, he is living the life of a Turkish pasha. A roof over his head, warmth, food, company. But for some time he's had daydreams of Skellig and climbing to the top of the southern peak and looking down at the swirl of the sea, the horizon stretching to dark infinity. The Quaker Meeting House event has been his only talk, or rather, non-talk, in Limerick; yet his purpose for coming to the city was to speak to people. He prays for a new year that will bring fresh impetus and direction to his life, and to the country. The formation of armed militias in the North and South have been unsightly scars on 1913. Surely 1914 will be better.

He and Douglas are holding the lapels of their coats together and tucking their chins into their scarves against the January wind. A freezing start to 1914. They make their way along yellow-lit roads to Cecil Street, where they will attend a public talk on the formation of the Irish Volunteers in Limerick. 'Better to know the devil,' Douglas had said in persuading him to go. Like Douglas, he abhors the idea of a recruitment meeting; but the epidemic of excitement in the city, and perhaps having some of his mother's Fenian blood, have made him curious.

THEY JOIN THE CROWD outside the Athenaeum Hall and file into a long rectangular room filled mostly with men of all ages and a scattering of women. Three small glass domes set into the ceiling lead their eyes to a night-sky artificially darkened by the wall lamps.

He and Douglas find two seats at the back, almost at the end of the row. There's a piece of paper on his seat. He reads the words with full attention: 'I, the undersigned, desire to be enrolled in the Irish Volunteers, formed to secure and maintain the rights and liberties common to all the people of Ireland without distinction of creed, class, and politics.' He puts it in his jacket pocket.

He becomes aware of an agitation in the gathering audience; there's a shifting around in the seats, unrestrained laughter, comments exchanged between companions but made for public consumption, heads straining to look at the stage or turning round to see who's entering the auditorium. By contrast, the aisle seat next to him is taken by a man wearing a felt hat and mackintosh who is keeping as still as a cat that's spotted something in the bushes.

The murmur in the hall grows louder, and sporadic clapping breaks out as three or four men walk on stage. One of them is tall and slender, and dressed in a pale suit and waistcoat that looks too summery for the month of the year; his luxuriant beard froths neatly around his mouth, cheeks and chin.

Douglas leans over and whispers to him, 'Sir Roger Casement'. He is surprised that a 'sir' would be urging the folk of Limerick to join a nationalist army.

Casement's words, spoken in a crisp English accent, induce a hush; the man next to him gets out a notebook and starts writing. Probably a newspaper reporter.

The main speaker takes centre stage. He is shorter but more solid than Casement and radiates neatness. His trim dark hair, not too long or short, and double-breasted suit give him the bearing of a civil servant. The master of ceremonies introduces him as Pádraig Pearse; barely has the name left his lips when Pearse begins talking. Dispensing with pleasantries, he announces that, 'Volunteer companies are springing up in our towns and country places.' He pauses and directs his gaze to the back of the hall: 'Dublin has pointed the way. Galway has followed Dublin, Cork has followed Galway, Wexford has followed Cork.' Again he pauses and the audience knows what is coming next: 'Now it is time for Limerick to follow suit.' A cheer goes up, and the man sitting next to him scribbles away, his left hand shielding his notes.

Pearse waves his hands to dampen the noise. 'There is again in Ireland the murmur of marching, and talk of guns and tactics. What this movement may mean for our country no man can say. But it is plain to all that the existence on Irish soil of an Irish army is the most portentous fact that has appeared in Ireland for over a hundred years.' He allows a silence to increase the tension. 'Home Rule may come or may not come, but under Home Rule or in its absence there remains for the Volunteers and for Ireland the substantial business of achieving Irish nationhood. And I do not know how nationhood is achieved except by armed men; I do not know how nationhood is *guarded* except by armed men.'

Again cheers erupt and heads swivel in flurries of excited comments. He looks at Douglas and then at the man on his other side, who meets his gaze by putting his hand over his notebook and staring at him with disconcertingly pale grey eyes. He turns back and sees that Douglas's head has sunk, always a sign of his discomposure. Douglas points to the stage: 'He's a trouble-maker this one. An Irish army! Dear God deliver us.'

Pearse gestures for silence. His voice gathers more intensity: 'In every generation we have renewed the struggle, and so it shall be unto the end. When England thinks she has trampled out our battle in blood, some brave man rises and rallies us again; when England thinks she has purchased us with a bribe, some good man redeems us by a sacrifice. Wherever England goes on her mission of empire we meet her and we strike at her; yesterday it was on the South African veldt, tomorrow it may be in the streets of Dublin. We pursue her like a sleuth-hound; we lie in wait for her and come upon her like a thief in the night; *and some day we will overwhelm her with the wrath of God.*' One man rises to his feet and others follow his lead, but Pearse waves them down, a smile of gratitude and intoxication lighting up his features.

Some brave man. He feels the same excitement as when he heard Annie Besant. He can remember her words, 'Where an idea is burning in the hearts of the people... some great man is born in whom that idea takes shape, who carries it to realisation.' She was talking about a world teacher—poor little Jiddu!—but who does Pearse have in mind? He can see a glow coming off his head. He realises it is an aura, like the one Jiddu saw on him; but this one is a deep orange colour. It is the first aura he has seen, and it worries him that a man talking about armies, blood and sacrifice should be emitting such a light. Perhaps only he can see it?

He doesn't know why he looks around, but he sees two men at the door, big fellas with caps on, talking to each other and pointing in his direction. The next thing they have lurched forward and one of them has grabbed the man sitting next to him and yanked him out of his seat. The two of them thrust the man against the wall and one of them prises the notebook from his fist before they frog-march him outside; virtually nobody notices.

He is shaken by this ejection, but Pearse's words distract

him. 'So when England talks of peace, we know our answer: "Peace with you? Peace while your one hand is at our throat and your other hand is in our pocket ? Peace with a footpad? Peace with a pickpocket? Peace with the leech that is sucking our body dry of blood? Peace with the many-armed monster whose tentacles envelop us while its system emits an inky fluid that shrouds its work of murder from the eyes of men? The time has not yet come to talk of peace."'

The hall erupts and Pearse is nodding his head, as if he is conducting the noise with it. Douglas turns to him: 'Let's go. I've had enough of this.' But he is too hypnotised by Pearse's conviction and rhetoric. The man has a peculiar force that seems supernatural. Everything he says revolts him, but his words make his heart beat faster in a thrilling way; and it's as if he can hear the hearts of everyone in the audience beating faster too. The thought of an Irish army defeating the British! Half a million desperate men against garrisons of a few thousand? It suddenly seems so plausible.

The deep orange glow around Pearse's head seems to be radiating towards the back of the hall. 'It would appear that the impossible has happened: the young men of Ireland are learning again the noble trade of arms. When we stand armed as Volunteers we shall at least be men and be able to come into communion with the virile generations of Ireland. The only question that need trouble us now is this: will the young men of Ireland rise to the opportunity that is given them? We have a year before us: the momentous year of 1914. The Movement has no politics, but it stands for Irish liberty against English domination, and sets itself the duty of arming the young men of Ireland in defence of Irish liberty. It is a great opportunity for the young men of Ireland, the young men of Limerick, to be given. *A year is theirs in which to make history.*'

As Pearse sits down the audience rises as if on the end of a giant see-saw.

Douglas and he look at each other and slip out before the exit becomes jammed. The street is empty except for four policeman at the other end of the street, making their way towards the hall, and someone lying on the pavement. As they pass him, he sees it is the man who was sitting next to him. He stops and bends down. The man's right eye is puffy and closed but the left one stares at him, even more pale grey than before. Congealed blood above his top lip. He props the man up against the wall. Douglas is pulling at his sleeve: 'Pat, there's constables coming our way. They'll know we've been in the hall. They'll think we're Sinn Féiners.' Douglas pulls him harshly. He looks into the face of the man as if to express his regret at having to leave him; the eye stares up, cold and glazed, like the eye of a dead predatory fish.

They half walk, half run, home. Inside, Douglas lights the gas beneath a kettle of freezing water; he dreams of a mug of his mother's Jameson's.

'I never heard the like,' says Douglas. 'That Pearse fella's going to start a rebellion single-handed. He must've read that poem by your Yeats friend. Romantic Ireland's not dead yet, and more's the pity I say. He wants to be another Tone or Emmet. Haven't we enough soldiers on the streets without more drilling?'

Douglas looks out of the window as if to spot a line of soldiers passing by. 'Don't care if they're Irish soldiers. Soldiers are soldiers, and guns are guns. What's the point of a gun if you don't fire it? And what can we ordinary folk do about it? Less than forty Quakers in the city. Someone has to do something, say something. Some brave man! We'll have to have you back at the Meeting House, Pat.'

'Why would they rough up a newspaper reporter?'

'Maybe he writes for the *Chronicle* and they deem it too loyal for their liking.'

They stare at the fire and take turns to quote bits of Pearse's speech and bemoan the idea of the Volunteers.

HE GOES TO BED and lies awake. Pearse's phrases range through his mind. Sacrifice, blood, trampling, sleuth-hounds, tentacles, virile generations... some brave man. The thump of the words diminishes, but he is left with the image of an eye staring at him through the darkness with the intensity of a baleful star.

He takes Douglas's paper-knife and slits the envelope and takes out a single sheet of watermarked paper. He looks at the bottom of the page and sees the name Jiddu Krishnamurti.

20 March 1914
Shanklin
Isle of Wight

Dear Patrick,

I am hoping this letter will discover you. Your aunt Faith comes to meetings of the Order of the Star and I was talking to her and we talked about you. She said for me to send a letter to your parents' home in Ireland. So I have done this. I wanted to know how you are and what you are doing. It was very good to meet you in London and I have been thinking much of our conversation. It seemed to me that you were a seeker and, if I may say so, an 'old soul'. It is rare to come across this.

I have not been very busy being the Maitreya! I was taken off to Sicily in January for the warm weather. A strange thing happened when I was there. I was in my room alone and meditating and I felt a presence in the room but knew there could be nobody there. When I opened my eyes I saw an Indian man with a glow around him, an aura. I knew immediately it was the Lord Buddha. I bowed my head and he told me I had to find my own way in life. When I asked him what that was, he did not reply but looked at me and smiled. Then it was as if I had woken up again and he had gone. It is most mysterious, but I find I am having strange experiences all the time.

We are living on the Isle of Wight for the moment. It is very cold here but Nitya and I go for long walks to keep warm. Mrs Besant is in India, helping the country in her many ways. Nitya and I are being looked after by theosophists—members of the Order of the Star. In particular there is a kind woman named Lady Emily Lutyens, who comes down from London to see us. I have been reading English poets, Shelley and Keats. Keats says 'I am half in love with easeful death' and I think of this a lot. Do not worry. I am not planning on killing myself. That would never do for the Maitreya! But I wish sometimes the studying for Oxford would stop. Many people have hopes in me and this is a burden. They are good people. They are kind to me. I do not want to disappoint them and the work is important.

I hope you are finding your way in Ireland. In England there is talk of war, even here on the Isle of Wight. I do not follow political developments but I am aware of anxiety in everyone. It's not just in India and Ireland! We must help people to live in a spiritual way, without hating their neighbours or treating them as inferior beings. It is urgent don't you think? Perhaps you can do something in Ireland? Talk to the people—in the streets, in the fields, wherever you can. Be a light to yourself and people will notice. Please write to me, if you wish, at the address above.

Your friend,
Jiddu Krishnamurti

PS: I have given my first talks. The very first one I was so frightened that I talked from behind the curtain!

The letter makes his heart beat faster. It feels like a rebuke for not carrying out the aspirations he had had on leaving Skellig; or it's like a summons, a call to action, an antidote to Pearse's war cry. He realises how much Pearse has affected him. The man looked like a bank employee, with his suit, neat hair, pinched face and odd-looking eyes; but he could have had the long tangled hair, sack-cloth robe and sandals of an Old Testament prophet the way he stirred the audience. Since his rallying call to the young men of Limerick, the city has been echoing with marching footsteps and military orders: British ones during the day; and, at night, those of the new Irish Volunteers.

He knows he must respond to this new martial spirit, even if only to tell Jiddu that he has tried. He will go out to the city markets with a soapbox. He will tell anyone who will listen, that preparing for war brings about war—the law of magnetic attraction. He will speak about Home Rule, about the Volunteers and the necessity of breaking down divisions between people. From the market places he will progress to anywhere where a crowd can be found. He will try to be like George Fox—dogged, fearless, filled with the holy spirit; he will wait outside churches after services and speak to congregations. If a letter written by a teenager can touch him so much, who knows what sort of an effect his own words, spoken with conviction in the open air, can have?

He is standing on a box by the gate of the Protestant cathedral of St Mary's, which is more the size of a parish church. The low ancient building, sunk solidly into the ground, is closed off from the world by an old stone wall and hedged in by venerable trees and tilting gravestones.

Sunday worshippers are now filing from the building, perhaps forty or fifty of them. He wants to talk to them about the divisiveness of churches. The prospect of speaking to an unwary audience is making him especially nervous, but he has to try. He raises his hand to catch their eyes as they pass him, but person after person either looks away, or gives a theatrical frown, as if he were a beggar or tinker. His words never get past his lips.

Eventually, as he is picking up his soapbox, he sees the minister approaching him.

'Good morning, may I help you?'

'No, Father.' His heart isn't in it. He wants to go home.

The minister visibly relaxes and looks at the blue sky with narrowed eyes, his cheeks pulling upwards to reveal yellow teeth. 'He maketh his sun to rise upon good men and evil.'

'And raineth on just men and unjust.'

'Ah, Matthew 5:45.'

'That's correct, Father.'

'You know your Bible?'

'A little.'

'Good man, good man! I haven't seen your face before?'

'I'm from Galway.'

'Well, you're welcome to join us in this place of worship.'

'Thank you, Father. Let's say I'm not a great one for the inside of a church.'

'You're a Wesleyan?'

'I have loyalty to no church. My father is a Quaker, my mother a Catholic.'

'Very unusual I must say! A house divided against itself. Perhaps a middle way between Quakerism and Romanism might be... the Anglican communion?' A hint of a smirk.

'Are there Catholic and Protestant graves in this burial ground?'

'Certainly. Those Catholic families buried before the Reformation have been allowed to continue to use this sacred ground as a resting place.'

'Tell me this, Father, which graves are nearest heaven—the Protestant or Catholic ones? Or is it that the sun shines upon both alike, and the blue sky bends over all?'

The minister's top teeth bite his bottom lip. 'I suppose your point is a fair one. Are you an evangelical?'

'I'm not anything, Father. Just one who is seeking truth.'

'We're all seeking truth, sir. Simply a matter of how it's done. We have our ways, and others have theirs. And I suppose we shall find out which is right on the great day itself. And how grim if the wretched Mohammedans were right in their assumptions, or the Buddha's followers.'

'Or unlearned folk who believe in God but not in priests and religions.'

The minister's face turns stony and his pink-veined nostrils flare as he opens his mouth to say something; but his thoughts cannot find the right words and instead produce a nod of the head before he walks through the gate.

THE FOLLOWING SUNDAY: HE is standing outside St Munchin's Catholic church. A bright morning with an east wind skimming off the river directly behind him. Mass is still underway. Outside, huddled by the door, a couple of men are snatching a few words between ritual puffs of cigarettes. He is determined to do better this time, be more assertive.

The congregation is emerging, blinking at the sunlight. He takes up his stance on his soapbox, says a little prayer and shouts, 'Good morning!' at the first passers-by. A few people pause. He seizes his chance: 'Does God see double?' He repeats the question and his riddle draws more people into a small group of listeners. 'Does God see double? Or is his vision single?' No one replies. 'You are Catholics and you come here to St Munchin's; and if you look across the river you can see a Protestant place of worship. Does anyone know the name of it?'

A young boy shouts: 'St Munchin's! 'Tis the same name as ours.'

'Correct. St Munchin's. There are *two* St Munchin's in Limerick. Did God make twin brothers and give them the same name, but made one Catholic, the other Protestant?'

He is expecting a reaction, even if only a laugh or two, but no one says anything.

'If religion is to have worth, should it not unite rather than divide people? Catholics believe Protestants will burn in hell. And Protestants ignore and despise Catholics.' He can see three or four people are thinking about this. The rest are irritated or angry. 'Does the Holy Spirit inspire us to form separate religious groups and persecute each other?'

Someone shouts out, 'Tell that to the Protestants! 'Tis them that needs manners.'

The words stir up shouts of support. He glares at the shouter: 'I *will* tell it to the Protestants. I will tell it to everyone. St Paul said that in God there are no men or women, no Irish or English, no Catholics or Protestants, no rich or poor. We are all one people. All of us. If you are wounded, I bleed. If I am grieving you feel my sadness.'

'If an English soldier is bleeding I'd let him bleed!'

The voice provokes laughter and cheers. People drift off, until there's nobody left but himself.

Douglas is shouting at him even though he's just sat down at the same kitchen table. Stabbing the newspaper with a finger, his landlord repeats: 'The Austrian Archduke's been shot. By a Serb.' The windows are inviting June light into the room, but Douglas continues staring into the dark valley of the newspaper.

'Austria's spoiling for a war with Serbia. If they invade, Russia backs the Serbs. If Russia backs the Serbs, Germany backs the Austrians. And you know what that means? Britain joins the war. And France. I'll tell you Pat, we're facing Armageddon. We need to rally the forces of peace. We need to *calm people down*.'

Without thinking, he suggests to Douglas that he might speak in the Meeting House again. Douglas embraces the idea: 'We'll arrange it. This mess in Europe is putting fire into everyone's bellies. Our new *Irish Volunteers* don't need any more encouragement. We Quakers have to stand up and be counted. We'll arrange it. We'll get an audience for you this time. No more of your soapbox sermons outside churches with no one listening to you. A proper advertisement in the *Chronicle*. Then you can tell everyone to drop their weapons, stop drilling and go back home and look after their womenfolk and children. Just pretend you're George Fox.'

EARLY AUGUST. HE IS walking down the stairs, hoping to leave the house before Douglas pounces on him. But Douglas is there at the table, brandishing the newspaper and looking like a child on Christmas day. 'They've done it Pat. Germans have invaded Luxembourg. Crossed the Moselle and headed to the city. Tens of thousands of them, it says here. The Grand Duchess couldn't do a thing. Ordered the surrender of her army. Know how many troops she had? *Four hundred*.'

IT SOUNDS LIKE A yell uttered from downstairs. He stirs from his bed; Douglas is shouting his name. It is the sixth of August, the day before he is due to speak at the Meeting House.

Douglas is at the bottom of the stairs and lowers his voice into a portentous baritone: 'Pat, we're at war. It's done. We're in the war.'

He has been expecting the news, but it is still shocking to hear it. The empire at war. A full-scale war. Not skirmishes in the colonies but modern nations fighting with millions of soldiers and the latest weapons. He feels seasick.

Downstairs, he sits like a criminal being sentenced while Douglas reads out bits from the newspaper. 'They're quoting the English press. The *Mirror* says a war fund of £100,000,000 was voted in the Commons in five minutes. *£100,000,000* Pat! German airships flying over Belgium. Huge crowds at Buckingham Palace singing "God Save the King". Crowds in Fleet Street carrying Union Jacks, watching the bulletins and singing the "Marseillaise". A crowd outside the German embassy booing and hissing. The king's given a message to the empire: "I shall be strengthened in the discharge of the great responsibility which rests upon me by the confident belief that in this time of trial my Empire will stand united, calm and resolute, trusting in God." What do you think of that, Pat? Will we stand *united, calm and resolute*? Can you see Mr Pearse and Mr Eoin MacNeill and their Irish Volunteers doing all those things for His Majesty?'

He breaks away from Douglas's fevered face, and pictures huge German airships floating like an armada of great whales across Europe.

S eventh of August, the day he is due to give his talk; he is trying to distract himself by walking around town. He heads towards St John's Castle and passes crowds in the potato market; he senses the herd excitement of war in faces and murmurings. When he comes to St Mary's Cathedral, scene of his failed soapbox oratory, he decides to go in and sit quietly and compose himself.

The interior is empty apart from an elderly woman sitting at the front, her head bowed in prayer. He flits around the dank interior of the church—glancing at the altar, organ, pulpit, candles, memorial slabs, flowers, flags and other trappings—then sits in a rear pew, well away from the woman. But the latter spots him and comes over to talk. She is tall, with a flat black velvet hat pinned to a silvery bun. She uses her umbrella as a guide for her feet, as if she is clearing undergrowth. She sits down. 'Have you seen the squint?' When he says he hasn't, not knowing what she is referring to, she gets up and gestures with her hand.

In the north side of the church she comes to a halt and points. '*Voilà*, the squint. It's medieval.' He sees a rectangular slit in the wall, almost like the opening of a postbox. 'Not many churches have one. We're proud of ours. It was for lepers. They weren't allowed inside the churches.' She lowers her voice: 'Just as the *Vicar of Rome* prohibits his flock from entering our churches. Pollution.'

'What did the lepers do with the squint?' He crouches and peers into the slit.

'The wretches lined up outside the church during the service. When a bell was rung they'd take it in turns to thrust a hand through this slit.'

The woman demonstrates this by thrusting her own hand through an invisible slit.

'Can you imagine? The priest waiting there and seeing this horrible white *thing* flapping at him! He'd drop the host into the hand and watch it depart whence it came. Then the next hand appeared, and then the next. Pretty rum, don't you think? Not very *Christian* to keep those poor devils outside. What was it the evangelist said about our Lord—Luke, chapter five? Jesus came to a place where there was a leper who knelt down and begged him to heal him and Jesus said "Be thou clean," and the leprosy left him.' She looks at him more intently. 'I haven't seen you here before. Are you from out of town?'

'I'm from Galway, ma'am, and I belong to the Society of Friends.' He decides not to mention his Catholic side.

'Quakers. I see. A strange group of God-fearers if you don't mind me saying so. As long as you're not joining those *ridiculous* new Volunteers.'

'I won't be joining them, ma'am; but they're not ridiculous. They are serious men and no better or worse than other men in arms.'

'By men in arms, are you referring to our soldiers?'

'*Your* soldiers.'

'I see. That sounds like a Fenian sentiment to me. You should be careful what you say, young man. That way of speaking can land you in hot water nowadays. My son works at one of the barracks. I'm not allowed to divulge which one. But let's just say I hear what goes on. A word in your ear, sir, don't be criticising the soldiers. Remember that if war with Germany comes to these shores we shall be fighting to save the skins of all Irish men and women, irrespective of creed. So, there it is. And now I must leave you.'

She gives a nod and makes her way to the door. He watches the framed rectangle of light darken as the door closes.

HE SITS IN THE church for an hour or so before leaving. On Nicholas Street he hurries away from the orchestrated sounds of drilling at the Castle up the road and makes his way to People's Park; there he finds a bench and gathers his thoughts for the talk.

AT SEVEN O'CLOCK HE makes his way slowly to the Meeting House. When he turns into Cecil Street he sees a large crowd up the road. Two RIC men are monitoring the situation. They ignore him as he walks past. At first he thinks it must be a Volunteers enlistment, prompted by Britain's declaration of war. Then he sees women among the men. Perhaps a demonstration against the war? But there's no shouting. Everyone seems orderly. When he approaches No. 36 he realises with consternation what they are doing: coming to hear him speak.

He resists the urge to keep on walking past the crowd and go home. The door is open and someone is stopping people from entering. Those at the back are craning their necks. He moves into the crowd, worms his way to the front and sees Douglas standing inside the door, arguing with a woman whose hat brim extends the width of her shoulders. He catches Douglas's eye. The latter lurches forward and guides him into the house. 'Must be war fever,' Douglas says, perspiration beading itself in his whiskers. 'Never seen the like.'

He says to Douglas: 'What exactly did you say about me in the advertisement?'

'Only that you were a "religious man" who would talk about the war and healing the divisions in our country.'

' "*Healing* the divisions"?'

He squeezes through the packed hallway towards the meeting room. Ernest is guarding the door, his mouth speaking to a woman, his eyes swivelling around the room and appraising the situation. Even though the windows have been opened, people are still flapping bits of paper and hats.

Ernest sees him and calls out: 'Patrick, dear boy, look at all these people! What are we going to do with all these people?'

Every chair in every row is taken and the remaining spaces around the room are filled with people standing; it's like an Underground train.

'I'll keep it short. Those who can't get in can listen outside. The windows are open. I'll raise my voice.'

He eases his way to the lectern and chair at the front and faces the audience. The conversations diminish to a murmuring, then the silence of expectation.

He's never seen a fuller room. Elderly men and women at the front, including a man at the end of the row whose head keeps nodding, as if controlled by strings. At the back, by the door, Douglas is standing next to Ernest, and in the middle, two Catholic priests are sitting beside a Church of Ireland rector.

'Good evening, ladies and gentlemen. It's a warm evening and some of us won't want to be standing too long.' The audience respond with an impatient shuffling.

He senses their war-generated agitation and need for reassurance, yet he knows he has no reassurance to give. He watches the gloved hands of women wafting air onto their pink brows. *Why don't they take their gloves off?* He becomes conscious that the silence is too long. All his prepared thoughts have vanished; he waits for new ones to come. He sees Douglas at the back, his shiny head tilted to get a good view. He has a flash of Douglas reading the newspaper to him and takes a deep breath: 'Austria has declared war on Serbia. Russia has declared war on Germany and Austria. Britain has declared war on Germany. Germany has declared war on Belgium and France. Who will be next? Which will be the next country to declare war? Spain? Sweden? *Ireland?*'

A rogue laugh rings out from the middle of the room and has the strange effect of settling him down. He feels himself entering a dimension of light and calm. He knows the words will come to him; it's as if he can operate at two levels: he can articulate the thoughts slipping into his head and at the same time look around and see reactions without being disturbed by them.

'What makes us go to war? How can we wave off our sons and husbands at stations knowing their trains will take them to the deadly fields of a foreign country? Knowing their loss will darken the rest of our days?'

A woman at the front brings out a handkerchief and blows her nose.

'Is it to protect our countries? Is it to protect countries who are too small to protect themselves?'

157

A voice shouts from the back: 'It's to protect the bloody British Empire.'

Exclamations of 'Shame!' hiss out.

He raises his hand. 'I have no wish to talk about empires, British, German, or French. Or Roman. Empires are designed merely to serve their rulers. There's no argument there. But why does a country invade another one in the first place? For land? For power? Because they imagine they can rule that country better themselves? Or is it something else? Is it that... the desire to be bigger, stronger, more powerful, rich, popular and so on is the way we all live? I mean *all of us.*'

The two priests exchange looks as if realising they're late for mass.

'This desire is not just the vice of politicians, kings and their lackeys, the soldiers and policemen. It can be found in a baker who's pleased his rival's shop has closed down; the priest who is envious of a colleague's popularity; the person who enjoys malicious gossip about his neighbour. It is found in *all of us*, you and me. Governments are created by people like us. Their decision to invade another country merely reflects our own nature, but on a grand scale.'

His passion surprises him and the audience. A man starts clapping but then thinks better of it. He can see an uneasiness in their hot faces, worried faces, annoyed faces. They came to hear him speak about peace, not the source of war being in themselves. He waits for thoughts to return.

'We can blame the Germans till we're blue in the face. And when we've finished, we can blame the Serb who shot the archduke. And we can keep on blaming someone else. Take Home Rule. We can blame Parnell for falling in love with a married woman. John Redmond, for not pushing the British hard enough. Mr Carson, for raising an Ulster army that's making the British hesitate about granting Home Rule. We can blame the British government.'

Someone shouts out, ''*Tis* their fault. Been their fault for seven hundred years.'

'But is the answer to raise armies? Are the Volunteers the

solution to the problem? Or will they only add to it?' Isolated cheers break out. 'And I mean *both* sets of Volunteers, loyalist and nationalist, north and south.'

He pauses again. 'So, what can we do to help this country? In the first instance we can restrain ourselves and others from joining armed militias. Then we can stop blaming other people. As long as we think the problem is someone else's doing and not our own, we will never get anywhere.'

He continues speaking, but after a while a woman standing by the wall faints. Those standing next to her fuss round, propping her up and fanning her face. Ernest signals to him to call a halt to the proceedings.

Before he can do so a woman at the front rises to her feet and pulls up the girl sitting beside her. She shouts out, as if the volume of her voice will stop him leaving: 'Sir, you'd be a wise man, I'd say, and have the power in you. The newspaper said you were a religious man, and my little girl is gripped by pain in her head, drives her to screams in the night, and us after going to Knock and not a thing they could do about it there. Prayin' to Our Lady, we were, and still my Deirdre's eyes'd full of pain, and her head full of pain, and the Lord knows we're believers. The newspaper said you'd be doing the healing. I beg you, sir, lay yer hands on her as our good Lord did.'

He curses Douglas's advertisement; then he wonders how he could have missed the woman—her crumpled hessian smock and brown flat bonnet tied tight are at odds with the gentility of almost everyone else in the room. Her daughter looks about twelve years of age in her grey tunic and white socks, her hair trimmed short. She looks at him as if the dim light of the room is dazzling. A silence has fallen in the wake of the woman's plea for help. He doesn't know what he should do; then he remembers Jiddu telling him he had the power to heal. He has never put it to the test. The woman has brought the girl right up to him. Everyone is watching. He has to try something. Without knowing why, he reaches out his hands and holds the girl's. 'Where exactly is the pain in your head?'

The girl doesn't answer.

159

'It'd be everywhere,' the mother says.

He presses his thumbs into the palms of her hands and shuts his eyes. The words of a psalm come to his lips, *He healeth the broken in heart, and bindeth up their wounds*, and he repeats it softly again and again, concentrating on the touch of his hands against hers. As the words roll off his tongue he begins to feel something like the calm and joy he experienced on Skellig Michael welling up inside; with an act of will he directs this sensation away from his heart and into his arms, where he can sense it move along into his hands then into the girl's. His own hands feel unusually cold, icy even, but he attributes this to the contrast with the patient's. He keeps his grip steady on her flesh and continues the prayer. Then he feels a warmth enter his fingers and spread to his wrists. The heat increases and seeps up his arms; it is as if he has lain in the sun for too long— a harsh prickly heat burning the skin of his shoulders and neck. He keeps holding the girl's hands, still pressing in his thumbs. The sensation of heat begins to subside, and as it does so, he loosens his grip.

The girl's face has changed, her muscles relaxed. She looks up at her mother: ' 'Tis gone.'

The woman's face is theatrical and her voice increases in pitch: 'Holy Mother of God, I haven't seen ye lookin' like that since the Lord knows when. 'Tis a miracle!'

He sits down, aware of the woman kneeling in front of him, reciting something in Irish; aware of faces looking at him, as if they've never seen him before; others are talking all at once, and the words blur into each other. He can't quite believe what has happened. He feels exhausted and closes his eyes. He can hear Ernest and Douglas chivvying people out of the room.

When the noise has subsided he opens his eyes—the room is now empty apart from Ernest, who comes over to him and shakes his hand. Ernest's neat white hair lies like a layer of snow on his head, and his hand is beautifully cool. 'Quite something, Patrick, quite something. Goodness, that woman and her daughter! I never knew you had the gift of healing. You'll be the talk of the town. We'll speak again another time—you look worn out—I'll let you out the back—there's a crowd at the front.' He allows Ernest to guide him to a door.

He is leaving the building, breathing in the night air, steadying himself. All he can see is the face of the girl… and the mother kneeling at his feet. He has no idea how he made the girl's pain go away. Perhaps it will soon return?

He heads home by back roads. In Wickham Street the outlines of a group of men ahead prompt him to turn right into Mulgrave Street. The open market area is usually swathed in darkness at this time of the night, but now it's lit with small oil lamps. He stops. He can see a regiment of ghosts: about a hundred men are walking up and down, dressed in overcoats, marching in formation, their boots and shoes soft on the ground. They are holding hurleys, ashplants and other wooden implements as if they were rifles. Volunteers! He becomes semi-mesmerised by the rhythm of their steps. He hasn't seen the Volunteers close up before. Irish men, drilling like soldiers; an Irish army; it seems incredible. Pearse's words come raging into his head and he feels a pang of dismay and—he's ashamed to admit it—pride.

A small spurt of flame along the street distracts him. Someone is lighting a cigarette and in the brief glow he can discern the green caps and uniforms of two RIC men. The policemen spot him and walk towards him purposefully; he wants to set off in the other direction, but he's feeling too tired; besides he has nothing to fear from them. When the two men arrive, they stand either side of him and begin to search him. One of them pulls out a piece of paper from his jacket, unfolds it, reads it and shows it to his colleague: it's the Volunteers' leaflet he picked up from Pearse's talk.

The men handcuff him and lead him into the centre of the city.

He is walking into a room that has a table and three chairs, a fire place, and a clock on the wall. A policeman pushes him towards one of the chairs and leaves the room. Another policeman returns with a colleague, who is smaller and older and has a salt-and-pepper moustache. His lips bear a pained expression, as if he is suffering from a headache or stomach cramps. He is reminded of the face of the girl he's just seemingly healed. The two men sit opposite him; the older man, presumably the sergeant, is holding a mug of tea.

'You were caught carrying seditious material. What is your name?' He speaks with a sharp Northern or Scottish twang.

'Patrick Bowley.'

'Address?'

'I'm living with Douglas Newsome in St Harry's Mall.'

The sergeant gestures to the constable, who inspects a sheaf of papers. 'Newsome, Douglas. Quaker, sir.'

'Residing with a pacifist?' The sergeant spits out 'pacifist' as if a fly has flown into his mouth. 'You're not from here?'

'Galway.'

'You've come down here to make trouble. Loitering by an illegal parade and carrying seditious literature.'

'I picked it up from the Athenaeum. The parade is not illegal.'

'It is if we say so. I know where you got the leaflet. Didn't throw it away, did you?'

A long silence. The sergeant sips his tea, his steamy breath rising to the ceiling.

It's the first time he's been inside a police barracks; fear has desiccated his mouth and tightened his stomach.

'We've had three good constables set upon, beaten up, since Mr Pearse spouted his treason. Someone is going to pay for that. We need information. Where are the Volunteers getting their guns from?'

'I don't know. I have nothing do with them.'

'I think you're lying. Before your arrest you were addressing a crowd in premises on Cecil Street. We saw the

162

advertisement in the *Chronicle*. We had someone there. Your sentiments were pacifist at best; at worst pro-Germany, a country we're at war with. You were then found attending a so-called Volunteers' parade.'

'I was speaking at a Quaker meeting house. I was not attending a parade. I was on my way home. I have nothing to do with any organisation, Sinn Féin, Volunteers, none of them.' He is holding onto his chair to keep his voice steady.

'Who mentioned any organisation? The Volunteers in Dublin recently received a shipment of guns from Germany. We need information on the Limerick lot. Who's giving them guns? Who's controlling them?'

He does not reply.

'Answer the sergeant's question.' The constable gets up and stands behind him. He remains silent; he doesn't know the answer. The sergeant nods and the constable lashes out with his fist and knocks him off his chair. He lies there for a moment, in shock, then gets up, shaking. A terrible pain in his cheek; his eyes watering. His lips are quivering, like a little boy who is trying not to cry. The constable is flexing his fingers.

'Where are the guns coming from?' The sergeant's tone has darkened. His cheek now feels numb yet roaring with pain; he's too frightened not to reply.

'Don't know. Told you. I've nothing to do with those men. Don't know if they've guns or not.' He hears the jerky note of desperation in his voice.

In one swift movement the sergeant throws the contents of his mug into his face. The scalding liquid hits his skin and he yelps. He tries to stand up but the constable presses down his shoulders. The sergeant leans forward. 'Listen carefully. I have men on the street being spat at, cursed and threatened. We are not going to stand by while hundreds of layabouts are drilling and arming themselves. I'm giving you three minutes to tell me where the guns are coming from. If not, I'm handing you over to my superior. He's on secondment from Dublin Castle. They like to send instructors down here to teach us provincials their wicked ways. His name is Smith. An ordinary enough name you may think. But his nickname is Razor. Believe me, you'll save yourself a lot of bother if you start helping us.'

His face is stinging with heat, his cheek throbbing. The clock ticks. He doesn't know what he can say to placate the sergeant. Three minutes.

The sergeant leaves the room, shaking his head. Almost immediately the door opens again and another man enters. He is average height and dressed in a double-breasted suit. He takes out a silver case and lights a cigarette. His cheeks contract as he sucks in the smoke. The man scrutinises him and says nothing, then moves closer and looks at his face more searchingly. He braces himself for some act of violence and tries not to shake. The man backs away and stands facing the fireplace. Then he turns round, nodding his head. 'I've got it.' He speaks with a soft English accent. 'I've bloody well got it! Do you know why they call me Razor?'

He fears the consequence of remaining silent: 'I don't know why.'

'I have a razor-sharp memory.'

The man taps his temple as if pointing out the exact spot where his memory is located.

'And do you know what I've just remembered? It may be your lucky day Mr Bowley. Back of the Athenaeum. Pearse's address. I was sitting next to you, taking notes on Mr Pearse's speech—until I was removed without my consent. And I'm pretty sure it was you who looked into my eyes when I was lying in the street, the worse for wear. I suppose I should be grateful those Sinn Féin thugs didn't do me worse damage. I think you wanted to help me. Your friend wanted to scarper. You see, I never forget a detail. That's how I ended up in this line of business. Intelligence work can be disagreeable. But a good memory helps you up the ranks.'

He stares at Smith's face but the light is too dim to see whether he has those pale grey eyes.

'You'd better tell me your story.'

'I'm a pacifist. Brought up as a Quaker. The Friends here invited me to speak about the war. That's what I was doing. I took a short-cut home. I saw the Volunteers.'

'What about your pro-German rhetoric? What are we, servants of His Majesty's Government, supposed to make of that in a time of war?'

'It wasn't pro-German. It was against all violence.'

'How do you explain Pearse's leaflet in your jacket?'

'I put it in my pocket and forgot to remove it. I'm against all Volunteers. All factions.'

'And the army, presumably.'

He says nothing.

'So, when the Germans arrive on this island, bayonetting babies and raping women, you'll politely inform them that you disagree with their actions?'

He says nothing.

'I can see my point of view better than I can see yours.' He blows smoke from his nostrils and smoothes it away from his eyes.

He feels he must say something. 'Violence isn't the answer. Militias aren't the answer.'

'I agree about militias. But there must be law and order.'

'So that the empire can hold onto its possessions.' He wishes he hasn't said that.

Smith takes a drag of his cigarette and sends a plume of blue smoke towards the ceiling: 'You sound like Pearse.'

He says nothing.

'Tell me. What do you make of Pearse's elegant essay on "the coming revolution"—published end of last year.'

'I know of no such work.'

'Really?' Smith takes folded papers from his inside jacket pocket. 'Let me read you a sample. It may explain why we take an interest in those who keep Volunteer leaflets about their person. First of all he has a bit of windy religiosity: "I do not know if the Messiah has yet come... the people itself will perhaps be its own Messiah, the people labouring, scourged, crowned with thorns, agonising and dying, to rise again immortal and impassible." '

As he listens to the words Smith is reading, he can see

Pearse's neat figure on the Athenaeum stage, his head surrounded by that deep glowing light.

'Cracked-up nonsense, but in the wrong minds it might prove inflammatory. This is rather more to the point: "Bloodshed is a cleansing and a sanctifying thing, and the nation which regards it as the final horror has lost its manhood. There are many things more horrible than bloodshed; and slavery is one of them." There you have it. Dangerous tosh. Mr Pearse is gunning for a martyrdom, if you ask me.'

He says nothing.

'What are we going to do with you? That is the question.'

Smith saunters up and down the room, hands in pockets. He stops and gives out a heavy sigh. 'I'll tell you what. We're going to let you go. I don't think you're a rebel in the making. I've seen a few of those in my time and somehow you don't fit the profile. You have the look of a... *priest* about you, if I may say so. Can't really see you gun-running or joining some band of clowns who think a bit of marching with broomsticks will turn them into soldiers. I'm giving you the benefit of the doubt. This time. You need to be careful Mr Bowley; promoting your pacifism, hanging around rebels and carrying silly leaflets isn't a good idea at all. Your name will be put on the list. Count yourself lucky. We're having a wretched time of it at the moment. Everyone thinks they're a rebel. Down to me, I'd shoot the likes of Pearse and Casement straightaway. No messing around. Just get rid of them. But we have to go through the correct procedures. You Irish must laugh at us. Forming your own Volunteer army in broad daylight. That's what I call democracy.' He lets out a grunt, like a belch. 'I apologise for my constable and sergeant. They're under pressure. They report to people like me, who expect them to be thorough. If you're mixed up with any unsavoury characters I should desist if I were you. Keep away from the likes of Pearse. He will drown in his own rhetoric, but he might take others with him. "The people will be the Messiah, scourged, crowned with thorns, agonising and dying, to rise again immortal." You see, he's got me at it too.'

Smith walks over and points to the door. 'Do we have an understanding?' He nods. 'I don't want to see you ever again, Mr Bowley. Believe me, if I do, I will show no mercy.'

HE LEAVES THE POLICE station and just past the front of it he sinks to his knees; his whole face is in pain and his teeth start chattering even though the night air is mild; he thinks of what might have happened, and is shocked by the depth of his fear, his cowardice. He forces his legs to move forward.

WHEN HE REACHES GEORGE Street it is as if he's crossed the border into a friendly country. He runs towards the canal and arrives at Douglas's house. He pushes the door open and collapses in a chair. Douglas ministers to him, while he tries to relate what has happened, forcing down the emotion until it becomes hiccups and snuffles.

He is on a train to Achill Island. The carriage feels self-contained and so safe. Outside, the west of Ireland sweeps away into the distance: endless dry-stone walls enclosing oblongs of fields and scatterings of cows; hoof-churned mud by iron gates; cottages with whitewashed walls made blotchy by rain and wind. And no one to be seen.

After his interrogation his one thought was to get away from Limerick. To go somewhere remote enough to take stock of his life—to be as far away as possible from the daily bulletins of war and the exhilarating dread animating the people of the city. Most of all, to forget the faces of those policemen.

The train stops at Claremorris. A few passengers holding bags, sacks and battered brown suitcases get off, including a soldier, who stands on the platform jerking his head around to see if anyone has come to meet him. A long whistle from the guard initiates the slow creaking of the carriages and the train begins to slip into its huge mechanical rhythm. The station buildings move into the past along with the soldier, who he now sees is holding a long white stick.

The man sitting next to him is reading a newspaper with the headline: 'Marne: Germans Falling Back. Franco-British Successes in Great Battle. Check to German Advance.' He tries not to think about what the headline is concealing: mangled corpses lying in the mud; mothers and fathers with a vast new emptiness in their lives.

They arrive at Westport. He gets out and changes to a smaller train for the final part of the journey that will take him to the farthest point west and the Atlantic ocean.

A blast of a whistle jolts him from his thoughts; the train lumbers off towards Achill, the island which, because of a land-bridge, isn't quite an island.

As they follow the northern side of Clew Bay towards Newport, he sees flashes of images of that strange day in Limerick. The leper's 'squint' in the church. His talk at the Meeting House and all those hot faces. The little girl in pain—the heat in his hands was not an illusion; she said the pain had gone. Could he do it again? Was it just lucky timing—the girl was getting better anyway? Perhaps he should try to heal people and forget his soap-box? Suddenly he's back in the police barracks, staring at Razor Smith.

The shock-dark of a tunnel clears his mind; then daylight leaps back and he sees they are crossing a river and coming into Newport. A shudder of a stop. Slamming of metal on metal. After shedding more steam and smoke the locomotive stirs into motion again and is soon shaking off clusters of cottages. How wonderful not to have another conversation about the war with Douglas, dear old Douglas, who seemed to be trapped in a childhood world of lead soldiers.

THE TRAIN COMES TO the end of the line. Achill Sound. Twenty or so passengers get off and divide themselves into groups to board two of the three jaunting cars. He takes his seat and the driver drapes an unnecessary rug over his knees. His body adjusts to the new rhythm of horses' hooves and wheels crunching into the patina of dried mud. Within minutes they are crossing the land-bridge; on either side the sea is low, with swathes of dimpled sand poking through the water; in front, high bare hills rise against the sky.

The car rattles along, a wheel sometimes sinking into a puddled hole, the thud of hooves giving a false impression of speed. The sky is dropping all around them, an incoming grey tide around soft islands of white cloud. Everywhere he looks there is a wilderness of boggy moorland and shapeless hedgerows lit by the fiery dots of fuchsia; in the fields, the isolated figures of crimson-shawled women are bearing creels of turf on their backs, as if they are carrying the world. Small silver lakes appear, irregular gaps waiting for jig-saw pieces. He sees a pyramidal peak rising above low hills and knows they must be approaching Slievemore mountain and the village of Doogort.

The road turns inland and white cubes of houses appear in the shadow of the mountain. He remembers Douglas telling him how Doogort was founded by a Church of Ireland minister called the Reverend Nangle, several years before the great hunger—to convert the Catholics of Achill and start a Protestant colony. The colony lasted for a few decades then petered out. But the houses of the colonists remain.

The car stops at the Slievemore Hotel. He is tempted to stay there for the night, but another car is ready to take passengers farther south to Keel, where he has decided to stay. He looks at the rows of whitewashed buildings, some dilapidated, and imagines hardy Protestants going around the island, knocking at doors and being listened to politely by the peasants, who, after their visitors had left, would probably cross themselves and sprinkle holy water.

He gets into the car for Keel. Away from the jagged presence of Slievemore, the landscape softens; within half an hour he sees the Atlantic meeting the bottom edge of the sky.

They stop at a small hotel, a neat two-storey building with a slate roof, its entrance facing inland in the direction of Slievemore, and its back braced against the ocean wind. He enters. A woman wearing an apron and deferential in the way of a servant fetches the proprietor, who introduces himself as Thomas. He's shown a small room with a single bed facing a window that frames the sea and evening sun. There's just enough space for a chair, desk and a wardrobe. He slings his case onto the chair and lies on the bed.

He wakes in semi-darkness and goes downstairs to the bar. Thomas is talking to an old farmer, whose strands of hair flop forward whenever he looks down to pick up his whiskey. The farmer shifts on his bar-stool and scans him up and down without inhibition. ' 'Tis company we have. Where're you from, boy?' He tells him he is from Galway and a carpenter by trade. The farmer grunts as if he were being told something he knew already. Thomas's wife, a silent dark stocky woman named Bella, offers him supper and disappears to prepare food. The farmer dominates the conversation, occasionally allowing Thomas to throw in a comment before continuing his flow, which before long turns to the war.

'Bloody Germans will be running this show before I'm

seventy-three. You'd think we'd've had enough of the Protestants telling us what to do on Achill.'

'Ah, Gerry, Nangle and his fellas have long gone,' Thomas folds his arms.

'Thank the Lord and Blessed Mary. *Nangle* making soupers of us all.'

'He saved many from starving, it's said.'

'In return for Protestant souls,' the farmer cackles, turning to him and looking him up and down. 'And what about you, young fella, are you with us or a *Nangler?*'

'I don't follow any particular religious path,' he says.

'An atheist then.'

'I'm not. I believe we are all part of a divine plan.'

'Divine plan is it? Sounds Proddy talk to me. Their divine plan is to come back to haunt us with the building of this railway. Lords and ladies from Dublin and Belfast. Come to watch us peasants digging the fields. Walking around with their canes like slave-owners in *Mississippi*.'

Bella appears with a tray. She hands him a plate: a fish with its head still on, a boiled egg and three potatoes. He eats as slowly as he can, resisting the urge to shovel the food in. He listens as Thomas and the farmer expostulate and grunt their way through local news, including who has joined the Rangers or Fusiliers. Then they turn to John Redmond's decision to support Britain in the war and how this has caused the Irish Volunteers to split into two groups, loyalists and nationalists.

'Making of a civil war there,' says the farmer. 'Eoin MacNeill and his band of Volunteer lads would never be fighting for England, no matter what.'

Thomas thinks about this and says: 'There'll be no fighting between us in the south. It's Carson's army in the north is the worry. Signing a covenant with their own blood.'

'John Redmond's the king of eejits,' says the farmer. 'Supporting the empire! Fine words never killed the pig.'

'But you can see what Redmond's driving at,' Thomas says. 'If we're supporting England in the war, how can they refuse us Home Rule afterwards? 'Twould be shocking if they did.'

'The English'll find some other way to pin us to the floor. They'll let us die in French mud then tell us we're not fit to govern ourselves.'

Thomas continues to be the voice of reason: 'They've passed the Bill. They can't go back on that.'

'Passed the Bill alright. But not going to do anything about it till the end of the war, sez they. Scared the empire will crumble.'

He is finishing his supper when a couple enter the bar. The man, probably in his late thirties, has a narrow face with dark horizontal eyebrows and barely an indent on the bridge of his nose; the strength of these features is offset by large watery eyes and lips pursed into a rosebud. His companion's age is less easy to gauge; her broad hat is pulled down over her forehead and her eyes look away from the company; her mouth is set, as if in resistance to a thought. The couple hesitate as if they're not sure whether to join the company at the bar. The woman looks pretty and refined and, as if sensing his attention, she returns his gaze. The couple don't linger, and he hears the stairs creak beneath their combined weight.

'Quare folk,' mutters the farmer.

'Artistic folk, Ger, artistic folk,' says Thomas. 'Painters.'

'German spies more like. We're told to look out for them.'

He goes outside. He can hear the sea and smell fire-smoke. He walks down to the shore, where his boots leave neat prints in the mush. It is mild for late September. He strolls and watches the waves tumbling and withdrawing like slithering white serpents. It is too dark to go far. He retraces his steps towards the glow of cottage windows and at last feels that he has left Limerick behind.

A STILL EVENING AT the start of October. He is walking westward towards the village of Dooagh. The sea is crashing down on his left and a strange glow is coming from the bridge over the stream. He can see a figure standing there, dressed in white, with orange-coloured lanterns arranged on the wall beside her.

She is wearing a large hat and standing in front of an easel. Her paintbrush is poised, like the beak of a heron. He instinctively moderates his step so as not to disturb her. He guesses that it is the artist woman. When he is a dozen yards away she looks round, broken from her trance, then turns back to her painting. He wonders whether he should stop or keep going. He compromises. He calls out, 'Decent evening for the month that's in it,' and does not break step. He hears her say something indistinct in response. After a hundred yards or so he looks back and sees the glow lighting up her smock. The sea distracts him, as does the hastening transformation of the landscape into darkness. A half moon projects enough light onto the track to keep him from stumbling. By the time he turns back and retraces his steps, she has gone. It's as if he's seen a ghost.

THE FOLLOWING MORNING: HE is in the empty bar, about to go out on further explorations, but the rain is lashing the windows. He takes a seat and shuts his eyes. When he opens them the stolid figure of the male artist is standing there, wearing a tweed jacket, a cape draped over his arm. His eyes are bulging at the rain. He introduces himself as Paul Henry and says that he and wife, Grace, are staying on Achill for a while.

'Looks like the rain's setting in.' Henry greets these words by peering out of the window and grunts to verify his assessment.

'I'd say the solitude would be good for your painting.'

'Precisely. Solitude. And light, mountains and lakes.'

'Is that what you paint?'

'I paint things that have been here before us and will remain after the last creature has left this planet. Wars come and go, but sky, sea and cloud are constants. That's what art does. Makes the world eternal, freed from the cycle of growth and decay. Isn't that right?'

The mention of a cycle reminds him of Nietzsche and the book he read, and re-read, in Faith's flat. He finds himself saying: 'Was it Nietzsche who said life was like a sandglass? Time runs out, then the glass is turned over and it all begins again. Might take thousands and thousands of years but every thought, every pain and pleasure, everything that has made you what you are is repeated. We may be repeating this very moment here!'

Henry looks at him as if hearing the name Nietzsche uttered on Achill were outlandish, then says: 'Perhaps history *is* coming round again. After all, as my pious brother keeps telling me, it's the same situation here in Ireland as it was in Palestine at the time of our Lord. Two empires, British and Roman. They had a procurator, we have a Lord Lieutenant. They had their freedom fighters—the Zealots—and we have the IRB. They had their rival sects, the Sadduccees and Pharisees, we have Church of Ireland and Catholics. The Jews kept threatening to rebel, so do we. Their rising came in 69.'

Henry's words jolt him. The same conditions! The cycle coming round again. It jogs his memory of William Yeats's words at Tulira Castle about cycles of civilisation and how the moment when one ends and the other begins a man of destiny appears. And isn't that what the theosophists believe too?

Henry continues: 'When is our rising going to come? Who's going to lead it? Mr Pearse? Mr MacNeill? Larkin? Connolly? Who's going to stop it? So perhaps Mr Nietzsche's sandglass idea is correct. I try to stay away from such thoughts. That way madness lies. The only antidote to war is beauty. I paint Achill—not the Achill that decays but the Achill that remains incorruptible. And what is incorruptible can be subject to no cycle or repetition. Look at us here… we could be the last survivors on earth and we wouldn't know it. Just us and the landscape, in communion. Nothing turbulent apart from the passing of clouds, changing the light. Rather beautiful.'

He notices a softening of Henry's face as he says these last few words. Then his features return to their set lines and thickness. The rain intensifies and the windows become squares of runny greyness. Henry nods at him and disappears upstairs.

He stays sitting where he is, imagining the mountains and the sea, magnificent but lacking all human warmth. He thinks of Palestine and Ireland, the Roman and the British Empire. The rebellion by the Jews.

EVENING; THE RAIN HAS cleared. He goes for a walk and sets out west towards the glimmer above the distant hills. He sees the familiar soft orange light. This time he decides not to disturb the painter. But as he is approaching the bridge Grace Henry puts down her brush and palette and turns to face him. She adjusts her hat as if to look at him more clearly. He goes over to her and utters a greeting, which she reciprocates with a voice that has a slight Scottish accent. Her eyes are full of concentrating thought, her light blue smock bright in the glow. She stares at him as if she, or he, has committed an indiscretion. He waits for her to say something, since it is she who has turned to address him. But she says nothing, as if there is too much going on in her head and she doesn't know where to start. She looks several years older than himself and has an attractive, womanly figure, though it is difficult to picture her smiling. She turns her head to the painting she is working on as if about to introduce it to him as a companion. He looks at the canvas and sees a night-time scene, a mountain in the background, presumably Slievemore, silhouetted, a blob or two of clouds over its summit, and a road running from the bottom edge of the canvas up to the mountain. The road is moonlit, like a river of light, or a mountain stream, with telegraph poles bordering it like a line of stripped trees. Tucked in beside walls and moulded into the fields are whitewashed cottages either side of the road. He feels the silence of the painting, the stillness of the depicted night, and the lack of people or animals. Just sky, cloud, mountain and human dwellings. He tries to picture people in cottages staring at hearth fires, but there's no trace of smoke in the painting, as if the cottages are deserted or it's the dead of night and the fires have gone out. He shivers and feels an urge to hold Grace's hand, as much to absorb its warmth as to convey to her the human touch her painting lacks. But he doesn't reach out. Both of them stare at the picture.

'The road starts somewhere before the canvas and ends somewhere near the mountain,' he says, hoping she will talk about it.

'I'm calling it the *Long Grey Road*. What emotion does it give you?'

'Distance. The picture is about distance. Between us and the world. Distance between people.' She stares at the painting, considering it in the light of his words. He continues: 'It's as if the viewer is God looking at his creation. We're looking down on the road. The cottages are small.'

'The Long Grey Road of Distance,' she says.

'Looks lonely, the picture. There's no life there.'

She turns away from the picture and looks at him. He keeps his gaze on the painting, wondering whether he has offended her.

'It *is* a lonely picture,' she says. 'We're like the flight of the sparrow in the Saxon tale.' He waits for her to explain. 'My husband torments me with it. A medieval poem I believe. The bird flies into the banqueting hall from the deep cold night. It enjoys a moment of light and heat from the winter fire. Then it returns to the deep cold night. That's what our life is like.'

He looks again at the painting. The road leads from coldness to coldness. Or from nothingness to the darkness of the mountain. Yet there is a viewer. That is taken for granted in the point of view. There is someone looking down on the scene. He has called it God. But it might be a human being. A painting implies life, even if it is only the life of the painter who has painted it. As he looks into the picture he feels the sensation he had when he was staring at the ballet dancers at Tulira: the world around him erasing itself, or disappearing from the corners of his eyes, and the edges of the painting drawing him into its reality. At first he instinctively resists, but then he thinks better of it and allows himself to enter the scene gradually. He finds himself emerging on the street the painting depicts, a grey evening and the street so silent he wonders whether the world has come to an end. He walks along and begins knocking at the cottage doors just to hear the sound of voices; just to hear the sound of knocking. He is getting colder. At one cottage he opens the door and in the dark interior he sees a bed with blankets heaped on it. He climbs under the blankets to regain warmth; a drowsiness comes upon him. He is drifting off when he hears a gentle knock at the door and is too soporific to respond. He is dimly aware of soft footsteps and the blankets being lifted up and a draught around his body. Somebody gets into bed beside him. He feels the warmth of a body, a clothed body; fragrant cotton. He turns his body to face the one lying beside him, still too sleepy to react. Someone's breath touches his cold face; then lips touch his, almost as a kiss. He wants to move deeper into the warm face but he is too sleepy to stir. An arm pulls him gently and he feels more warmth from the other body. The lips again touch his mouth and stay there. A tongue slips between his lips and infuses his body with heat. He wants to consume that tongue and enjoy the warmth forever; he wants to pull the body against him and feel its solidity; but he cannot move his arms.

'What are you thinking?' Her voice pulls him out of the painting.

'Nothing. I was imagining myself in the painting.' He looks at her, suddenly embarrassed.

'I do that,' she says. 'Sometimes I wonder which is real. The painting or this terrible world. Do we paint what we see or wish to see? Or what our soul insists we see, though we would prefer to ignore it?' Her sadness has a hint of bitterness, and her tone makes him feel sad too; the picture looks cold, grey and dead.

Then a thought comes to him: 'There *is* life in your picture,' he says. 'The *telegraph poles*. That's where it is. In the wires. I can hear the voices. They're speaking to each other.' He pauses and she looks at him. 'They're telling each other news of births and deaths, of war and migrations, of uncles and aunts, horses and cows.'

She twitches her head, as if she's heard something in the

177

distance. 'They're connecting us to the world, aren't they?' she says. 'To the cities. To London and Paris.' She says the word Paris with a strange excitement. 'I lived in Paris once. I was happy there.'

They stand side by side and the silence between them deepens to the extent that he feels under a spell. He does not know how to break it without appearing insensitive. He looks up at the sky and sees a huge break in the clouds revealing clear dark blue space. He senses Grace doing the same. The night skies over Achill are the darkest he's ever seen. The depths of stars seem to pull him into their midst. A shooting star catches his eye. 'Look,' she says, her tone full of youthfulness, 'did you see it skiting there?'

'Yes.'

'And did you wish? It's too late if you haven't. It has to be done on the instant. I have a wish ready in case I see one. I'm often here in the evenings.'

'I did wish. I had an encounter, in Limerick, with a woman and her young daughter. She had a pain in her head. It's a long story... but the mother believed I cured her girl by the laying on of hands. I wished that the girl is still cured. It's been on my mind.'

'I hope it comes true,' she says and, after a pause, she reaches out and takes his hand. He thinks she is going to shake it to say goodbye, but she simply holds it, with her eyes cast to the ground. He can feel the warmth in her skin, even though their grasp is light. Then, almost simultaneously, they withdraw their hands and he bids her goodbye. She nods her head and looks at the sky, as if waiting for another star.

HE IS LYING ON his bed and letting his thoughts subside. It is a week or so after his conversation with Grace Henry. Achill is becoming familiar. The distant hush of the sea is washing away Limerick, Galway and even tenacious London. The war seems like a story someone has made up to pass a winter's evening. He has no impulse to stand on his soapbox and, like the Reverend

Nangle, harangue uninterested passers-by or peasants in the field. With this admission his spirit becomes lighter. Yet Grace Henry is disconcerting him. There is something in her soul crying out to be nurtured; and his own soul has recognised it. He thinks it prudent to move to Doogort before Christmas.

HE STARES AT THE letter and Jiddu's handwriting. It has been forwarded from Keel to his new accommodation in Doogort. He opens it and pulls out a creamy sheet of paper.

The Old Rectory,
Bude,
Cornwall

Dear Patrick,

Please, many apologies for not replying to your last letter sooner. I was very happy to receive it and I am wondering how you are on Achill Island? I am disturbed that you had that horrid experience in the police station in Limerick, but I am greatly cheered that you healed the little girl with the headache. Of course it is natural, as you say. It is a gift we all have and have lost. We can recover it. That's what Theosophy teaches. I told you there was the power to heal in you! Please send me more of your news.

You said you were going to move from Keel to Doogort. Is it more to your liking? I enjoyed reading your stories about all the turf-cutters, shepherds, kelp gatherers, cowherds, etc. and I laughed when you said you thought many believe that you are a 'spoiled' priest, or a poet, spy, friar or tinker. Perhaps you are a bit of all those things?

I am now living in Bude in Cornwall in the old rectory there. It has been cold this winter but the days are brightening fast, thank heavens. Nitya is studying hard to get into Oxford, but his eyes are bad and he is lonely. I am still supposed to be trying for Oxford too, but my brains are not up to the task. We study Sanskrit, Latin, algebra and other subjects from a tutor. We go for walks on the beach and in the lanes nearby. My joy is a motorbike that was bought for me. I have a gift, I am told, for mechanical things. Not as good as healing, I think!

Lady Emily visits occasionally. Mrs Besant is away in India speaking for Home Rule. My training as the Maitreya continues. The Masters who live in the Himalayas (but nobody communicates with them except for Mr Leadbeater) are pleased, I think, of my progress. I find it difficult. I know I ought to be interested in the work but at the present moment I am afraid I am not. I am trying hard to do my duty.

Lady Emily brought us a friend, a white Siberian dog, to keep us company. There is no one of our age for us to be with. I think Mrs Besant knows that I am very attached to Lady Emily, like a mother. She wrote to me and said: 'Your happiness lies in the work, and you will be restless and unhappy if you turn away from it. Nothing else will last, you will find. A man called to the highest service loses "the lower life", and if he is brave enough to let it go, he finds a splendid and changeless happiness.'

This war is a terrible thing. I want to work in a hospital for the soldiers, but I am told that they are hostile to Indians and other dark-skinned people being there. I do not think the Germans are as bad as the English newspapers are saying they are. I hope in Ireland the war is not having too much of an ill effect. Sometimes I think I would like to stop being the Maitreya and have a different life. But then I think Mrs Besant is right. I will be restless if I turn away from the work.

Please write to me soon in Bude. It gives me pleasure to think of you moving from one place to another.

Sometimes I think I am a prisoner. Please keep telling people that violence is not the way to progress. I am terribly anxious to say this, but I have no one to say it to.

With much affection,
Jiddu

PS: I never said thank you for copying out the words of Nietzsche. Living the same life again would perhaps explain déjà vu and the feeling that you have met someone before, when you know that you haven't? I discussed it with Mrs Besant a while ago. She agrees that we do live innumerable times but says we can escape the cycle by making ourselves totally selfless. When the Buddha reached nirvana he escaped the pattern of being born again and again.

He puts the letter back in the envelope. He can see Jiddu in Cornwall with a shiny motorcycle and a big white dog standing beside it. He feels guilty that he isn't using the freedom he has been granted, while Jiddu is trapped in Bude, and trapped by the colour of his skin.

SUNDAY MORNING. A KNOCKING on his bedroom door. He hears his landlord's voice: 'Mr Bowley, we've some folk outside. I don't know what it is, but they're wanting to see you. Looks urgent, whatever it is.'

He puts on his clothes and walks downstairs. Through the window he can see a group of a dozen people and two horses and carts.

He walks outside and a woman steps forward and begins talking at great speed. 'Sir, Kelly'd be my name—I'm a widow—my husband was taken off by the fever two years or more, and now my son's sick—has the look of death about him. The doctor says there's nothing to be done—and I went straight to the priest and he was all shaking his head and saying words of a prayer but Eugene hasn't stirred a limb at all; and, well, news of his sickness was going around the homes of Keel and there's a woman, a lady painter like, who says there's a good man on this island who may have the gift of curing about him...' She carries on talking and he can see the process that led up to her coming to see him.

The woman turns round and points to one of the carts to indicate which one her son is in. Before he can tell her he may not be the healer she hopes him to be, she has crumpled to the ground and is gripping him around the calves. He looks at the black scarf wrapped around her head and then at the others who have accompanied her. The men are holding their hats in front of them. The women's eyes pierce him from within their shawled faces. He can feel the grip around his legs being tightened. He touches her on the head. 'I can't do anything if I can't move.'

She lets him go and keeps her head bowed. He reaches down and takes her cold hand and raises her to her feet. His heart goes out to her. Her blotchy eyes crease with the effort of keeping the tears at bay; he put his arms on her shoulders and feels her spasms of weeping. He disengages from her. 'We all have to die, and when and how are a mystery to us. You've brought family and friends with you. Whatever happens, these people will help you.'

He walks over to the cart where the woman's son is lying with his head poking up from under a blanket. He looks to be in his teenage years and is lying motionless, as if asleep. He has a notion that holy water might help, or at least allow him the time to think what else he can do. There is no water, so he licks his finger and makes the sign of the cross on the boy's pale forehead and throat. He does not stir. He makes gentle circular movements on the boy's temples with his fingers. He pulls back the blanket, unbuttons the boy's shirt and makes a similar circular movement over his heart. At the same time he intones a simple prayer, 'Dear God, please heal this boy, if it be your will.' The boy does not stir, as if his soul is standing at the crossroads of life and death and can't make up its mind which road to take.

He isn't sure what to do next. He keeps on making crosses and circles on the boy's head and chest, but the boy doesn't stir; then he stops repeating the prayer and listens. He can hear the silence of the bystanders and distant rumble of the sea. He waits and listens, and then a thought, like a voice, tells him what to do, and it's insistent—he bends down to the boy's ear as if to whisper something, but instead he bawls out: 'In the name of God, wake up!' Almost immediately the boy sits up, as if startled by a nightmare, and a cry rises from the onlookers. The woman yelps and runs over to her son, who is taking deep lungfuls of breath, as if he's surfaced from the bottom of a lake. The boy looks around him, trying to grasp where he is and what is happening.

He hears a woman shout, 'Jesus, Mary, Joseph!', repeating the words as though she thinks no one can hear her. He turns to see who is speaking and wants to say it was probably just a case of the boy being comatose, that his shout merely activated his body in some way; but as he swivels his head, he sees people averting their eyes from him, as if he were an evil magician.

He says a few words to the widow, who can hardly be distracted from her son, and walks back to the guesthouse, conscious of people stepping away from him. He passes his landlord and walks upstairs to his room.

He lies on his bed. His legs are trembling. He had no idea that he was going to do what he did, or what the outcome would be. It had just happened. For a moment he'd felt possessed by—a voice, spirit? Now he knows he will have to leave Achill—word will get round and he'll either be mobbed by every sick person on the island or, who knows, stoned as a black magician.

THE EVENING BEFORE HIS departure from Achill; he is walking to Keel. An early quarter moon is lighting up drifts of cloud and obscuring, in its immediate ambit, the stars that can be seen in clusters in the eastern reaches of the sky. He reaches the straggly outskirts of Keel and walks towards the bridge and sees orange lamps ahead of him; a white-smocked figure stops painting well before he reaches her. She has a scarf wrapped tight over her ears and a wide-brimmed hat pulled down on top.

'Good evening Mr Bowley. We haven't seen you for a good while, but I've known you've been in Doogort.' She comes over and guides him, lightly touching his elbow, to her painting, the same one he saw months before. The silvery-grey road still leads from darkness to darkness. 'I'm calling it *The Long Grey Road of Destiny*. That's what it is.' She gestures at the road with her paintbrush and traces its course from the bottom of the frame upwards. 'We're all on our little roads and we can help one another but cannot alter someone else's journey. We may think we can.'

He wants to add something profound, but all he says is: 'I'm leaving tomorrow.'

'I suspected as much. I knew you would come and see me one last time before you left. You have good manners. So, you're here. I will miss your presence. You may have guessed that it is lonely being here.'

She looks down, as if to search the ground for words, then looks up at him, the moonlight a sheen on her scarf. She touches his hands with hers, and they have great warmth, as if they were her only bodily outlet for it. She eases herself towards him and raises her face as if to allow him to kiss her on the cheek. After a hesitation she gently presses her head into his chest. He folds his arms around her and holds her body until she looks up, regaining her composure. 'I won't see you again.' He feels moved by the finality of her words, and wants to contradict them; but he cannot find the right reply and says nothing. He puts his hands on her shoulders, kisses her on her cold cheek, then kisses her lightly on the lips. Her eyes are closed and there's a faint but unmistakeable contentment in her expression. He kisses her again on the lips and feels them part slightly; the tip of his tongue, despite his best intentions, gently parts her lips further for a delicate communion with her own tongue. Almost immediately, as if they both decide at the same time this intimacy is a mistake, they pull their faces away. He gives her a last kiss on the forehead, then turns to walk back to Doogort. After fifty yards he looks back and sees her staring at her long grey road.

He is back in Westport, boarding a jaunting car. The buildings are greyer and lower than Limerick's, and the town's regular pattern of canals and bridges gives it a reassuring sense of orderliness. Union Jacks are fluttering from poles projecting from hotels and brightening the windows of victuallers, pharmacies and other shops. The horses pulling the cars have red, blue and white ribbons tied to their harnesses. Men in huddled groups are smoking and reading newspapers with headlines about the war.

He has returned to the world.

The car heads out west to Croagh Patrick, skirting the calm waters of Clew Bay, and arrives at the bottom of the mountain. The driver shouts: 'Straight up, ye can't go wrong. And ye can see America from the top.'

His heart lifts when he sees the mountain rising before him, its cone disappearing into a landmass of cloud. It's St Patrick's Day, 1915, and there are swarms of pilgrims.

The start of the climb is gentle enough. The path is rocky, crumbling in places, but nothing to halt his progress; he exchanges greetings with pilgrims who are picking their way down or overtaking him on the way up.

Soon he is high enough to appreciate the depth of the ravine on his right, as sheer as anything he encountered on Skellig.

After half an hour he gives his lungs a rest. He takes off his hat, and the wind flies at his hair. Clew Bay has become the size of a grand lake. Clouds drift apart and the sun begins silvering ringlets of waves. The hundreds of tiny islands are like green and grey stepping stones.

He resumes the climb and reaches a level stretch that gives him respite before the final ascent. He sits on a rock and watches an elderly woman circling a cairn on her knees while murmuring prayers. Again he looks back and this time Clew Bay has shrunk to a pond with lily pads. A wisp of cloud wraps him in damp fibres. He thinks of Moses in the wilderness of Sinai, climbing the mountain to meet God amid smoke and thunder and lightning. Here there are only swathes of cloud at eye level, coming and going.

Climbers pass him, disappearing into the mist; the greyness evaporates and he can see two contrasting panoramas either side of the saddle: the waters of the bay to the north, and a sea of green fields to the south. The world has been stripped back to rocks, stones, mist and the constant movement of people ascending and descending, talking to each other, encouraging each other. His heart goes out to these strangers, each one likely to have a story to tell: a sick husband or wife, perhaps, or a dying parent, or a son sent to France.

He is starting on the final stretch of the incline and the stones underfoot are bigger, rounder; the slope seems as steep as the side of a pyramid and the mist becomes so dense it is impossible to know where the edges of the mountain are; it's an act of faith to pull one leg after another over the slippery rocks, with a sheer drop lying in wait. He thinks of Skellig and the steepling southern peak and is glad to be with other climbers. A woman, descending slowly on her backside, looks up and blurts out, 'Don't be giving up now, just a few more yards.' Her words press air into his lungs and distract him from the drop; he keeps going and within a score of steps his trajectory is suddenly horizontal. He has arrived.

The clouds have shut off every possible view; the only movement is that of pilgrims processing in and out of a small chapel at the far end of the tiny plateau. He sits on the shale and lets his mind become like the mist around him. Achill arises from the white screen; Grace Henry's lips touching his; the sick boy who was brought to him. He pictures Grace's painting, with the moonlit road running up to Slievemore mountain and bordered by the empty cottages. He thinks of the world he is returning to, soldiers boarding trains at stations, soldiers returning home, newspaper headlines of battles—his imagination takes him off to mud and trenches and corpses—the ground beneath him seems to lurch and he lunges for the stones either side of him. He wants to hug the earth and stay still. He grips the stones until his fingers hurt. He can sense Ireland slowly rotating around him behind the

cloud. If only he could find some bearings in the landscape…
but there's nothing but whiteness. He says a prayer to himself,
heedless of the meaning; the rhythm of repeated words begins
to slow his heart down. He fights every intrusive thought.

He looks up to see a man with a flat cap and an unlit pipe
wedged in his mouth cresting the summit and leading by the
arm a woman, who is laughing, out of relief or joy. They hug
each other without heed to anyone or anything, and he watches
them as if behind a screen, as if they are doing something that
will never happen to him again.

He is in his shed back home in Galway. Bridie is calling out to him and opening his door; she hands him a letter. He sits on his bed and opens it. It simply says, 'Please come and meet me at the address above.' It is typed and sent, unsigned, from the Eglinton Hotel in Salthill, only a couple of miles away.

At first he suspects a trap. The memory of his interrogation in Limerick is still glowing. Then he has a flash: Jiddu. He's run away from Bude and escaped to Ireland. Of course! Hence the secrecy. He is on the run from the theosophists.

HE HURRIES THROUGH LANEWAYS and reaches the promenade and its open skies, keeping one hand on his hat until he reaches the Eglinton.

Inside, he is about to tell the woman behind the desk that he is expected by one of her guests when he sees a woman sitting on the other side of the room. She seems young and is dressed in black. He has a sudden thought it is Grace Henry. When the woman sees him she stands up, comes over and extends her right hand, while lifting her veil with the other. He shakes her hand and forgets to let go as he sees what seems to be a phantom standing in front of him.

Agnes. Dear God, Agnes. He stares at her like a village idiot and hardly hears her apology for not signing the letter and saying that she wanted to see his reaction to her presence without him having any warning. He starts blathering about something, anything.

He leads her out onto the promenade and they walk away from the city, half-shouting above the wind and taking it in turns to relate their stories.

She tells him that Dominic was killed in action. 'Tenth of September. The Marne. I was horribly shocked and sad. Father was heart-broken. But, and God will hardly forgive me for saying this, it was also... a release. I've spent half a year feeling guilty about it. More than guilty. My life has felt pointless... confused; my spirits have been low. Father kept saying it was time for me to get on with living and he'd do anything to help me. I said I wanted to go to Ireland... to see you. He agreed a change of location would do me good, but that it was too soon—propriety. I insisted it was the only thing. Your aunt, Faith, lent me her support. In the end he consented.'

She talks on and on, not knowing how to end her story. When she mentions her honeymoon in Scotland he feels barely controllable jealousy; but he rallies when she describes how quickly her spirits sank after the initial novelty of being a wife. How curt her husband became; the endless things expected of her; being unable to express her views on anything without his irritation or patronising smile. He discouraged her from playing the cello; he would not countenance any talk about suffragettes. Her world had felt like a cage, and her father pretended not to notice.

He thinks of Dominic paying for his taxi cab home after he was beaten up; and of Dominic lying in French mud. Even more he thinks about putting his arms around Agnes and kissing her, facing Galway Bay.

THE FOLLOWING DAY. HE'S called round to the Eglinton and collected Agnes for a long stroll and another long conversation. He realises how ashamed he feels of his city's grey façades and cracked or boarded-up windows; potholes in the roads; the hordes of idlers and ne'er-do-wells who crowd round doorways of banks, pubs, churches and shops. How different from Wimbledon it must seem to her. But she is blind to the city's warts and has talked more vivaciously than he ever remembered. 'It feels so free here,' she says, more than once. 'Too much of it and I won't be able to go home.' He wants to say, 'Free—only if you have money,' but he cannot bear any hint of sourness.

He shows her the inside of St Nicholas's and relives his disastrous sermon there; he is tempted to lead her to the pillar behind which he kissed Nora. They go to the city hall, where he tells her about the suffragette meeting and the boorish intruders. In between city sights, he tells her what he has done, said and thought since London. He speaks of Skellig Michael; the letters from Jiddu; Limerick, Pearse and Casement, and his arrest and interrogation; his escape to Achill, and the boy he apparently healed. She listens and occasionally touches his arm to encourage or console. She seems to be entranced by anything that is different from war-heavy London.

NEXT MORNING HE RETURNS to the Eglinton and escorts Agnes to his home. He feels more nervous than ever before. Supposing Joe looks her up and down with his special scrutinising look? Supposing Bridie hasn't been able to resist a tipple? Supposing Agnes shows disdain for a house that's more than respectable by Galway standards but humble compared with her Wimbledon home?

He has told his parents only that Agnes is a woman he met in London through Aunt Faith and that she is recuperating after recently being widowed. It is a happy coincidence that she has decided to stay in Galway for a few days.

He opens the front door and Joe and Bridie are waiting for them in the parlour. Joe steps forward and shakes Agnes by the hand, his eyes trained on her appeasing face.

'You're very welcome to our home, Miss Chaigneau. I am sorry for your trouble. The loss of your husband.'

'Thank you, Mr Bowley.'

Joe flicks a smile on and off and shifts uneasily to the side to allow Bridie to come forward.

Bridie offers no hand to Agnes but simply puts her arms around her. 'Yer very welcome, dear—Jaysus you've come a long way to get over your misfortune, but there's nothing like a journey to take the sting out of a sadness. Come here and take the weight off your feet. Ye'll have a cup of tea.'

As the two women disengage he can see that Agnes is close to tears. She sits down and he takes his place next to her, reminding himself that his parents do not know his feelings for her. She is just the daughter of Faith's boss; she is just a young widow in mourning.

Bridie reappears with a pot of tea. 'Will ye not have a drop of something stronger in it?' Joe, who is standing by the fireplace, turns his head down towards the turf smoking away in the grate.

'That would be lovely!'

He can't believe Agnes's assent. 'You do know my mother is referring to whiskey?'

'Of course. What else would 'something stronger' be? My late husband taught me some bad habits.'

Bridie lets out a cackle and fetches the bottle of Jameson's, pours a neat tot into the cap and tips it into Agnes's tea. 'Yer a girl after my own heart, and I'll have one meself, to keep ye company. A drop of the strong stuff does wonders for the nerves.'

The conversation flows, but almost solely between Agnes and Bridie, while he and Joe retreat into themselves and listen politely or follow their own thoughts.

'So yer mammy died when you were young?'

'Yes. We have photographs of her—'

'She'd've been a beauty, I'd say—'

'And I can't tell whether I can remember her or just the photographs.'

'Must have been hard for your da bringing up a young girl.'

'I had nannies and governesses. He managed. Our house has always felt like a place of... strangers. Father buried himself in his work and in theosophy.'

Bridie doesn't react to 'theosophy'. Joe looks over at him with a quizzical look, and Agnes sees him.

'Theosophists believe religions should bring us together rather than divide us. There's one supreme spirit and we are all equal brothers and sisters capable of becoming true spiritual beings. To help us do this God sends a world teacher at different times in history. Jesus was a world teacher.'

He sees Joe raises an eyebrow at this and prays his father

will be gentle. He is relieved, somehow, that Agnes hasn't mentioned that the current world teacher is a young Indian man.

Joe directs his undivided gaze on Agnes: 'We in the Society of Friends believe jesus was a 'world teacher' alright... We also believe he was, and is, the *Son of God*. And you speak of equality—we Friends have a proud tradition of that.'

Bridie loses her smile for a moment, divining how things might develop; she heads off trouble by offering Agnes more tea. The conversation turns to the weather and the city and, inevitably, the war. At the mention of the war everyone's thoughts turn to Dominic and Agnes's loss; Bridie is dabbing her eyes with her sleeve, and Joe's face softens.

HE AND AGNES ARE leaving the house and walking to Eyre Square. He feels ecstatically relieved. Joe behaved himself—just. Bridie was at her best. Agnes seemed to enjoy their company. Nevertheless, he can feel his stomach muscles still struggling to relax.

They walk in companionable silence to the Railway Hotel and find a snug in the main bar. He orders a pot of tea and plates of stew.

'No whiskey in the tea, this time.'

'Your parents are very good people. Kind people.'

'What else did Dominic teach you, apart from drinking whiskey?' He means it as a genial remark, but somehow it doesn't sound that way.

'I'm afraid that's as wicked as it got. Whiskey in tea. No other guilty secrets. And what about yourself? What wicked secrets are you hiding?' She smiles coyly, half jesting, half probing.

He's been thinking for a while how much he should tell her about the things he has disliked about himself, things done and not done. The last couple of days have been a mutual rush of exchanged life stories and a determination to maintain an enchantment between themselves; he hasn't wanted to introduce any discordant notes. Perhaps now is the time to test the water. Better to be honest now than later.

'I haven't told you about the publishing party where I met Dominic.'

'Dominic told me he found you on the street, in a sorry state. I felt terrible. I felt that if I'd been there it might not have happened.'

'He did a kind act. Put me in an taxi cab. But there were other things that happened before then.'

She holds her cup of tea, poised to drink it, but too distracted by the imminent revelation. He tells her, haltingly, about the encounter with the prostitute. He tells her about seeing Nora at the party, and how she was the first woman he kissed. For good measure he tells her about the time he paid a sixpence to touch a woman's breasts in Galway city. The only thing he doesn't reveal is his last meeting with Grace Henry. Somehow that feels as if would be a betrayal of Grace's privacy. At least, that is what he's telling himself. It will have to wait for another day, or never.

He doesn't know how Agnes will react; and it looks like Agnes doesn't know either. He can see her eyes working through the details. Probably moving from one scene to another. Which is the most objectionable? Kissing Nora in a church? The more he thinks about the various incidents the more vile he feels; he can see them through her eyes. What was he thinking of allowing himself to be dragged into a prostitute's lair? Did he half want it? Is drunkenness his only defence? Does self-pity come into the reckoning as a defence? But why hadn't Agnes *bloody well written to him* as she said she would? That might have made all the difference. He wouldn't have gone to the party and got drunk, and not… and not.

As if reading his mind, Agnes says: 'I should have written to you. I tried but the words wouldn't come. Then I thought I'd go to the party and do the brave thing and tell you face to face what my situation was. But when it came to it I couldn't bear to see you in company, and with Dominic there too. You've no idea of the pressure put on me to be engaged to him.

And he was charming too. Good looking. Well off. Well mannered. My father presented him to me as a solution to all the difficulties in my life. It was wrong. I knew that. I think my father secretly did as well. Dominic barely hid his scepticism over theosophy—of course he was careful; he knew father's feelings on the matter. I should've told you all this in writing. The least I could've done. I can see how it would have affected you and why you drank too much and had that encounter with that woman. Sounds like the beating you got was more than enough punishment for any lapse of morals or judgment.'

He takes this as a sort of forgiveness for his actions. He feels unburdened. He was dreading telling her. And she hasn't even mentioned Nora—perhaps too negligible? Kissing a woman is hardly a sin, even in a church.

He smiles at her, in gratitude and relief, expecting the same from her. She puts her tea cup down. 'But paying sixpence, stone-cold sober, to touch a woman's naked breasts is *disgusting* and damned immoral. Do you think women let men do that unless they're desperate?'

He stares at her in horror—half-hoping she is feigning outrage. But her expression is steady and her cheeks are flushed. Her unexpected condemnation makes him feel slightly nauseous. Perhaps this is the moment when they will part and never see each other again? Why did he ever touch that woman? Why did he ever tell Agnes? He can feel his world collapsing.

Agnes continues glaring at him. 'But I will say this. I admire your honesty. I know you know you did wrong. And I appreciate it took courage to tell me. It makes me trust you. And now you will trust *me* the more because I have let you know my true feelings about it.' He can see her eyes softening; she moves her hand towards him and he feels her gloved fingers close ever so slightly around his.

On the day before Agnes is due to return to London, he leads her to the harbour front and the old Spanish Arch, and there, in the shadows of the great curved stone arch, fully confident of his acceptance, he kisses her. As his lips touch hers he's aware that this is a moment like no other—more all-consuming than when he first kissed her in Wimbledon. He can feel the lack of uncertainty in his own emotions flowing into her body, and receiving the same from her.

It takes them a while to regain sensible speech.

There is really nothing more for him to say now except, 'Will you marry me?' But just as this thought enters his head, the words Mrs Besant uttered to Jiddu stop his tongue: 'Your happiness lies in the work, and you will be restless and unhappy if you turn away from it.'

At that moment, beneath the arch, his ecstasy turns to self-hatred, as if two opposing parts of his soul have sprung up and are pressing against each other, engaged in a life-and-death struggle. He holds her tight, digging his chin into her shoulder, and says nothing.

THE CARRIAGES OF THE Midland Great Western train edge the platform with their metallic green.

They have arrived early and sit on a bench. He wants to say how much he is in love with her and doesn't want her to leave. He wants to ask her for her hand in marriage. He has rehearsed the words; but the other voice is fighting him, insisting he is a loner, a wandering hermit. He remembers the moment in London when she broke away from him, knowing she was destined to marry Dominic. He slips his arm through hers, as if to root her to the spot.

They watch porters load suitcases and trunks onto the train; she is leaving and nothing has been resolved. He feels as light-headed as he was on Croagh Patrick and grips her arm too hard. She is looking at him, waiting for him to speak. Again he wants to say *I love you*, but what he says is, 'I'm frightened.' He has invested so much emotion and thought in an imagined future with Agnes. Her sudden reappearance in his life has seemed like a miracle—surely a sign that fate is telling him what to do? Not fate, but God? But has it been too sudden, too easy? Can his life be switched so quickly and dramatically? Does he just give up his faltering preaching mission forever? And what would he say to Jiddu, semi-captive in Cornwall, longing to preach peace and help in hospitals—'Dear Jiddu, you'll be happy to know that Agnes and I are to be married'?

His head feels as if it will spin off his neck and onto the train tracks. The sudden volley of train doors slamming shut sounds like gunfire—he has a flash of the ordeal in the Limerick barracks; he can feel himself trembling. Agnes is looking at him, waiting; he buries his head in her shoulder, partly to hide his distress and partly to feel the softness of her body; her gloved hand touches his ear and she is murmuring something, barely audible against the hissing of steam and the shrilling of a whistle. He realises from a surge of passengers and shouts from the guard that the train is finally about to leave. He pulls his face away from her coat.

Agnes glances at the train, at her travelling bag, and his face and says, 'I'm not leaving you like this.'

He gabbles back: 'You have to. You'll miss the boat.'

'I'm not missing the boat. You're travelling on the train with me.' She rises, pulls him up, tells him to take the bag, and leads him to the nearest train door.

He doesn't know what she intends: 'I can't go to London!' The words sound feeble and weak of faith.

She shouts with the force, but not the tone, of anger: 'You're not. You're coming to Dublin to see me off. I have money for tickets. We can talk on the train. I'm not leaving you like this.' Her passion and authority brook no argument: the plan has been divulged and has to be adhered to.

THEY TAKE SEATS IN a first-class carriage, almost empty. A long echoing whistle induces the first lurch and the train lumbers forward; soon the smoke is clearing from their window.

His thoughts and feelings spill out in words in measure with the increasing distance from Galway, but his stories are disjointed and repetitious. He again describes being drawn into the painting of the ballet dancers, healing the girl in Limerick and the boy on Achill. 'The whole thing scares me. I don't know whether there's a power that comes to me, or what. I don't want to preach against the war any more. I want to love someone. I want to have a home. I'm not Jiddu; I'm not a theosophist.' He stops, as if the next thing he's about to say is too painful to utter.

She waits, her hands folded on her lap.

'I'm not… *Jesus.*'

He can see she is taken aback by his vehemence. She holds his hand, as if he were a child. She makes soft soothing sounds. Then she says: 'You're not going to be Jiddu. Or Jesus.' He gabbles on about what Paul Henry said about ancient Palestine mirroring present-day Ireland, and gives her a garbled version of Nietzsche's idea of life repeating itself.

Agnes tuts and coos, then when there is a pause, she says as a light remark to lift the atmosphere: 'It's not as if your mother was expecting before marriage and you were born in a stable!'

A wave of giddiness hits him from nowhere; he can feel his brain resisting terrible thoughts that have never occurred to him before. Words attempt to stutter from his mouth; his body stiffens with the effort of resistance. He sees the alarm in her face. He feels her strength reaching out towards him, trying to brace him. But it's as if he's drowning in fear; then she throws him an extraordinary rope that he grasps at, grips and pulls towards him.

'Patrick, listen to me. Jesus didn't have a wife.'

He looks at her face to see whether she means what he thinks she means. In confirmation she smiles—the sweetest, most beautiful spontaneous smile. He takes her face between his hands and kisses her. They can hardly bear to separate their lips.

The morning of their wedding in Wimbledon. He has woken up far too early and is lying in bed in his old bedroom in Faith's flat, but his stomach makes him feel he's on a boat. A voyage into a new life! All he has to do is to get to the local Friends' meeting house by noon; all he has to do is give a declaration of marriage in front of the congregation.

As he lies there fantasising, the early morning sun lays a golden stripe across the wall. He gets out of bed and pulls the curtains: Wimbledon Common, dawn-moist and green, its trees heavy with leaves. Wimbledon Common. Who would have thought it possible he'd be back here in these circumstances?

When he arrives at the meeting house he sees his parents, arm in arm, already waiting at the door. It's strange seeing Joe in a three-piece suit with his hair combed back; and Bridie with her fiery hair tamed by pins and protected by a dark green bonnet that matches her dress. They look a handsome couple! He goes over to greet them and finds that he, as much as they, find it almost impossible to articulate meaningful words. They smile and embrace him, then Joe shakes him by the hand and wishes him good luck before leading Bridie inside.

He follows them in and sees a scattering of guests. Hugh is talking to an elderly couple and breaks off to come over to him.

'Patrick. I don't know what to say! I remember when we first met, at the Tagore poetry reading, you said to me something about our souls being made of love—well, I must admit, it wasn't what I was expecting to hear from a young man such as yourself, and I was rather impressed by you and your bearing, even if it suited me at the time not to show it. I had another way mapped out for my daughter, but with hindsight…. What I will say is this: if your and Agnes's souls are made of love, then each day will be a constant welcome to you both.'

He finds himself unable to reply for fear of loosening too much emotion. Instead he shakes him by the hand, slowly and mechanically. They both turn away simultaneously. He scans the room and sees Agnes sitting at the back by herself, having a quiet moment. She wears no veil and her dress is close-fitting, ivory in colour. He joins her and holds her hand. He knows the wedding ceremony will simply be part of a regular Friends' meeting. No music, no fuss, not even a priest. God alone joins couples together.

ALL THE GUESTS HAVE arrived, and it is time for Agnes and him to proceed to the front and sit down in chairs facing the gathering. He can see Bridie in the front row, the ribbon of her bonnet cutting into her double chin, her eyes welling up; beside her, Joe and Faith are sitting stiffly, the male and female forms of each other. Next to Faith is Hugh, debonair, a white carnation in his lapel, overdressed for a Quaker ceremony.

Silence; a long beautiful silence.

He feels he could stay in the silence forever, but also knows that at some point he will have to get to his feet and make the required declaration. He waits and wonders when the moment will come—and then it does: he finds himself standing and saying, 'In the fear of the Lord and in the presence of this assembly—Friends, I take this my friend Agnes to be my wife—promising, through divine assistance, to be unto her a loving and faithful husband, so long as we both shall live on earth.'

He sits down and Agnes rises and makes her own declaration and resumes her seat. He cannot believe it is finally done. They are man and wife.

The silence regains its momentum.

He and Agnes continue sitting there, waiting for friends or relatives to stand up and give words of encouragement or tell exemplary stories about them—but only if moved to do so by the holy spirit.

The silence feels as if it has become unbreakable.

Then a male voice rings out from the back. It's loud and clear and has an Irish accent. He knows immediately whose it is and can't believe he hasn't seen him already, and wonders how on earth he arrived here.

'My name is Douglas Newsome of the Limerick community of Friends, and Patrick lodged with me for some months up to the outbreak of this catastrophe that has stricken Europe...'

Douglas! Dear old Douglas! Joe must have told him about the wedding. He has come over here specially. Good God. Now the marriage feels truly blessed.

Douglas continues to speak about him, telling the assembled how he was a model tenant and what an impact he made on Limerick with his soapbox preaching. Douglas builds up a head of steam in his inimitable way and the names of Fox and Bunyan ring out. 'In truth, I confess I do not know his wife, Agnes, but she's a fortunate young woman, and may God guide their lives in all things, especially in these tragic times, and may they bring light wherever they step.'

THE RECEPTION IN THE adjoining hall is marked by wartime and Quaker austerity—huge beige pots of tea and a small wedding cake. He circulates, introducing people to each other, and sees Hugh talking in earnest to Joe, probably explaining what theosophy is. He goes over to Douglas and embraces him.

'Well, look at you, m'lad.' Douglas clearly wants to shed a tear or two but is hanging on. 'Do you remember the state you were in after that police grilling? Remember that? Almost the last time I saw you. And now... Well I never. Your Agnes is a beautiful woman. She has a soul, that one.'

Douglas fires questions at him—what has he been up to since Limerick, what does he think about the war at the moment, where are he and Agnes going to live, will he come back to Limerick...?

He puts a hand on Douglas's shoulder: 'Sufficient unto the day is the evil thereof.'

'You're right, Pat. There's a lesson for us in that. But don't be staying too long in London. Lord, we need all the good folk we can get back home. Pearse is stoking things up. He gave a mighty speech in Dublin—funeral of O'Donovan Rossa. His words alone must've recruited thousands of Volunteers—cursed are the troublemakers, for they seed strife. We need strong voices, Pat. John Redmond is losing confidence. The warmongers are seizing their chances.'

'Ah, my days of the soapbox are over, Douglas. I'm a married man. I have to earn a living. A wife to support. Besides, no one really listened to me.'

Douglas thinks about this and can't hide his wistfulness. He puts on a smile: 'Of course, Pat, you're right. I was never a one for the marriage myself, and it must be another world when you're in it.'

'It *does* feel like another world, alright.'

He and Agnes are disembarking from the train at the small town of Ballina, not too far from and not too near Limerick. It is August 1915 and they are on their honeymoon.

They walk along the long narrow bridge that stretches across the shining surface of Lough Derg and joins Ballina to its sister town, Killaloe. They stop halfway on the bridge, the invisible county border between Tipperary and Clare, and he feels as if they are physically crossing from one life to another.

The lake stretches north as far as the eye can see, sweeping away Wimbledon, London, and the war. To the left, the high enclosing hills make him think of the Switzerland of his imagination; and on the lake itself, solitary fishermen sit in motionless coracles; a steamboat is puffing towards them, taking passengers from Portumna down to Limerick.

They continue walking the remaining hundred yards to Killaloe and find a guesthouse at the top of a street that rises away from the lake. He can hardly believe he is with the woman he loves and disengaged from what he imagined would be his life's task. He smiles at the memory of ritually breaking up his soapbox. He is now free to be a husband and, God willing, a father. He has a woman he can touch, kiss, make love to, share his life with. He thinks of his marriage declaration: 'Friends, I take this my friend Agnes to be my wife, promising, through divine assistance, to be unto her a loving and faithful husband, so long as we both on earth shall live.' It gives him satisfaction to repeat that, like casting a benevolent spell on his life.

As they reach the far end of the bridge, he knows he has finally reached the mainland.

THAT NIGHT, THEY LIE in bed in each other's arms and listen to the street sounds wafting in the open window. There is nothing to say and the silence is like that of a Friends' meeting in which everyone has been touched by the holy spirit at the same exquisite moment.

THE FOLLOWING MORNING THEY and the other passengers in the jaunting car are wafting air against their faces with their hats. They leave Killaloe and head north for Tuamgraney, the next village on the western side of the lake and the first stop on their honeymoon itinerary.

Every so often they pass through waterfalls of green whenever branches interlace over the road. Agnes remarks how everywhere seems so green—in the light in the hedgerows with their mossy stones, in the fields beyond, in the tall beeches and dark pines and even the shadows they cast. She gestures at the soft green of drooping nettles, the defined green of bracken and ferns, and the spiky green of grasses. At this moment the lough seems like the glittering eye of an emerald Ireland drifting farther into the Atlantic, putting distance between him and Agnes and the carnage in Europe.

IN TUAMGRANEY A SMALL crowd has gathered to meet the car; the indigents quickly assess the new arrivals and home in on him and Agnes. He gives them coins and receives loud praises in return. They find a room for the night.

Later in the day they are strolling arm in arm up the road that leads to Ennis. They come to an overgrown field, half a mile out of town. The field is unusually hummocky. An old woman, a black headscarf knotted tight beneath the folds of her chin, is holding a bunch of wild flowers and pausing by the gate. She turns to them. 'Me nan would be over there.' She gestures to a corner where a hawthorn stands protectively. 'She was laid to rest there, but God alone knows whose bones they really are. 'Twas a dark time alright. The hunger.' He surveys the rest of the bumpy field: he suddenly sees that he's looking at an informal cemetery, its contours mapping the bodies of the dead.

The woman looks Agnes up and down. Agnes smiles, and the woman takes this as a sign to elaborate on the story she has begun. 'Thousands dead for want of a scrap of food. Couldn't fit them in St Cronan's graveyard. Brought the bodies here instead. Pouring out of Scariff workhouse they were, cartloads of bodies with the flesh shrunk on them. Folks hadn't the strength for the burying—they'd just be throwing beach sand over the bodies. God himself must have been digging the pits. No priest to say the rites. Not enough coffins. They'd a few boxes with hinges on the bottom. They'd lift a fella into the box, lower him down then pull a handle and the bottom fell open and yer man tumbled into the soil.' She points to a corner of the field. 'Over there's the angels' plot, for unbaptised children, God rest their souls.'

The woman pauses to look at Agnes' reaction and softens when she sees the trail of a tear on Agnes's otherwise impassive face. 'There'll be another hunger with this war—tearing our menfolk from the fields.' The woman crosses herself and enters the field.

He watches her lay her wild flowers on the mound of her grandmother; he holds Agnes by the arm and leads her away; and he thinks of Pearse and his anger, and, to his own surprise, his heart goes out to him and the Volunteers, drilling with their broomsticks.

A RELIEF TO BE arriving next day in the village of Mountshannon, a few miles north of Tuamgraney. With its main street of neat slate-roofed houses and prominent Church of Ireland church, the village looks too orderly for the wilds of Clare. A track leads down to a small harbour from where they look across the lake to the distant shoreline of Tipperary.

THEY ARE SITTING AT a table in the parlour of their landlady, Mrs Andrews, a Protestant widow. She is standing with her back to the window, hands on hips, a slender woman with white hair and a black hair comb matching her black clothing. Her eyes dart around within the sepia hollows of their sockets, as if her thoughts have been animated by the arrival of two paying guests.

He asks her about Mountshannon.

'Protestant village. Just bog, rock and trees here till the 1700s, then a gentleman by the name of Alexander Woods bought the land and built the village. Flax and linen we had then. Evil times came; most of us Protestants died out or went off to seek their fortunes. Full of Catholics now. We've had to learn to live together. Times are hard. A few folk would still be making linen. There'd be a bit of fishing, and visitors going out to see Holy Island. We've had to learn to live together.'

She asks them what they are doing in Clare. He tells her they are on their honeymoon and she says: 'The Lord help us! Who'd be mad enough to get married at a time like this?'

He is sitting with Agnes in a rowing boat, a day trip to Holy Island, a tiny islet barely a mile away from Mountshannon's tiny harbour; their skipper and oarsman, John-Joe, is singing a tuneless song with gusto. Their vessel is low in the water and the fine spray from the oars freshens their faces.

Within minutes they can see the island's slender round tower rising up above the trees.

They clamber onto a rudimentary jetty and follow the path that leads them through a corridor of high unruly bushes. They emerge into open ground beside St Caiman's roofless chapel and a graveyard full of horizontal slabs, set in the ground like paving stones. The rooks, flecking the trees like large black leaves, greet their arrival.

He wishes John-Joe would go away, so that he can lie down on the grass with Agnes and kiss her, undo the back of her dress and touch her pale skin. But it is as if John-Joe senses this and keeps tight to them, prattling away about the weather and the war.

They walk over to the western edge of the islet and John-Joe guides them to a well, a few yards from the lake. It is enclosed by a circular stone wall as high as a person's chest.

' 'Tis holy alright, as you'd hope.' John-Joe looks down into the water, his coat draped over his shoulder by a single finger. 'They say if y'see your reflection in it, all yer aul sins will be forgiven.' He looks at John-Joe to see if he is serious, then lifts Agnes up so that she can lean over the thick stone rim of the well and peer into the dark water.

'Clear as a mirror,' she announces.

It's his turn. He looks down into the well and sees the sky reflected in the still water as a slash of brightness, and patches of duckweed peppering the surface. He focuses on a spot and watches the outline of his face; the dark gleaming light has a strange beauty—in its stillness and the way it's contained by the curve of the well. As he stares into the depths, he feels as if he is being drawn into a tunnel to look more closely at his own face. He then has the sensation that the face he is looking at *isn't his.* He peers with more effort, trying to make out the features. They look familiar; and suddenly he has the sensation that the face is looking down on him, not vice versa; he can almost see it properly, but the water is too dark. He glances up to break the spell and looks down again. The face is still there.

'Are you seeing anything?' says Agnes.

He doesn't reply.

John-Joe, perhaps sensing he has seen something, says: 'There'd be tales about the well. They say if the water moves agin' the movement of the sun there'll be a storm rising; I've heard a spirit lives in it—but 'tis only seen at times of danger or death or mourning.'

He again stares into the water. He can almost see the eyes in the head, but not quite; the hair looks black and slicked back, or is it just dark strands of weed? The face itself is white, like a corpse's. The eyes are looking at him as if the face is about to say something. He listens. The mouth moves and he hears the sound of an utterance, low and indistinct. He wants to stay longer, to hear the message, but he can sense John-Joe and Agnes are restless; Agnes is saying something. He looks at the face for a last time and almost thinks it is familiar.

He heaves himself back to the ground. 'I saw my face all right. Just wanted to make sure. Shiny and stainless it was, you'll be glad to hear.'

IT's THE EVENING AND Mrs Andrews is in the parlour singing a hymn. They are about to tiptoe upstairs when she shouts, 'Will ye not join me for a cup of something?'

They sit down and take the offered tea cups; he smells the whiskey before he sees there's not a drop of tea in the cup. Mrs Andrews nods her head as if to indicate that it is, indeed, whiskey, and that they should drink it. He takes a sip and savours the tang. Agnes does the same.

Mrs Andrews looks out of the window at the dimming light outside. 'Lost my husband years back but not before he'd driven the empire into Davey, our son. Davey was always for the flag. Mad for the soldier's life. The Fusiliers. Shipped off to France to God knows where. Now he's back. In the hospital in Naas with no eyes to be seeing anything with. May as well be two pebbles. And his breathing's like an old sow's. The Germans gassed him and his soldier friends. Harmless bit of bonfire smoke, he said. Until it started burning their eyes, lungs, and they not knowing what to do or think, just that they couldn't breathe; running as fast as they could, zigzagging like rabbits and dropping like flies, and everyone holding their throats or yawning wide to get more air. Says he saw nothing but a blur and felt a raw burning in his lungs; yelled for help— yelling and flapping like a schoolgirl, he says. Someone grabbed him by the arm and kept him running.

'They tried to help him but his eyes were gone. No use to the army any more. The Germans did their bit and the British did the rest. Packed him off back home, and what use is he to me now? Sitting in a hospital all day and him not bothering whether the curtains are pulled open or pulled closed, not letting in a blade of light. He's dead to me. He's not my son any more. *He's not my son.*' She puts one hand over her eyes and raises the cup to her mouth with the other: 'All I'm saying is, where was God when that gas was choking our fellas to death? Where was he when my son's eyes were burning up? What use is God when he lets this kind of thing happen?'

He looks at Agnes, who is staring at the floor, her shoulder blades rigid. He knows all this talk of war is making her think of Dominic.

What he wants to say to Mrs Andrews is: 'I don't know where God was, and I don't know why he lets those things happen to your son or to anyone else. God lets us do what we want, not what he wills. We cannot start a war and then say: "God, we've started this war, we're killing people, gassing them, why did you let us do it?"'

He doesn't voice his thoughts. He goes over to Mrs Andrews and lays a hand on her shoulder and lets her convulse.

NIGHT-TIME. HE WAKES up with Agnes shushing him and gripping his arm. He's had a nightmare. He was on Holy Island leaning over the side of the well and looking into its reflection. He saw a face looking up at him—he leaned over as far down as he could to get a good look at the face—two hands lunged at his shoulders and pulled him into the well—he remembers the shock of going underwater and trying to beat off the hands, the struggle to hold his breath; he kicked and kicked and twisted his body but felt the air leaving him—as if he were being gassed—and a sense he would have to let go and resign himself to his fate—then he heard Agnes's voice calling him and her hand shaking him.

THEY ARE LEAVING MOUNTSHANNON next morning. Mrs Andrews shakes their hands: 'The drink got the better of me. I go to Naas hospital tomorrow and the thought is killing me. Someone's got to stop the politicians telling folk we're winning this war and it's grand to be fighting in it. It's not even *our* war—Redmond is fooling himself. Dancing to the British tune will do us no good.'

She turns away and closes the door and he and Agnes make their way to the jaunting car bound for Portumna, at the northern tip of Lough Derg.

The sun is trying to beat its way through thick cloud and the horses' hooves provide a steady stable rhythm. The lake is too far from the road to be glimpsed, but they sense it lying beyond the straggly greenery of trees and hedges, or behind a house, or down the various tracks that lead off from the road.

Portumna has a pervasive sadness in the streets. The castle glowers behind its walls, trees and gates. A huge grey-walled workhouse in the centre of town still holds the memory of cholera-ridden families. Even the beggars seem to lack the energy to importune them for money. They decide to stay only one night and take the morning steamboat back to their starting point, Ballina and Killaloe, several hours across the lake.

EARLY MORNING. HE AND Agnes are on the quay, stepping into the ferry. They climb to the open railinged deck and squeeze onto a bench at the front, beside a pile of trunks, cases, bags, hampers and a cage containing a somnolent rust-coloured hen. At nine o'clock a seaman dismantles the gangway, the ship's bell rings out and steam pours out of the tall black funnel. The vibrations increase and they move off, paddles slopping off the river with the easy motion of a watermill.

THE DAY IS DRY with patches of clear sky expanding and contracting among the clouds; and the tree-lined banks of Clare to the right, and Tipperary to the left, draw nearer or recede at different times during the journey. He can see the passengers are a mixture of day-trippers, off-duty British officers—judging by their pastel jackets and trousers and straw boaters—and working men in woollen waistcoats and flat caps, some accompanied by women with bucket hats, pulled down against the breeze. There are children picking their way around bags and adult legs.

On a bench opposite them, four men are talking their way through a flask of whiskey, which is poured carefully, at intervals, into tin cups. They all look like middle-aged clerical staff, dressed in long coats and felt hats, except one, who is a priest. Perhaps brothers or cousins on their way back from a funeral. The drink has amplified their voices.

One man is making a point, or continuing a story that has been interrupted: 'The Finglas Road was as packed as any other I've ever seen in Dublin; you couldn't turn without bothering folk around you; four black horses, plumed; magnificent. O'Donovan Rossa, God rest his soul—sure, he'd never have imagined the fuss. Thousands gathered in Glasnevin cemetery. Couldn't get close enough to hear what Pearse had to say at the graveside, but I have his speech.' The man pulls out a newspaper cutting from his coat.

While Agnes closes her eyes in a momentary pool of sun, he leans forward to hear Pearse's reported words, suddenly remembering that Douglas had mentioned the speech at the wedding.

The man draws his head back from the cutting in order to read it: 'Here's how it ends. "They think that they have pacified Ireland. They think that they have purchased half of us and intimidated the other half. They think that they have foreseen everything, think that they have provided against everything; but the fools, the fools, the fools!—they have left us our Fenian dead, and while Ireland holds these graves, Ireland unfree shall never be at peace."'

The man's three companions remain silent. One says, ' 'Tis powerful stuff alright. 'Twould rouse a man into battle.'

The evening after their arrival in Ballina; they are sitting on a bench near the bridge over the lake, watching the steam of a departing train bloom and disperse; pedestrians are crossing the road between the flow of horses and carts. He cannot see the lake directly but everywhere there is a sense of its reflected light.

They are back where they began.

He is disquieted; not only is the honeymoon over, but he keeps picturing Mrs Andrews's son Davey. He can see him lying on his bed, eyes pointed towards the ceiling and watching the gas cloud making its way towards him; he can hear the screams in Davey's head as if they were in his own. He thinks of Jiddu wanting to join a hospital and not being allowed to; he knows how lucky he is. He is not English and has no duty to serve in the army or become a stretcher bearer. He has the promise of a new life, away from war, politics, rhetoric, and any Volunteers; away from preaching. His only duty is to be a quiet, inoffensive woodworker, supporting his wife and raising a family. *That's all he has to do.* And he can do it—as long as he can close out the world and its sadness. Agnes will help him; she wants to stay in Ireland. London, she has been saying, is like a giant hospital ward. The fit and able men are either in France being shot to pieces or training somewhere in the country, ready to be shot to pieces. The city streets are filled with widows and bereft mothers, beggars, cripples and others unfit to serve king and country. Her father is increasingly living in a world of his own that includes the invisible theosophist Masters in the Himalayas. Then he thinks of Pearse's funeral speech: Ireland unfree shall never be at peace; he thinks of Mrs Besant's words to Jiddu: 'Your happiness lies in the work,' and he dismisses both from his mind. But he cannot dismiss the face he saw in the well.

The setting sun breaks clouds into fragments of light; at the far end of the bridge Killaloe is descending into silhouettes.

Behind their bench a dog begins barking and growling. He turns round to see a large black mongrel working itself into frenzy at the approach of a man, running towards them. The man pants up to them. He and Agnes stand up, on guard. He can see the man is young, in his twenties, and should be good looking—but his mouth is twisted down on one side, as if he is trying to scratch his chin with his lip. He is prematurely balding and his eyes seem frustrated with everything they swivel to look at. The man stares him in the face and screams: 'Don't send me back. Don't you bloody well send me back.'

A woman comes over to them and the young man calms down when he sees her and listens to what she has to say to them: 'Gallipoli he means. Gallipoli. Ned Reagan's his name. He was in the Fusiliers. He lives here, in Ballina—his mother won't have him in the home with all the screaming and shouting and God knows what. 'Tis terrible, God love him. When he looks at some folk he thinks he's seeing his commanding officer.' The woman crosses herself and walks away.

He holds out his hand to Ned, who regards it like the snout of a dangerous dog and keeps his own hand in his pocket. 'Ned. Tell me what happened at Gallipoli. I'm not your officer. No one is going to send you anywhere.' Ned squirms. 'Ned. Give me your hand. I want to hold it. I want to help you. I'm not going to do anything to you. I'm not your officer. You're not going back to Gallipoli. You're safe here. This is your home. These are your people. Give me your hand.'

He keeps speaking in what he hopes is an authoritative but soothing voice. Ned whips out his hand and the wrist is a shiny purplish stump. He hears Agnes's intake of breath and there is a pause before he regains his own composure.

'Tell me what happened. I heard a lot of men died before they landed on the beach.' At the mention of 'beach' Ned crouches down. A long silence. He doesn't know what to say; then Agnes speaks: 'Go on Ned. No one can hurt you here.' Her intervention makes Ned raise himself up. 'You can tell me, Ned.' Agnes looks so calm and peaceful, so beautiful, that anyone with the most terrible of mental wounds would spill forth their story to her.

Ned looks at her and says: ' "Twas us and the Hampshire

lads.' He pauses and his shoulders relax, his eyes are calmer. Agnes beams a soft smile of encouragement. 'Inside the ship, we were. Off the coast. Early in the morning. They let the side of the ship down and 'twas dark as far as the horizon; quiet as a church. Sergeant Harrington steadied us. Said we were to land on the beach and take position there. Said we'd be grand if we kept our heads down, held onto our rifles and prayed to God. We got the order. Headed for the gangway. That's when it started. Bullets ripping round us. Whole shore packed with Turks—and sure you couldn't see one of them.' Ned is breathing faster and Agnes tells him to take his time. He looks at her with frightened eyes. 'Men tumbled off the ship. Threw myself flat on the gangway and heard the screams. There was a man drowning, his pack dragging him down. Someone kicked at me, roaring. I got up, bullets pinging the ship, and jumped into a boat and there were other fellas in it. One was shouting anything that came into his head. Just stupid fucking rubbish coming out of his mouth. I lay flat. Saw nothing but heard screams coming from the water and the banging of guns. Rifles, heavy machine guns, shells. Turks had 'em all coming at us— don't know how we got near the shore. Stopped twenty yards out, in the shallows. Someone shouted swim for it and there were splashes. I jumped and went straight down, sea up my nostrils. Bobbed up and heard someone screaming to God he'd been hit. Dragged down again, my pack a terrible weight. I got the knife from me belt and cut one of the straps and kicked down. The pack fell away. I rose up again, lungs fit to burst. I wanted the silence of the water because of the screams. Wanted to stay under and die but couldn't do it. So I kicked out for the shore and lay by the edge. Crawled on my stomach. Bullets puffing up the sand round me. One hit my hand but I keep going. Found a dip in the beach and weren't there three men in it already? One of them had teeth chattering like he was doing it as a joke. The other two had their faces in the sand. We listened to the shells and the little thudding sounds. One man must've raised his head to see what was what because there was a wash of something hot and sticky on the back of my neck and it's his brains. I'm lying there, next to the fella with his head blown off. Don't dare breathe, let alone move. The sun came up, high and hot, and the guns stopped. We lay there hour after hour. I don't know what happened. I remember the thirst and that the fella with the teeth died. My hand was a mess of blood and I wrapped something round it. Someone came to us. Men with stretchers. Pulled us out and gave us a good looking over. They say I fainted.' Ned stops to wipe his cheeks.

He does not know what to say to Ned. He must say something, but nothing comes out. He wants to heal him, like the boy in Achill or the girl in Limerick. Then he hears Agnes say: 'You've suffered more than is right for anyone to suffer in a lifetime.' He looks at her and marvels at her authority. 'I know what suffering is. My first husband was killed at the Marne. We were married for only a short while. Our life was before us. Nothing can take away what happened to you. But you can change how it affects you. In time you'll recover your spirits. You won't forget Gallipoli, but it will fade. Your mother doesn't know what to do with you and all your screaming. But you won't be doing that any longer. Promise me that, Ned. No more screaming. Your mother has had enough of it.'

Ned stares at Agnes as if he is seeing the Blessed Virgin Mary and slowly walks away.

The day before their departure from Ballina. He and Agnes are trailing up the main street and looking for a path that will lead them into the Tountinna Mountains. They are going for a last long walk, in search of 'the graves of the Leinster men', the apparent resting place of a group of legendary Irish warriors. They pass a row of terraced cottages and find a donkey track heading up the mountain.

With every step the view of the lake gains in majesty. It is a day of broken clouds, and shadows sweep across the lough's surface before the light returns and the water shimmers as if it were a new divine element. He looks back and sees the arches of the bridge connecting Ballina and Killaloe like a large stone frozen in the process of skimming across the water. On the other side of the lake, mountains rise in crinkled grey colours, and he remembers the first full day of their honeymoon and the road they took from Killaloe to Tuamgraney and the hedges and trees casting green onto their faces.

He had imagined a cool mountain breeze fanning their faces as they progressed, but the more they climb the hotter it becomes. The sun is a ball of clouded radiance high in the sky and his shadow refuses to part from him. Farther up he gazes down at the lake and imagines he is a fish slipping through the waters. It looks so inviting; small boats lie stationary near the shore of the western side. A passenger vessel is steaming north towards Portumna. He fancies he can see tiny Holy Island with its mysterious well in the distance, but it is hard to be certain.

Eventually they reach a part of the track that stays horizontal for a while and he feels his calves and lungs rejoicing. He pauses and lets Agnes go on; before long he hears her shout—she is pointing at something in the undergrowth.

When he joins her he sees a vertical slab of prehistoric stone poking up between long feathery grasses. On further inspection they find there are other stones, flat on their backs in a rough circle: the Leinster men's 'graves'. He had imagined upright stones with ogham writing on them, or mysterious Viking runes or a worn Latin inscription.

They sit down on the grass several yards away from the stone circle. Agnes lies on her stomach with her feet pointing towards the stones, while he flops farther away, facing them. He then gets up and sits inside the circle itself. He begins to pray: he prays for his new life.

He feels an extraordinary ease and wonders whether it is connected with the hallowed circle—it is like sitting in the centre of a stone sun with its stone rays laid out on the grass. There is a sense of timelessness, or of the present time and its attendant worries and concerns evaporating before the powerful atmosphere of the place; he feels as if he is in the presence of, and has been accepted by, ancient ancestral spirits—those who first created this mountain sanctuary.

That was more or less the last of what he remembers with any clarity. What happened next Agnes tells him as they later climb down the mountain.

She was lying there, she says, feeling sleepy; beyond her eyelids the world was brightness, birdsong and the soft burring of insects. She drifted. Images came and went: their steamboat heading for Ballina; the grey crumbling houses of Portumna; Ned, the Gallipoli soldier. Her thoughts gave way to a benign blankness, between sleep and wakefulness.

Something made her open her eyes, probably a sudden brightness, as if the sun had dissolved any remaining haze. She raised her head and saw that he seemed to be glowing with pure white light—as though he were an angel: she shielded her eyes and told herself it must be him; the light wasn't reflected but emerging from his body and flowing over it, almost like a liquid. It was hard to distinguish any features on his face. The light intensified and seemed to pour off his body and make shapes either side of it. Now it looked as if there were three radiant figures standing there and made even brighter against the sky by a swathe of cloud blocking the sun; the figures seemed to commune with each other, and she thought they looked like people she knew, who'd come to comfort and encourage them.

She didn't know how long it lasted; time had become an

indefinite present moment. Eventually it was as if the light was being recalled. First one, then the second, radiant form seemed to merge with the central figure; and as the light diminished, she saw his familiar features being restored and a diffuse radiance around the contours of his body. His face looked happier than it was possible to describe.

THEY ARE LYING IN bed in their guesthouse. He is unable to explain what happened to him on the mountain except that he feels he's been irrevocably altered in some way; he can now recall feeling as if his body was changing into light and his heart opening up, like the fingers of a clenched fist peeling apart; and then his consciousness was obliterated; he has no memory of what happened next. The way Agnes described it made it sound similar to the Knock apparition, and he wonders whether the theosophists' 'invisible Masters' in the Himalayas have bodies of light. Now, an inner peacefulness is oozing from the pores of his skin.

He knows it is merely a question of who will be the first to say what is in their minds.

'You have to go back to the work. Jiddu was right. You will be haunted otherwise.' Agnes's words are rushed, peremptory.

He puts his arm around her: 'Can't do that. I'm married to you now. We're going to settle down.'

She returns his arm to him. 'I've been thinking about Mrs Andrews's son; and Ned at Gallipoli. People like them need help. We all do. It is not the right time to settle down and have a family. That can wait.'

Her words, spoken from the heart, befuddle his thoughts and lower the force with which he says, 'I'm not going to go off, wander the country and leave you!'

'No. You're not going to leave me. I married a man who had principles, who wanted to help his people. You have to get another soapbox. You have to keep telling people what you've been saying... that war is evil and starts at home. It doesn't matter if nobody listens to you. I'll be beside you. I'll listen to you. Hiding away in a house in Galway *is a falsehood*.' Her tone is such that he finds himself dismantling, there and then, the painstakingly constructed image of his new domestic life.

He knows she is right. He has to finish what he's started. But where it will all end, God knows… he remembers the words of Paul Henry on Achill Island. Two empires, British and Roman. Their procurator, our Lord Lieutenant. Zealots, IRB. Sadduccees and Pharisees, Church of Ireland and Catholics. The Jewish rising in 69. *When will ours be?* He recoils from that thought, but cannot avoid the image of Jesus in the painting on the wall opposite their bed. Jesus has a crown of thorns on his head and is carrying his cross through the streets of Jerusalem. As he gazes at the picture he gradually feels himself being drawn into the frame, into the hubbub of the street, and tries to resist with all the concentration he can muster. He can feel himself in the crowd, watching Jesus stumbling along, crushed down by the weight of the crossbeam; and now he can see the hill of Golgotha looming up ahead and the sun breaking through the storm clouds. Three crosses are silhouetted against the sky. Women are wailing and shrieking. He grips Agnes's hand, presses her wedding ring and pulls himself out of the painting. He kisses her on the lips and strokes her cheek. He kisses her again. She guides his hand to her breast and doesn't notice that his fingers are trembling.

Next morning he remembers the dream he'd had in the night: he was staring at a wall with an almost life-size crucifix on it. The face of Christ was looking at him. Its wooden mouth dropped open like a marionette's and it said, in Pearse's voice: 'I do not know if the Messiah has yet come.'

PART THREE

THE PILGRIMAGE

He is peering at a map of Ireland with his father, who has folded his arms and tucked his hands under his armpits. Bridie and Agnes are sitting either side of them, making a tight horseshoe around the fireplace, blankets over their knees, keeping December at bay. He can sense Joe is excited that he and Agnes are going to walk from Queen's County in the centre of Ireland, to Dublin. They will do this in the early spring of the new year and march like pilgrims or preachers of old—like George Fox or John Wesley; along the way he will talk to people about peace, violence, and bringing an end to war.

The journey will be done in easy stages, no more than twenty miles a day: from Joe's cousin's house in Stradbally they will head eastwards to the coast then northwards to Bray, thence to Dublin. There they'll stay some days in Monkstown with Douglas's brother, Benjamin Newsome. They will start at the end of March 1916 and arrive in time for Easter. 'It may all come to nothing,' he says, addressing the fire. 'But we have to make the effort. Otherwise we'll be wondering for the rest of our lives.'

Joe rises from his chair and feels moved to shake him by the hand and give him words of encouragement: 'As Bunyan says, "What God says is best, *is* best, though all the men in the world are against it. It is always hard to see the purpose in wilderness wanderings until after they are over."'

Bridie adds a cautionary note, anxious for Agnes's welfare. Joe will have none of it: 'Our daughter is twenty years younger than Countess Markievicz, and if she's half as hardy, she'll be able for a march to Dublin.' Joe turns to Agnes: 'As the countess says, "Dress suitably in a short skirt and strong boots, leave your jewels in the bank and buy a revolver." I'd say you could do without the revolver.'

IN EARLY MARCH 1916, he receives a letter from Jiddu.

Dear Patrick and Agnes,

Thank you for your letter and the news that you and Agnes are going to walk a long way to Dublin and speak to people about the evils of war. I must say when I read this I felt aggrieved I could not be walking with you! I have tried to 'do my bit', as they say, during this time, but still no hospital will have me, and Mrs Besant says I must concentrate on my 'real' work. I am beginning to wonder what my real work is. How I wish I could go out into the world and do something like you are doing! Nitya and I are still in Bude. I'm working hard to take the examination for Oxford, but my tutor is frustrated with me. I do not like to say this to Mrs Besant or Lady Emily. They will find out when I fail the examination.

I do not know what is happening with my life. Nitya is still very unhappy. Mrs Besant and Lady E love him of course, but their affection is more directed to me. We are cooped up like hens, except when I go out on motorcycle rides—sometimes I wish I could just keep going to Scotland or even Ireland. Mrs Besant is more involved than ever in the Home Rule business in India. I do hope you will succeed in helping Home Rule come to Ireland. Tell the people to be patient and courageous. If they use guns, their opponents will use guns. If they use words their opponents will use words, but their own words will prevail, because they have truth and justice on their side. There! You can see I am truly the world teacher! May the 'luck of the Irish' be with you on your enterprise and I wish I were there with you. Write me a letter if you can.

With great affection,
Jiddu

It's the last day of March, 1916. Queen's County is draped over them in a low-lying cloud. With a large canvas bag slung over his shoulder, like a soldier off to war, he leads Agnes out of Stradbally and they settle into a rhythm of walking, desultory conversation and silence.

By the time they reach the hamlet of Ballintubbert, a few miles into their journey, the day is clear enough to see rounded hills rising in the direction of Athy, their first port of call. The sandy surface of the lanes is cratered with potholes made dark and silvery by overnight rain, and the leggy, battered verge grass glitters; blossoms on the blackthorns, as soft as ballerina dresses, lift their spirits.

Yet his euphoria at starting the pilgrimage after months of planning is soon being mitigated by the flat, featureless Kildare countryside. Behind the hedgerows, the fields range away in a level monotony, barely relieved by clumps of ancient trees. Already he misses the intricate stone walls of Galway. This land of the Pale has decent cultivation in it and pasturage; but it is not cultivated enough. Half-hearted, somehow.

They have arrived at the small smoky town of Athy and are heading up the main street to the bridge, where they lean over and watch the Barrow sliding towards them, its waters swollen by rain. A Union Jack flutters above the squat Norman tower of White's Castle at the east end of the bridge. Clouds that have been low all morning release fine drops of rain. They take shelter in a doorway.

When the rain eases they head for the market place, where he will begin his first speech. He takes up an elevated position on the steps of the fountain and gathers his thoughts while watching pedestrians strolling through a drizzle as fine as clouds of silvery midges; around him are ranged various handcarts full of mounds of cabbages, potatoes and turf; women in long cloaks squat around little collections of sellable things: a dozen tin cans, bits of crockery, old curtains, a battered saucepan, two round loaves of soda cake. Some of them hold babies to their chests; little children are splashing in puddles and throwing handfuls of mud at each other. Three or four men, smarter looking, with country caps, have gathered round and are waiting for him to say something. One is holding a notebook. He hasn't spoken in public since Limerick and he feels shy and awkward. Agnes has turned away, as if she fears she might hinder his concentration. He clears his throat to gain attention. Almost everybody is ignoring him, except for the beggars and urchins, hoping for money. He reminds himself how lucky he is to be free to speak—unlike Jiddu, marooned in Cornwall.

'Fellow Irishmen and women, people of Athy, we live in a world turned upside down. War stalks our cities and homes like the angel of death, snatching off our loved ones. Not like the war in '98, with farms burned and men and women hung from gibbets. But a war that nevertheless spirits away our sons and husbands. Those who should be digging fields at home are digging trenches in France; and those who board troop trains to the cheers of their loved ones are returning in boxes to the accompaniment of tears and wailing. War is stalking us. And not just from abroad. Thousands of Irish men, Protestants and Catholics, have been drilling here in this land with weapons, as if the only way to resolve a dispute is through fighting.

'And there's another sort of war, perhaps even more injurious: its weapons are injustice, hatred and ancient resentments, and the battlefields are our cities, towns and villages. Workers are besieged by their employers; women are attacked on all sides for having the insolence to demand they should be allowed to vote for those who govern them. But these and other ills won't go away by violence. Violence breeds only more of its spawn.'

He carries on, pointing out how priests of different countries at war are invoking the same God to be on their side. Eventually he runs out of thoughts and words. The clutch of listeners drifts away. He is left with Agnes and a toothless beggar, who is looking up at him with a beam of a smile, as if grateful for being told a great truth. He feels a moment of gratitude and love towards the wretch, who holds out his hand for money. He gives him a coin and says, 'God bless you'; the beggar shakes his head in bafflement and points to his ears.

THEY ARE SETTING OUT from Athy, next day. A weight slips off him as they leave the sad crumbling main street and cross the bridge and head out of town. The rain is light enough to freshen their faces but not soak their clothes; long straight hedgerows channel them along the road that leads northeast to Dublin.

THE AFTERNOON IS SLIDING into evening by the time they reach the outlying cottages of Ballitore, an old Quaker village that reminds him of Mountshannon; he wonders how Mrs Andrews fared at Naas hospital with her son. The Ballitore houses are sturdy, smartly painted and well maintained. No stray dogs ranging around and sniffing at refuse.

They find the house of an acquaintance of his father's, a schoolteacher named George Pim, to whom he had written months before. George turns out to be as quiet and as orderly as his house; his questions and answers are prefaced and followed by a narrowing of his eyes and a large puff of his pipe—the smoke from which serving as the outward expression of his emotions.

Later in the evening, George gets out a map and asks them about their journey and purpose and nods unpredictably at various details. He shows more interest in their footwear than their message of peace. He and Agnes cannot get warm beside the turf fire and are longing to go to bed; the day's walking has seeped up from their aching feet to their heads. But George shows no sign of fatigue; and his wife, Clare, starts belabouring them with her thoughts, her eyes becoming slits behind her spectacles and her fingers closing to small fists, as tight as the bun pinned at the back of her head. She is full of old-fashioned Quaker zeal: 'It's the drink that softens a man and lets the devil come in. And sometimes I'd be thinking there's devils enough gnawing away at this country. They turn British hearts to stone, and Irish hearts to fire. And as for the madness in France, we've had lads coming back in coffins—and who's brave enough to explain to their mothers what they were doing in a foreign land? Defending small countries like Belgium, they say, but Belgium was lost long ago. The men of Europe will shoot each other to death and only then will they stop.' George says nothing. But he does give his pipe a big puff before folding up the map, as if to bring a halt to the evening. He shows his guests to a spare bedroom upstairs.

They are nearly too tired to take their clothes off.

THEY ARE SETTING OFF from Ballitore, the morning clouds higher and more three-dimensional, the mizzle replaced by dry air but also the threat of a downpour.

It isn't long before vistas of level boggy fields reduce their conversation to silence; he is becoming aware of the sound of his boots on the road, the satisfying grind into the mushy surface, the slight creak of leather; the hedgerow that looks so uniform from a distance reveals infinite spiky textures of green and brown; verge grass bends over to the road in silvery clumps; here and there the hedges have been reduced to low bare twiggy boundaries; occasional lines of giant skeletal trees frame vistas of the empty fields.

The rhythm of footsteps cannot erase his first creeping doubts about their enterprise. It is only their third day; but nothing has happened except the talk in Athy, attended by a deaf beggar and one or two others. The packed meeting house in Limerick seems like an aberration. He wonders whether they should just take a train to Dublin and protest outside the Castle, like the suffragettes would do. Chain themselves to railings, shout slogans; even break a few windows.

On first inspection, Dunlavin looks much more like a town than the prim village of Ballitore. The main street is broad, with a post office, a bank and RIC barracks. A road slopes off down to the left, to a market square dominated by a domed courthouse. A crowd of people, perhaps thirty or forty, are standing near it, perhaps waiting for the result of a court case.

A woman with a shawl and bare feet and a face that seems to be made from decaying autumn leaves comes up to them and demands to know who they are. Agnes explains briefly what they are doing, whereupon the woman exclaims to the skies in an alarming way: 'Pilgrims, ye are. Marching for peace. Stopping all the wars!' She runs off to the courthouse and he and Agnes can hear her encouraging others to come over. She soon returns, shouting at the top of her voice. She is followed by a gaggle of curious souls in her wake.

He and Agnes are surrounded. A man with a shirt buttoned to the top but no tie, and a beard that grows only under his chin, and hair only on the sides of his head, shouts out: 'She says you're marching to Dublin to tell everyone about peace. Peace! That's what Redmond says he's bringin' us, peace and Home Rule! We can bring peace to this country alright if we'd the guts for it. Three million of us and how many soldiers and constables keeping us herded in our pens? A couple of thousand? If we picked up knives and pitchforks at the same time we could be freeing this country for good. The British don't have enough eyes, hands and guns. Just one good patriot leader, that's all it needs. I'm telling yez, we get rid of the bloody British and there'd be peace alright. The Big House brigade and their cronies won't be staying around making tinpot laws and sentencing us to death for pinching apples from their orchards. They only get away with it because they can whistle up the constables or soldiers but if *they're* not here to help them, they'll be running back to Albion. Ireland is *our* country. A country that must be purged of all *foreigners*. 'Tis holy soil we have, made pure by the footprint of the Gael and by the saints of the Holy Roman Church. There's going to be bloodshed, and it won't be ours filling up the rivers and canals, I can tell you.'

The man glares at him, daring him to reply. He has few teeth and his agitated tongue has worked spittle up the sides of his mouth, forming a thin foam around his top lip. The other townspeople say nothing, not wishing, or daring, to break the mood.

He glances at Agnes, as if to excuse himself in advance, and is taken aback by the look in her eyes, which, he realises, is reacting to the expression on his own face. His voice breaks out like a slow stream of icy spring water: 'Is this what you all think? Or is this fella speaking for himself? He says we should go on a rampage and kill everyone he thinks is an enemy. Will we kill the local policemen first? Who among you will stick a knife in a constable? And who will be the first to tell the dead man's wife what's happened? And after the policemen, who's next? The landlord? Then his family. Then his agent. Then *his* family. And maybe the landlord's workers, because they've been taking his shillings for as long as anyone can remember. *Who's next?*' The last two words he roars out. He scans the crowd as if every one of them is a murderer and one or two take a step back.

'Does no one want to say who's next to die? Well I tell you. We'll kill the Church of Ireland ministers, because they feed their heretic host to the mouths of traitors. And then we'll kill their families. And then it's the priests, because they haven't striven hard enough to stop the British from ruining our lives. And by the time we've finished all the killing there will only be us left. And *us* will consist of just one man—this man here!' He points at the man who began the argument, who wilts before the accusing finger and slinks away.

Another voice shouts out: 'Don't be minding John-Pat. He'd start a fight in an empty church.' It's a priest who's speaking; he looks about his own age, hair combed back, fleshy cheeks. 'The people of Dunlavin are a good flock, and we get on well enough with our Protestant neighbours. You've not

230

received the welcome you deserve. Come to the presbytery, you and your wife, as my guests.'

THE PRIEST'S SITTING ROOM has a large window, full of grey light, and various pieces of bulky brown furniture—a bureau, chairs and table. A carved crucifix hangs on the wall beside a framed photograph of Pope Benedict XV. He hasn't seen the pope close up before and he peers at his benign regal face with his gold-rimmed glasses perched between his thick black eyebrows and hooked nose.

The priest settles into a leather armchair: 'I heard mention of your pilgrimage to Dublin. Most unusual... most unusual. I'm told thousands journey to Lourdes, and many even go to our own Knock. I'm curious. Lourdes has its curative waters, and Knock has the vision of Mary to draw the faithful. Tell me, what does your pilgrimage have?' The priest now has a pudgy smile of satisfaction.

He still feels too exercised by the encounter in the town square to answer. Agnes explains what they are doing.

'I see...' says the priest, as if what he has seen is merely a flaw. 'We all want peace. But it has to be done within a structure. A process. Take St Ignatius—he was a soldier and knew how organisations worked; and his Jesuit Order has borne up well through the centuries. Look at the British Empire—it didn't happen by accident. You may not like it, but everyone knows where he stands. Look at the Church. A perfect pyramid of command, from Our Graciousness Pope Benedict down to the lowliest curate. To achieve anything you must have organisation and order.'

'In the Church,' says Agnes, 'what happens if there's a command you disagree with?'

'You obey it. The Church is the ultimate authority. And if a pope speaks *ex cathedra* he is a mouthpiece for the Holy Spirit. Who cannot be contradicted.'

'But what happens,' says Agnes, 'if a French Catholic priest blesses French troops and asks God to protect them before a battle, and a German Catholic priest does the same with his troops before the same battle? Whose side is God on?'

'Both must obtain permission from their superiors before they can do such a thing. They are supervised. That's the point. There's no room in the Church for *individuals acting on impulse*.' The priest has a strained smile on his face. He changes the subject. 'You walk to Hollywood village next?'

'Yes,' says Agnes. 'Then Glendalough. Dublin by Easter.'

The priest glances at his fingernails and returns to the fray. 'Isn't peace better achieved by adhering to eternal doctrines? By yourselves, your voices will be lost. You'll be voices crying aloud in the wilderness. Just think if you were in the fold of the church—'

'Which church?' His interjection is loud with residual anger. 'My father's a Quaker, my mother a Catholic.' He tries to keep his voice steady, in vain. 'My wife's father is a theosophist. Which church's *fold* do you suggest we should be in? Or are the churches the problem in the first place? Every town in Ireland has Protestant and Catholic divisions. If you cling to being a Catholic your Protestant neighbour will do the same—where's the Christian brotherhood in that?'

'Here we have mutual respect between our communities.'

'Respect! You believe a Protestant is a heretic, don't you? Surely it's an article of faith?'

'It is. But it's the same with them. They call the pope the anti-Christ.'

'They do. And how can there be fellow feeling between those who think the others are heretics, and those who think their neighbours follow the anti-Christ? Did Jesus say, "Love your neighbour, but *only* if he worships in exactly the same way as yourself?" This pilgrimage you're dismissing may end tomorrow, or it may reach Dublin unheralded. But it will be carried out under the authority of no organisation.'

The priest gets up without a word and shows them the door.

As with Athy, it is a relief walking out of Dunlavin. The Kildare landscape is now more familiar and breaking down his resistance to its monotonous views. There's something reassuring in the endless flat fields and little winding roads, with their scrawny hedges and spindly trees. The countryside may hold few surprises, but it is all the more restful for it. He feels ashamed at losing his temper at the man in the square and the priest. He attributes it to fatigue and frustration. He is worried that Agnes has been unusually silent. She has never seen him enraged before. He wants to say sorry to her, but something stops him.

After half an hour of walking and silence, Agnes says out of the blue: 'I was proud of the way you stood up to that priest.' Dear Agnes, offering an olive branch.

'I couldn't help myself.'

'But you also couldn't help yourself with that witless man in the square. You sounded as violent as he did. It was ugly, Patrick. I didn't like it at all.'

They come to a halt, he takes off his pack and faces her reproving look.

'I'm not saying your sentiment was wrong. Only that your voice... was that of a *murderer*.'

He wants to defend himself, retort that he was provoked. Then he thinks of Jiddu—having to answer hostile questions at the end of his talks, being insulted for being an Indian. Would Jiddu lose his temper? Perhaps. Probably not. They walk on in the company of an uneasy silence.

Hills are rising in the distance. He knows this means they are nearing the village of Hollywood, which stands at the western end of the Wicklow Gap valley. From Hollywood the road will descend through miles of wild moorland to Glendalough and the ancient monastery of St Kevin.

Rain is now falling heavily, slushing up the road and streaming out of potholes. They take shelter beneath a clump of roadside trees, but the knobbly branches only stagger the

233

rain and delay their soaking. By the time they reach Hollywood—no more than a scattering of houses—they are drenched.

They find a room in the inn and make use of the fire to dry their clothes.

NEXT DAY THE RAIN is remorseless. He looks at Agnes and her expression tells him they will stay another night. She seems down at heart and another day's walk in the rain won't improve things.

They sit in the bar all day beside the fire. Other travellers and guests join them; there is a gradual drift to merriment brought on by all-day drinking. Through the mist of cigarette and pipe smoke one of the guests comes over, holding a newspaper. 'Are ye the peace marchers?'

'Peace marchers?'

''Tis in the *Leader*. Man and a woman, answering to your description.'

The man hands the paper to him. He scans the article. Written by someone who had heard him speak in Athy and was unimpressed by his message. It is his turn to feel demoralised.

That night in bed, he listens to the rain spattering the window panes; Agnes is asleep; and a cloud of pointlessness has settled on his heart. *The world can go to hell.* Indeed, it is in the process of doing exactly that. Would they really regret it for the rest of their lives if they stopped their journey and returned to Galway?

The early-morning rain has eased to a mist, and the wind is swirling it around, almost letting in gaps of blue. The chill in the air has gone, but the road to Glendalough is pure slush and their boots are soon covered with sludge; there's a feeling of extreme wetness everywhere—on the grassy banks, cadaverous trees, and the clumps of yellow furze that appear like sudden fanfares to send them on their way.

Their spirits are relatively high after the smoky confinement of the inn; and the sun, straining to break through, at least offers the promise of warmth.

After three hours of solid walking, picking their way between brimming potholes and lumps of road, their optimism has waned. They stop and sit on a boulder. Agnes unlaces her boots and rubs her feet.

'A good rub won't make the blisters go away, I'm afraid.' His remark is intended to be light-hearted but it emerges with a heavy earnest tone, as if he's making a well-informed medical point.

'I'm not rubbing them to get rid of the blisters, I'm rubbing them as a spell to stop you making utterly commonplace remarks.' Agnes's eyes have flared into fiery points. Then the fire subsides. He sits and stares out across the valley: too many miles walking; too much rain; too little achievement.

'We have to keep going, love. We can't be caught at night half way there. It's the longest stretch. If we can do this bit, we can do it all.'

Agnes shrugs her shoulders: 'You go on… I'll catch you up.' Her tone still carries petulance, but he takes a chance and leans over and puts his arms around her and holds her. As they embrace, he feels his diminished energy trying to invigorate her.

Agnes puts her boots back on and they heave themselves up and continue on their way. The road ahead is trailing endlessly into the valley, and the clouds are banked high; the sun keeps teasing but refuses to appear. The countryside looks as if it will never wake up from winter, and he doesn't like to remind her they have another four or five hours of walking to do.

THEY ARE APPROACHING A low stone bridge over a rocky stream. Several men are standing there, all dressed in a similar garb: long coats, scarves tucked in, flat caps, walking boots. He sees that one or two are carrying shotguns. They have a surliness about them, like a pack of maltreated dogs; they range in age from mid-teens to late twenties.

At first he thinks they are hunters; then he has a thought they may be Volunteers, off on a drill. Without turning his face towards her, he tells Agnes to look ahead, not say anything and keep walking. He is worried about her English accent.

One of the men comes forward, stops them and takes his time scrutinising them. He has an air of confidence and power; his face is set with an expression of tiresome duty; his eyebrows, the colour of his curly hair, are like dark fur above his eyes. The man asks what they are doing. He tries to explain about the pilgrimage, and as he does so he notices that on the bridge there is a man who is gagged and has his hands tied behind his back. He notices, too, that Agnes has seen this.

The man in charge returns to a colleague and has a muttered conversation, all the while looking at him and Agnes. He wonders who the gagged man is. A spy? Thief? Rough justice? The man slouches over to them again and orders them to keep going on their way.

He knows he should say something about the prisoner. He feels cowardly; but also vulnerable, especially having Agnes beside him. The man tells them again to go, this time with menace, and he and Agnes walk arm in arm through the band of men, eyes straight ahead. As he passes the gagged man, he cannot help seeing his frightened eyes and he calls out to the ringleader, asking what crime the man has committed. The ringleader comes over, takes a pistol from under his coat and points it at his head. He hardly dares to breathe, as if a single breath could trigger the gun. The man says: 'If I tell you to go a third fuckin' time it will be the last words ye'll hear on this earth, you and your wife.'

He grabs Agnes by the arm and marches quickly away from the bridge.

After a hundred yards he turns round and sees the men trooping in single file across the moorland. Agnes bursts into tears. It's the first time she has wept so openly. She can't stop herself and he tells her to keep walking and puts an arm around her waist to ease her forward. He enters a reverie of leaping onto the moor and catching up with the men. There he is, panting in front of the leader, imploring him not to shoot the gagged man.

He comes out of the reverie. They continue on their way, but he is braced to hear a distant gunshot. When they have turned a corner they stop and he holds her. It takes them a while before they can speak to each other. He says: 'That won't happen again. From Glendalough onwards the roads are more public. Our journeys will be shorter.'

'Who were those *terrible* people?'

'Don't know. Volunteers? The IRB? A local vigilante group? A rogue Protestant militia?'

'That wretched man.'

'Agnes, if anything should ever happen to me…'

'What do you mean?'

'You saw that man with his pistol… He was one twitch of a finger away from killing me. Perhaps both of us.'

'Patrick, don't say that—don't *ever* say that! It won't happen. I believe we are protected.' Her words are more confident than her tone.

'I hope so. But if anything does happen… I want you to go to a spiritual medium. A good one. Any big city would have one. I want you to contact me. My spirit, I should say.' Even to himself he sounds slightly feverish.

'You know I'm not sure if I believe in that sort of spiritualism.'

'If theosophists believe in invisible spiritual sages living in the Himalayas, it's not such a big leap to believe a medium can

237

contact the dead. Anyway, you don't have to believe. All you've to do is promise me you'll do it. I was there when William Stead's son contacted him from the other side and I saw the relief it brought him. Who knows what goes on with these things and how it works? What I do know is that Stead was visibly comforted. Just promise me. It'll just make me feel easier.'

'I promise you.'

THE ROAD CONTINUES TO twist and turn down to Glendalough. The rain has held off and the darkening sky is serving to turn the furze into glowing crocks of gold.

Up till now they have never walked more than about twelve miles in a day. The strain of the extra distance creates the silence that oozes above the squelching of boots.

He cannot stop thinking about the gagged man at the bridge and the pistol aimed as his head; and he knows Agnes is dwelling on it too. His thoughts switch to the RIC barracks in Limerick and the sergeant drinking his tea. He forces his thoughts to happier scenes: the Eglinton Hotel, the marriage ceremony, their first honeymoon night in Killaloe.

The gusting drizzle confines their eyes to the road just ahead, or, when it lifts and reveals improbable spots of brightness in the sky, to the slopes rising in front of them. All the while they are descending into the deep wild glen; the road in the distance, when caught by a sudden beam of sun, gleams like a twisting stream.

It is late in the day when trees suddenly increase in number either side of the road, and the Glendalough Hotel appears on their right like a miracle.

THE MORNING AFTER THEIR arrival. He is stepping out of the hotel and heading for the monastic ruins, which merge with a lake, fields and slopes of the valley. Some trees are on the verge of greening, and the vegetation smells of freshness, of creation ready to burst forth.

He wanders into the compound of the dilapidated monastery. It reminds him of Holy Island on Lough Derg. He remembers John-Joe rowing them out and seeing the round tower waiting for them. The silence of the place, the isolated caws of crows. Here the stillness is similar, the round tower as impressive as Holy Island's. He recalls the story of St Kevin praying with his arms stretched out and the blackbird nesting on his hand and eventually laying an egg on it.

He walks through the gravestones that surround the tower and a broken chapel towards the lake. The steep slope set back from the water is dense with trees and bushes alive with raindrops like glittery insects. The lake is stillness itself. Not a breath of wind, just the croakings of birds floating above the glassy surface.

He sits down on a fallen tree trunk between the lake and the path, closes his eyes and reflects on the pilgrimage, his marriage to Agnes and the state of Ireland; a wave of unhappiness washes through him, a futility similar to what he'd felt on Skellig and, more momentarily, in Hollywood. Keeping his eyes closed, he breathes gently until a silence evolves into peacefulness. As if looking into the lake and penetrating farther into its depths, he can see something or somebody in the recesses of his psyche. He waits a little longer and a figure becomes apparent and gathers clarity; it is Jiddu! He is sitting on a motorbike, about to set off somewhere. 'Where are you going?' 'Nowhere! I have a motorbike and nowhere to go, and you have only your two feet, but are making a pilgrimage!' 'Are you still in Bude?' 'Yes. Rejoice in your freedom, Patrick. I don't know what I'm doing any more. Can the Maitreya feel lonely and sad and lacking in conviction? Doesn't that mean he is not the Maitreya? Keep telling them about war and hatred. When I have been talking to people here it has always been in a hall and they know what I am going to say because they are all theosophists. You speak to people in the market places and in the streets, and they do not know you or your message.'

A nearby blackbird lets loose a virtuoso string of notes and he instinctively opens his eyes to the brightness of the world. Over by the ruins he sees Agnes looking for him. He marvels at her steadfastness and endurance. He says as much to her in the shadow of the round tower.

She puts her arms around his neck: 'Do you think I'd rather be in Kensington wondering what dress to wear for an evening engagement? Patrick, I've never felt more alive.'

He hugs her so tight it goes beyond affection.

They set out early from Glendalough, accumulatively weary from the previous days; but his spirit is somehow lighter after his waking dream of Jiddu: he reflects on how lucky he is to be where he is, and with the woman he loves. Ireland may be under British rule; militias may be springing up; but, unlike Jiddu, he can still walk out of a door and go where he wants.

As if in unison with his mood, the sun springs through a break in the cloud and entices them along the road to Roundwood.

BY THE EARLY AFTERNOON they are arriving in the small town and being greeted by a gathering of folk, alerted perhaps by a newspaper report or someone seeing them at Glendalough, or both.

An elderly priest with a benign stoop, dim watery eyes and a gentle manner steps forward from the group and welcomes them, praising their enterprise. He invites him to say a few words in the church in the evening. It's the first genuine warmth he has felt from any priest or rector of any church and he wants to embrace the man.

JUST BEFORE SEVEN O'CLOCK, he and Agnes walk to the church, a short distance from the inn. He's had little time to rest and he now realises that the last thing he wants to do is speak to an audience. But he can hear Jiddu's voice reproaching him for not making use of every opportunity.

By the church entrance they pass four young men wearing long coats and flat caps with peaks thrust down over their foreheads; they are expelling breathy smoke from cigarettes with utmost concentration. They remind him of the gang they met at the bridge on the road to Glendalough and he tries to banish the thought. The men seem to tuck their chins into their coats and look down as he and Agnes pass them.

THE INSIDE OF THE church is smaller than its bulky exterior suggests, and cold. Weeks of rain and sunless skies have taken their toll on the fabric of the place; candle flames are merely reminders of absent heat. The audience comprises, he guesses, farmers, labourers, field workers, artisans and shopkeepers. Perhaps about thirty people.

After the priest has clapped his hands and given him a few words of introduction, he walks to the front, surveys the audience and says: 'Good people of Roundwood, I'll not keep you long. You've had a hard day's toil, as have we.' He sees a man at the back roaring a silent yawn. 'You may've heard that my wife and I are marching for peace in a time of war. The newspapers tell us we're fighting a just war against our enemies. But who are our enemies? We've branded the German race as the devil's children. We call them "Huns" to make sure we all know how barbaric they are. But millions of Germans are just like us: ordinary folk, like the people of Roundwood—farmers, shopkeepers—who hate war. Nor is it just the war between European nations we should be concerned with. There are men arming themselves for war in our own country. This does not have to happen. Everyone has a choice.'

A voice shouts out: 'The only choice we have is to remove the English by force of arms.' He thinks the speaker must be one of the men who was smoking outside the church, but he looks older and has thick unkempt hair; his accent is educated. 'Not as if we haven't given the English due warning. We've waited for Home Rule year after year. Centuries in fact. It kills them to pass the bill—and when they finally do, they tell us we've to wait till the war ends before it can be put into action! Well, there'll be no more waiting in this parish. We have men willing to die for *their own* country, not the empire. We'll do what it takes.'

The man's words have hypnotised the audience, and his passion has put his own tepidly-spoken offering to shame. Part of him agrees with the man. *If only* the English, *if only* Asquith... But if-onlies cannot be avoided in life. And killing people to gain a noble end? He is about to answer the interrupter when the latter walks out. He tries to pick up the thread of his argument, but all he can feel is the damp cold creeping into the smallest, deepest bones of his body. Agnes has her head down, her arms hugging her body, her knees squeezed together. An influx of exhaustion paralyses him; he tries a few sentences but stops half way and pauses too long; he sees four or five people leave—it's the young men with the coats and caps. He can hear himself apologising and bringing the proceedings to a close.

IT'S EARLY THE FOLLOWING morning, the sun still feeling its way into the sky. He and Agnes are leaving Roundwood. He wants to slip away unnoticed—he is still embarrassed by his curtailed performance the previous evening.

They have gone only a hundred yards past the last house when Agnes points to the ditch on the right. He sees a pale lump of something. It looks like a dead animal. They go over and both shout at once: it's a man in his undergarments, hands tied behind his back. His eyes are swollen; dried blood around his nose; something in his mouth, like a coloured rag. Agnes takes decisive action; she pulls out the rag, and it's a small Union Jack. She tells him to help her undo the knots. She feels the man's pulse. He is alive. Semi-conscious. Agnes runs back to the inn while he stays with the victim. He sees from the black hair that he was the man in the church who interrupted his talk. Who's beaten him up? The four young men at the back of the church? Protestants? Rogue police officers? Volunteers? Was the man a spy?

Agnes returns with a couple of local men, who carry the victim off in a wheelbarrow. He is expecting Agnes to look jittery, but her face is pale and composed.

They set off again, and do not talk about the incident. There's too much to speculate on, and neither of them has the energy or will.

They turn off the main Roundwood road and make their way northeast for Newtownmountkennedy, the town with the longest name in the country. Within a mile they find themselves on a causeway laid across a huge lake that appears from nowhere. It is like a miniature version of the bridge connecting Ballina and Killaloe. He has a sweet memory of their honeymoon and mentions this to Agnes, who flashes a smile of recognition, but her eyes are elsewhere. A stone wall allows them to lean and gaze south across the water. The water is glassy and soothing, and the banks around the lake are low to the water and fringed with bushes, sedge and trees that frame views of fields behind them; one has a horse in it, brown with a white patch on its forehead, immobile, staring at the grass. The sun is brightening the clouds and delineating ripples on the water. He allows himself to think about the man in the ditch. First it was the gang on the bridge with the gagged hostage; now this victim beaten almost to his death. It feels like the forces of darkness are circling them.

As if in tune with his thoughts, Agnes says: 'We have to bring our venture to its proper conclusion. Otherwise, as you've said before, we'll always wonder.'

He turns to look at her and follows the line of blue silk buttons that lead up from her waist to her neck; her face is pale from the cold spring morning, her lips pursed, as if holding in as much warmth as possible; her bobbed hair pokes out of her low round, almost brimless navy hat, in a neat fringe; he holds her and kisses her; he feels her body shaking uncontrollably, releasing terrible tension, and holds her for dear life.

AGNES IS WALKING MORE slowly. In a way he wants her to complain more; a little more self-pity from her would make him feel less ashamed of his own, swirling around inside and never finding quite enough air. He dawdles to let her catch up and takes her cold hand.

After a while they pause at a point in the road where the view ahead reveals a sudden clear descent to panoramic countryside. It reminds him of the moment on the road to Glendalough when they saw the whole valley laid out before them. Agnes says: 'Look at the colour of that cloud!'

He follows her finger and sees a vast horizontal dark blue-grey band.

'That's not cloud. That's the sea.'

He can feel an unstoppable smile breaking on his face like a wave from the deep. Once they reach the sea, it is simply a case of following the coast road up to Dublin.

THEY ARE LEAVING NEWTOWNMOUNTKENNEDY and heading east for Kilcoole and the coast. The fields either side of the lanes rise and fall in long gentle gleaming curves, but all he thinks about is the sea, the rhythm of the waves, the screech of gulls, the tang of brine in the air, Galway, Salthill.

IN KILCOOLE THEY PASS a lane that leads to the beach and are lured down it. It is an extraordinary feeling emerging from the adjacent cottages and facing immensity, the sheer volume of water, the crash and the hiss...

On the shingle he lies back, eyes closed; wave after wave loosens time and space, washing away all responsibility. As each withdrawing hush of the sea diminishes the immediate future, he resists thinking about their next stop, Bray. He opens his eyes; Agnes has taken off her boots and her hat, and her hair is bouncing around; she is staring outward but looking inward. Her face looks as pale as the sky. She senses his attention: 'Just reflecting on Tagore and Mr Yeats. Unlikely couple somehow.'

'If someone had said then, in Hampstead, that you and I would be sitting on a beach in Kilcoole as man and wife...'

They lapse into silence and listen to the waves. Just now, Bray seems like an impossible imposition. 'Sure, this is the life; will we not just go home to Galway?' His words are meant as a light or humorous remark. But fatigue has given them unintended weight and Agnes snaps out of her reverie.

'We could just do *nothing* for the rest of our lives. Live on my allowance. I could sew samplers and make bread and you could mend houses and build shelves.'

He knows he shouldn't respond, but can't help himself: 'Well, millions of folk do that! And they're none the worse for it.'

'We could let the politicians govern countries, generals lead armies… priests tell us how to worship. There's war in Europe, women are treated like irresponsible *imbeciles*, and the churches are patriotic and rigid. At least the theosophists believe there is good in *different* faiths. I know you think it's a queer business, but my father believes there's truth in it and he's a good man.'

He hasn't griped about the theosophists for a while and her mentioning them surprises him. He tries to stop the escalation: 'My aunt believes theosophy is a good thing too.'

'Well, she ought to know. You Quakers should be the last to criticise unusual sects.'

'I don't know their teachings well enough. I simply object to the way Jiddu seems to be a puppet.'

'He's a grown-up man for God's sake. He's not being held against his will. The time isn't right for him to go out and address the world. But it is right for *you*.'

Agnes folds her arms then picks up a pebble and throws it towards the sea. He lies back on his arms and watches the waves. The rhythm calms him and he closes his eyes. Then he hears what sounds like a crow belching a caw in his ear—he looks at Agnes in time to see her turn away to be sick. The first thing he thinks of is the Union Jack stuffed inside the mouth of the man at Roundwood.

He rubs her back as she leans over, coughing and spitting. 'I think it was the man,' she says. 'In Roundwood. Trussed up like some dead farm animal. It shook me more than I thought.'

They are walking into Bray. Although Agnes has more colour in her face, she is still relatively wan. Market day; crowds; carts piled high with potatoes and beets and pulled by docile battered-looking horses; men with all the time in the world, smoking cigarettes as if they were trying to find a new flavour in them.

As they advance, the crowd seems to part and rearrange itself either side of them, three or four bodies deep, and he gets a strong feeling they know who he and Agnes are.

By the time they reach the market place proper, the crowd has thickened further. He looks up at a drinking fountain in front of the market house. On its broad circular base rises a stumpy Greek column with a dragon-like creature on top, its wings flaring upward. Standing next to it, elevated from the ground, a small wiry man in a tail coat and bowler hat is shouting at them. He can't hear what he's saying at first, but then the words, 'Are youse the pilgrims the papers are telling us about?' become audible. He nods his head in reply and the man shouts, 'Come up here and give the people of Bray a few words of yer wisdom.' He is doubtful about giving a speech to so many people, but Agnes has the vexed look she had on the beach and shoves him onwards.

He climbs up onto the fountain and tries to remember John Redmond and Annie Besant and how they held an audience. He makes gestures with his hands and is relieved, and slightly alarmed, at the sound of people hushing their neighbours. He doesn't have time to think about what he is going to say.

'Citizens of Bray, we are in a crisis. They told us the war would be over by Christmas 1914. It's almost Easter 1916. And what will happen when it finally stops? It will break out again. It may be in a few years' time or twenty or thirty years. War does not change; it is us who must change. Not those across the Irish Sea or the Atlantic. Not those in London or Berlin. But *you. Me*. Ordinary Irish men and women. Carpenters. Farmers. Priests. Policemen.'

He has raised his voice; there is no wind and his words carry down the streets.

'There's war in all of us. We're fighting ourselves. We're fighting our neighbours, and even our friends and family. When we think a jealous thought, we are at war; when we harbour resentment we are at war; when we begrudge, we are at war; when we attach ourselves to a tribe—to a parish, a county, a country, a religion—we are at war. Until we loosen ourselves from *all our loyalties*; until we recognise that the moral purity we strive for masks our own anger and spite—until we recognise that, we'll fall into war after war. And believe me: the shedding of blood gains nothing by right. The mass killings in France are causing needless grief. If someone could promise that death and sacrifice would lead to permanent peace in the world—you might judge it fair recompense; but there will never be peace until we see the causes of war; and the causes of war start in ourselves.'

He comes to a halt. As he does so, the crowd heaves into life—people are shouting their heads off and he can hear words like, 'traitor', 'coward', 'Fenian bastard'. Then something thuds into his chest. It's heavy and hard, like a turnip. There is laughter mingled with a few cries of 'shame'. He is more shocked than hurt. Another turnip is launched and he half-ducks, even though the missile is not even close. He tries to spot his assailant, but all he sees is a scuffle breaking out, a messy brawl of fisticuffs and shoving. Agnes is beseeching him to get off the fountain. He clambers down; rough, angry faces turn towards him. He grips Agnes by the hand and pushes his way through the crowd into more open spaces. No one is following them. Instinctively he heads for the sea front.

The market has sucked so many people into its centre that the outlying streets are deserted.

Near the promenade they approach a large hotel with big sash windows. Three men and three women are walking up and down outside it. The women are in pale uniforms and the men are walking with exaggerated stiffness. 'They've got wooden legs,' says Agnes. 'Must be a military hospital.' She takes his arm as if to move him faster past the building. He vows that he'll never complain about sore feet again.

As they reach the promenade, the east wind blasts them with salty air. They lean against the railings and look out to sea and at the rounded mass of Bray Head jutting out to the south.

The empty horizon is a balm.

It's difficult to drag themselves away to a guest house, beside the Bray Head Inn. It turns out to be a cheerful place; clean and tidy. Their bedroom has plain white walls and large windows full of sea light.

A KNOCK AT THE door. The proprietress is calling his name. He's sure it's the middle of the night. Agnes is shaking him fully awake. More knocking. He climbs out of bed and finds the door; light pours in from the corridor. The proprietress is standing there with two men beside her. They're wearing uniforms. RIC policemen. She's talking gibberish at him. One of the men takes control, speaks calmly: he and Agnes are to dress and come downstairs. They do as they're told.

They're entering the sitting room and one of the policemen is standing in front of the hearth tapping his peaked cap against his thigh. 'Sergeant Hamilton of the Royal Irish Constabulary. I have orders to search your room.' He has a Northern accent. His colleague is presumably already upstairs. He isn't sure how to handle the situation; the memory of his interrogation comes back. Will he start shaking in front of Agnes? All of a sudden he hears her saying, 'How dare you disturb us at this time of night', and how dare you do this and that. The policeman says he has orders; he says there's a war going on and it's no time to tell people the Germans aren't the enemy. Agnes tells him their pilgrimage has no other purpose than to draw attention to the stupidity of violence. Her righteous indignation has cowed the policeman. Her voice sounds especially British, as if she is showing him her provenance and class. The policeman rallies. He says young men are dying in France to keep the country free and they could do without treasonous speeches.

The door opens and the other policeman appears and says he's searched their room. The officer rises from his seat. He leaves them with the words: 'If you really want to make a difference, learn how to use a rifle and point it at a German.' The policemen walk out of the room and the proprietress sees them off the premises.

He and Agnes return to bed. For ages they lie on their backs looking at the ceiling and holding hands. It's as if the sounds of the night have changed to a different key. No longer the whispering of the sea, but distant shouting, the trundle of carts and motor car engines, the whistle of trains and even the occasional gunshot. He is unnerved. It feels as if a series of warnings is being given to them. They can still take the first available train to Galway. Nothing to stop them. They've walked from Stradbally to Bray. They've made their point. No dishonour in abandoning the journey.

His decision releases a deep peacefulness and sleep creeps up and hovers over him. He drifts deeper. Then comes the dream he's had before. He is standing next to Agnes and John-Joe and looking down into the Holy Island well. The same face appears and this time he thinks he knows who it is. As he cranes his neck to look more closely, two large hands burst out of the water and grab his neck—he flails at them with his fists but his adversary is too strong—the hands throttle him and drag him into the water; he thrashes, splutters, seizes his assailant's wrists to push them apart, feels his air running out; he shouts and shouts and gains the heroic strength of the desperate; the grip around his neck loosens and the man's face loses its savagery; the assailant suddenly looks sad, and whispers, *Tell them to stop the killing.*

He wakes and finds he is sitting up; Agnes is holding his arm. She waits for him to gather his senses. 'I saw someone... in the dream... trying to kill me. I dreamed about him in Mountshannon too.' He doesn't know how to tell Agnes who the dream figure is—this time there is no mistaking the identity.

As he hesitates, she says: 'You've just seen Dominic.'

He stares at her through the darkness.

'You were shouting his name.'

He is too shaken to fill the gap she has left for him to say something.

She says: 'We owe him this journey. At heart he was a good man. Don't you see, his ghost is angry—we must lay it to rest.'

They are walking along the promenade in Bray. It's early morning and they are anxious to leave town before it wakes up; it's now only ten miles to Monkstown, their final destination. The police raid has made him feel as if there are spies peering through the curtains of every house they pass, noting his movements.

THEY CROSS THE RIVER Dargle and head north in the direction of the village of Shankill. Almost imperceptibly the landscape changes; hedgerows turn into high crafted stone walls, and fields become parkland with ancient trees and large houses. Horses and carts clop past them on the road, along with one or two motor cars and horse-drawn cabs and cyclists.

They reach the district of Glenageary before branching northwest for Monkstown and the home of Douglas's brother, Benjamin Newsome.

IT IS MID-AFTERNOON and the sun has become a diffused patch of brightness in the clouds. As they turn a corner of the road that leads to Benjamin's house, they see a young boy, evidently a look-out, who shouts with excitement because he knows who they are. The boy skips along ahead of them; they can see a small welcoming committee waiting up the road. As they approach the group, a man steps forward, takes off his bowler hat and yells out, 'Welcome to Monkstown! We've been expecting you. Our spies in Bray said you would be arriving about now.' He comes and shakes their hands as if to pump new strength into their bodies and introduces himself as Benjamin; he looks like a younger, more rotund version of Douglas, with the same shiny tanned pate and whiskery face.

Chattering away about the luck of the weather, Benjamin conducts them to the Monkstown Meeting House across the road. In a large white-painted, wood-panelled room, a long table dressed in a linen table cloth bears sandwiches and earthenware jugs of water and milk. The last thing he and

Agnes want to do is talk about their pilgrimage, but they are surrounded by eager deferential faces with scrubbed pink cheeks.

THEIR FIRST MORNING IN Monkstown. A beautiful relief for him and Agnes to be reclining in the sitting room of Benjamin's capacious home on Richmond Hill and not feel the necessity to go anywhere. Benjamin is fussing around in a kindly way. Large spotless windows look out onto a garden at the back, and a quiet street at the front. One wall of the room is lined with books. There are Turkish rugs on the varnished wooden floor. They are telling Benjamin about their journey and reading letters sent to them at Benjamin's address. One is from Jiddu.

The Old Rectory,
Bude,
Cornwall.

Dear Patrick and Agnes,
        May I offer congratulations on your long march. I hope it was not too sore on your legs and feet and that you told many people what you were doing it for. Even if only one person changes heart it will have been worth the effort of all the walking. Did you read of the terrible battle at Verdun? There have been services in the church for the soldiers of Bude.
        We see very few people and Lady Emily has been told *not* to come to see us because her presence is distracting to me and the 'great work'. The more they talk about the invisible Masters in the Himalayas the more I think they may be entirely wrong. Yet there must be some truth in the whole business? Theosophists are good, spiritual beings. At least they hate all forms of killing, and prejudice too—look at me, an Asian! And look at the insults Mrs Besant has received because of me.

I wish I could be with you both in Dublin. We have daffodils here, which make a jolly show of the graveyards and the little lanes. Nitya sends his very best wishes to you. Write and tell me how you are. I need someone to give me heart.

Your affectionate friend,
Jiddu

He puts away the letter, feeling so glad they did complete their pilgrimage—how would he have faced Jiddu otherwise?

He scans the bookshelves—he has missed the simple act of sitting down and reading. He finds a volume of the works of George Fox and opens it at random and reads out to Agnes: 'Dwell in the peaceable seed, which destroys that which causes troubles, wars, and fightings.'

Agnes murmurs agreement. She is absorbed in an article about the war that Benjamin has left out for them because it has been written by Annie Besant, who quotes a Quaker named Alfred Salter. Agnes reads out Salter's words: 'I must try and picture to myself Christ as an Englishman, with England at war with Germany. What am I to do? Am I to make myself proficient in arms, and hurry to the Continent? Look! Christ in khaki, out in France, thrusting His bayonet into the body of a German workman. See! The Son of God with a machine-gun, ambushing a column of German infantry. Hark! The Man of Sorrows in a cavalry charge, cutting, hacking, thrusting, crushing, cheering. No! no! That picture is an impossible one, and we all know it.'

He pictures Christ on horseback with a sword and helmet and cannot help laughing. Benjamin and Agnes are taken aback. He tries to stifle his laughter, but the thought of Jesus slashing at Germans is too ridiculous. Weeks of tension arise like a fountain, wobbling his shoulders, and he lowers his head in embarrassment to stop the convulsions. He tries to shake the laughter off with a feigned cough, but fails and drags Agnes down with him; at first in measured bursts, then violently, both of them rock with semi-silent laughter. He glances at Benjamin, who looks embarrassed by their behaviour.

He recovers a shred of composure and asks Agnes what Mrs Besant thinks about the war. Agnes wipes her eyes and scans the article. 'She says it's a "clearing of the ground, for the coming of the world teacher and for the new civilisation."' He says: 'I wonder if she's told Jiddu that the war is a clearing ground for him?' He can feel the laughter creeping up on him again, spluttering out, and he leaves the room.

He is on a train from Monkstown heading for the heart of Dublin. He feels slightly bereft but also liberated by not having Agnes beside him, the first time since their marriage. It was her decision to stay at Benjamin's house for the day and rest.

HE EMERGES FROM WESTLAND Row station into streets of perpetual motion—trams, motor cars, horses and carts, and pedestrians with no time to spare flow past him in a blur of drab colours and noise, reminding him of London. The only difference is the presence everywhere of green-uniformed men, the largest number of soldiers he has seen since Limerick.

He crosses the Liffey, makes his way to Marlborough Street and arrives at the steps of the huge temple-like Catholic Pro-Cathedral. Within the precincts, beggars, one or two of them on crutches or in army uniform, are importuning passers-by. Headscarfed women sit on the ground selling lacework as white as snowflakes, along with small carved crosses and painted eggs. Worshippers enter and leave the sanctuary, dwarfed by its classical columns; a priest appears at the entrance, takes the air for a moment before disappearing indoors.

He stands on the steps and begins to speak about the war, at first addressing thin air. As his voice carries, people gather, attracting others in turn. A man begins shouting something at him and he can't hear what he's saying. The man shouts louder: 'Sir. Conscription. There's talk of it happening in this country. We're obliged by law to obey the commands of our governors. Yet conscription to fight a war that's not ours is a terrible thing. What should we do?'

He looks at the questioner, who is well-dressed and sincere. He remembers the words of Alfred Salter and replies: 'If you were Christ and you received a conscription order, what would you do? Join up and go off to France and thrust your bayonet into a wounded German soldier?'

'That's not a fair comparison,' someone else shouts. 'Christ defends the weak, and the weak are the nuns of Belgium violated by German soldiers.'

'And what will Christ do? Machine-gun those soldiers?' The rhetorical question provokes protests; different voices start shouting and the meeting degenerates into a slanging match. He wants to calm everyone down, but finds himself just too weary to do so. Instead he listens to the shouts and heckles then eventually resigns himself to abandoning his first Dublin foray.

He makes his way back to the river, belabouring himself; he should have done much better; he was too tired—he should have stayed at home with Agnes. And the massive cathedral, looming behind him with its stately columns, was unexpectedly intimidating.

He steps into a train at Westland Row and, station by station, the great weight of soldier-teeming Dublin eases from his shoulders.

THE FOLLOWING MORNING: HE is again sitting in the train from Monkstown to Dublin, this time with Agnes by his side. With her moral support, he won't give up his preaching so easily. The carriage window suddenly reveals the sea and a vast grey sky, and his thoughts slide back to Galway and his old fantasy of living somewhere out in the county—a small place like Oughterard or Clifden, with Agnes and, God willing, their children.

WHEN THEY REACH THE cathedral he again takes his stand on the steps and begins to talk about war, violence and conflict; as had happened the day before, a small group of listeners gradually forms.

At first he is slow in thought and speech. Only when a voice cries out 'Pacifist coward!' does the blood flow from his heart into his voice. A passing cyclist and two policemen stop to see what is going on.

He has hardly finished speaking when questions are flung out at him. Someone asks what a Protestant is doing on sacred Catholic ground; another accuses him of being a German spy and wanting to undermine the war effort; another calls him a traitor to the Irish race and the memory of the heroes of 1798. A young respectable-looking woman walks to the front of the crowd and half-turns to face them. 'My husband is after dying in France. Fighting for the English, on French soil with German bullets in him. Tell me he lives again in a better place. Tell me I'll be seeing him again when I depart this earth.' She looks at him with a thin tight mouth and distress plumped in her cheeks.

He replies: 'I am no doctor of divinity. I'm not qualified to tell you what the churches believe. What do we know of the great mysteries of existence? Is there a hereafter?' He suddenly recalls the Wimbledon séance and William Stead's son's description of the afterlife. 'If there is life after death, will we have bodies like the ones we have now, or will we be insubstantial things? Or when we disappear from this world will our afterlife simply be the memories of what we were, and what we did, in the minds of those who remain?'

The woman turns her back on him, pushes her way through the crowd and makes off down Marlborough Street.

A man shouts out, and he can see he is a priest, young, groomed dark hair, a self-assurance about the way he tilts his head back at a slight angle: 'You are confused about life after death. There is only clarity in the Church. We face unprecedented problems in this country and we need a rock to cling to. The Church is that rock. In every parish there is a priest tending his flock, officiating over baptisms, marriages and funerals. If the country is a body, the Church is its spine, not to mention its heart and lungs. We are a force of strength and unity. You were unable to address that lady's question. You should have told her she would see her husband again. That is God's law.'

'Tell me this,' he says to the priest. 'Would you allow a Protestant to be buried in your parish graveyard?'

'They have their own places of burial.'

'But if they didn't?'

'It wouldn't be allowed.'

'Because?'

'Because the Protestants have departed from the true faith. Neither would they have a Catholic buried in one of their graveyards.'

'Can you tell me where in the *scriptures* it says, "Make sure you find out somebody's religion before you bury them"?'

'That is an ignorant and foolish thing to say. There are traditions. The Church is two thousand years old. It has rules, customs. They give it its strength, its power. If there were no rules there would be no Church.'

'Can someone believe in God and not be part of the Church?'

'People can believe what they want. We are the one true path that leads them to God.'

'Buddhists. Mohammedans. They believe in God. But you say they are on the wrong path?'

'They are. It would be a stain on the name of our missionaries to suggest otherwise.'

'Protestants, Buddhists, Mohammedans, Hindus—it's a distinguished list of those who—what? go to purgatory or hell?'

'That is the teaching. They believe the same will happen to us, no doubt.'

'They probably do. But they are mistaken?'

'They are. You seem to sneer about our lack of doubt. But you are peddling confusion. As I said, that woman asking about her husband—your answer should have been, "Yes, of course you will be united with your husband in the afterlife in the company of the saints." That would have been a consolation to her.'

He says nothing and can sense the faces waiting for his response. He cannot think of anything and is about to sit down or walk away, when he blurts out: 'But what if her husband were a Protestant?'

He watches the priest open his mouth to respond. The

crowd waits. He can see the man's lips tightening. He almost feels sorry for him. 'Damn you! There is a hell and you will find yourself there sooner than you think!' The crowd lets the priest pass through them and he strides to the cathedral door, hesitates, looks round, then disappears inside.

He waits for the murmuring to subside. 'There are good doctors and bad doctors. Good priests and bad priests. Anyone who divides people on the basis of religion, that same person will be divided deep in his being, and one half will hate the other.'

At this point he sees a woman at the back beyond the crowd stooping to put a coin into the hat of a squatting beggar. The woman looks humble, dressed in black, a shawl covering her head and most of her face. 'I've just seen a woman give money to a man over there.' People turn to see where he is pointing. 'I don't suppose she asked him first whether he was Catholic, Protestant, Irish, German or English. Charity is blind.'

He is about to expand on this remark but something makes him pause, possibly the shriek of a seagull; he looks up at the white toneless sky and feels it drifting towards him, or emerging from inside his head, blurring the faces of the audience; and there's a silence, as if he's underwater. He wonders whether it is the accumulation of fatigue or a delayed euphoria that is suddenly making him feel light-headed and losing gravity; he remembers the timelessness that crept up on him in the circle of stones, the graves of the Leinster men, overlooking Lough Derg. He feels as if he is rising from the steps of the cathedral, higher and higher, until he's looking down on the city, as from an airship; but he is held motionless and can see the tops of buildings and the tiny figures of people, crawling around the streets. Then he realises there is no river; the Liffey is absent; he is looking at another city and he panics for a moment, feeling that he has drifted to another country, perhaps another world; he can see what looks like the flat tops of houses baking in the sun, and the line of a city wall containing a maze of tiny streets or alleyways; he traces his eye along the top of the wall and sees that beyond one section of it there seem to be the contours of a hill; it looks familiar to him, and he can't think why; while he is staring at this scene the light strengthens, as if the clouds are thinning and sunshine is washing the hill with pale gold; as it does so it lengthens shadows from things on top of the hill that he hasn't yet noticed: the shadows darken and gain in clarity until they are imprinted unmistakably on the ground.

They have been cast by a line of three crosses.

He shouts and feels Agnes almost simultaneously yanking his sleeve. He sits down on the steps and she follows suit, taking his arm. He says to her: 'This is the last time.' She asks him what happened but he cannot tell her. He is aware of people drifting from the compound, including the cyclist and policemen. Voices behind him: two priests have emerged from the cathedral and are telling them to leave.

They have walked from Monkstown to Kingstown Harbour. Thursday before Easter. A large-funnelled ship has just left for England, its frothy wake streaming back and subsiding in the waves; sun-glinted seagulls are floating like small white angels and screaming like demons. They stroll along the pier over the glassy weight of the water and look back at the spires and domes of Kingstown. The wind is brisk and makes them blink.

'When shall we leave?' Agnes's casual question sounds to him more like, *Please can we go home*. His strange reverie at the Pro-Cathedral seemed to be symbolic of their journey's end and he is ready to leave Dublin as soon as possible. 'Tuesday. We'll go on Tuesday. Monday will be bad for travelling.' He kisses her on the cheek and holds her hand. They will start their new lives in Galway after Easter.

EVENING TIME: THEY ARE dining at home with Benjamin and various friends, neighbours and acquaintances of his. As guests of honour, he and Agnes are enthroned at either end of a table gleaming with silver cutlery and two triple-headed candelabra; red candles project a kindly glow onto the faces of the assembled. The conversations struggle to progress beyond talk about the battle of Verdun.

Two women sit on his left and right, both wearing long dresses of dark rich colours and glittery jewellery; their husbands are on their other sides. He can barely concentrate on what the women are saying; his thoughts drift off to the hospital in Bray with the men with wooden legs walking up and down outside, and then the visit by the RIC constables in the night. He looks down the table and catches Agnes's eye; he marvels that it takes only a second to convey and receive intense love and the knowledge that each knows what the other is thinking and feeling.

He bows to social graces and holds his attention long enough to make sensible replies to questions about the walk to Dublin and its purpose; he's aware that the women's responses are generally benign, if slightly patronising; then he tells the woman on his right, whose hair is a mass of black ringlets, as tight as bed springs, that he believes ordinary Germans are no better or worse than the French or the British; as soon as he says this, her furrowed brow indicates there will be repercussions; she repeats what he has just said to her husband, a retired gentleman with a Kitchener moustache, who asks his wife to speak louder and cranes his whiskery ear to her mouth. The man, his face the colour of the wine he is drinking, glares at him with disbelief fused with anger: 'If what my wife has told me is correct, you've no right to say such a thing. Damned impertinence in fact. One thing for pacifists—and I count Benjamin as a shining example of one—to drive ambulances and carry stretchers at the front; but to stay aloof from war, safe and sound in this country, and say that *the Huns* are no different from us is a damnable lie. Treason in fact. Nothing less than treason.' He can feel the hatred washing over him and for a moment he can almost hear the man's murderous thoughts.

He holds the man's gaze and refuses to look away; he knows he could mollify the situation by trying to explain away his words, but he feels too tired and suddenly low in spirits; nor does he want to back down before the man's mental and emotional barrage.

Eventually the man breaks off from what has become a staring contest and gets to his feet, dragging up his wife with him; the man mumbles excuses at Benjamin, who escorts them out of the room, while the rest of the diners, relaxed by drink, continue to chatter away.

The world has gone dark. A blindfold has been tied around his head and a hand is clenching his arm and guiding him. There's a steady rhythm of footsteps in front of him. They walk for a number of minutes and he has no idea in which direction they are heading. Noises of the night betray no specific location. He is being bundled into the back of a lorry.

He's desperate to remove his blindfold; his hands instinctively rise to pull it off and he receives a blow to the side of his head from something hard. He yells and wants to rub his head but fears they'll think he's reaching for his blindfold again. Engine roar, gear changes, acceleration; he dreads, to the bottom of his soul, what is going to happen. He can feel his temple already swelling up.

He recalls the hammering on Benjamin's front door in the early hours of the morning. Voices threatening to break it down. Benjamin shouting and soldiers bursting in, Agnes motionless, staring, and being threatened with a rifle butt to her face. He was especially alarmed that they were soldiers, not the RIC. But he knows it will be alright. They will soon see their mistake. He has committed no crime. They've mistaken him for someone else. They searched his room in the Bray guesthouse and found nothing. The worst they can do is fine him for anti-patriotic talk. Perhaps a week in jail. After all, they are letting the likes of Eoin MacNeill and Pádraig Pearse and their Volunteers *drill with guns*—and what is he doing? Preaching peace.

THE LORRY STOPS. HE is manhandled out of the vehicle and is standing on a hard surface. The wound on his head is throbbing. He tries to calculate where he is, given the length of the journey. But he doesn't know Dublin well enough. He is led into a building, then along corridors and down stairs, and pushed into a room. He thinks of the Limerick barracks and fights his rising panic. His blindfold is taken off: he blinks and squints at the room, which is small and empty apart from a chair and a central light. No windows. Two soldiers stand either side of the door. An officer—judging by his uniform and bearing—enters the room and asks him his name and address. He in turn asks the officer why he's been arrested and the latter looks agitated: 'Our information is you're a traitor. Undermining the war effort. Giving succour to the enemy. Incitement to riot. You're to be questioned.'

The officer and the guards leave the room. He is left in darkness. It must be Good Friday morning by now. He feels safer sitting on the floor, back against the wall, knees drawn up. He is exhausted, drifting from thought to thought; he shifts positions, semi-aware of falling asleep and of waking up. He is lying on his back with his legs straight out. The room is so dark he can't see his hand an inch from his face. He has a thought that he might go mad, but then remembers Bunyan, imprisoned for twelve years for refusing to stop preaching. If Bunyan could survive, so can he. He touches his body with his hands to make sure his invisible limbs are still there; the side of his head is still throbbing. He makes an effort to breathe gently. *They won't let him rot here forever.*

Footsteps pass outside from time to time; the sound is faint and he's not sure whether he's imagining them. Benjamin and Agnes will be coming to rescue him. Benjamin is respectable and well-connected. He must know people at the Castle! Agnes is English. That must count in his favour. An English wife.

THE DARKNESS IS OBFUSCATING his sense of time. He doesn't know whether hours or days are slipping past. He is hungry. It could be Saturday by now. He concentrates on Skellig—if he could survive there... He slides into a semi-somnolent state. He can see himself in a horse and cart with Joe, going up the avenue towards Tulira Castle. They are emerging from an avenue of trees and there it is, the castle. He is knocking on the door and it is flung open to reveal Edward Martyn in his smoking jacket and wearing little gold-rimmed glasses. The ballet dancers on the wall… Round the images go and the thought comes to him that his life is repeating itself in his head and that will be his fate, to stay forever in this darkness and witness his life repeat itself, the same joys and miseries, the same people, the same conversations; he is in a state of living death; or perhaps he *is* dead, stuck in a cycle that will be repeated over thousands of years, or forever.

He fights the panic, repeats a prayer; beyond the prayer is a voiced thought saying there is no escape; this is it; it doesn't matter whether you are dead or alive, because what is the difference? This is your punishment, your purgatory, the great recalling of everything you did and said, and didn't do or say. He feels that if he had a gun he would shoot himself just to get it over with, but then a voice tells him it would make no difference: in physical death the same repetitions would emerge. He rebels against this thought; he thinks of the Buddha reaching nirvana; he tries to think of his honeymoon and being inside the stone circle on Tountinna and the timelessness he entered, but he cannot recall it in any detail.

LIGHT GOES ON; DOOR opens. Three men enter, two guards and a burly officer, moustachioed, swarthy complexion. Could be Italian. He shouts at him to get to his feet. He stands up, totters, shields his eyes from the light.

'Mr Bowley. Our reports say there's going to be an uprising. Today.'

He doesn't know which day he is talking about.

The officer pauses to study his reaction. 'The IRB, Volunteers, or Citizens' Army—someone's starting a rebellion. That's what we've been hearing. We're arresting suspects. Tell us everything you know and we let you go. If you don't, we'll shoot you. Can I be clearer?'

A wave of light-headedness. The electric light is so bright he feels he's an inch from the sun. He cannot think what to say.

'You're on our files Mr Bowley. Seditious literature in Limerick. Going round the country saying the Germans aren't our enemies. Telling people not to fight at a time we need able soldiers.'

He says nothing. He struggles against queasiness by picturing Agnes and Benjamin. Surely they are working to set him free.

The officer comes over, grabs him by the neck and begins to throttle him. He tries to break the man's grip, but the man's hands are too strong. His lungs are bursting. He suddenly remembers his dream in which Dominic tried to strangle him and the thought impels him to stop resisting the officer—the latter is taken by surprise, loosens his grip and lets him splutter.

'We need to know what's happening here, in Dublin, and we need to know *now*.' The officer picks at his moustache as if to calm himself down. 'You can save your life if you talk. We have a priest who witnessed you praising our enemies outside the Cathedral. A sworn statement. And there are others. An RIC sergeant searched your bags in Bray and found a pistol. That could be a hanging offence.'

'I had no gun in my bag.'

'Your word against a policeman's. We could see what the courts think about that.'

The officer walks to the wall and stares at it as if inspecting a patch of damp. He turns round. 'What you peasant revolutionaries can't get straight in your fucking skulls is that the empire is *at war*. Thousands of men a week dying in mud to stop the Huns raping your womenfolk. And you have the bloody gall to promote treason under a sly pacifist façade.' The officer gives a deep sigh. His voice becomes quieter. 'Who are your contacts in the IRB? Where is the rising happening? How many men are involved?'

He tries to measure each word: 'I don't know the answers to any of those questions.' His voice is involuntarily shaky.

'We've intercepted a German telegraph. We know something's going to happen here in Dublin. We need to know exactly when and where. Then you can walk free. Perhaps you don't know that Mr Casement, Sir Roger himself, is in a cell? Found in Kerry a couple of days ago, trying to land guns from his German friends; a pitiful sight by all accounts. He's going to swing. But you needn't.'

He remembers the elegant figure of Casement speaking with Pearse in Limerick and can't imagine such a refined man would be gun-running; he almost chuckles aloud.

'You've heard the questions. You're going to wait here a little longer and think about the answers. If you happen to hear any screams, don't complain about the noise.'

The officer leaves and the light goes off again. The interlude of light makes the resumption of darkness even worse. He has a flash of standing on the pier at Kingstown harbour with Agnes, staring out to sea. How can he be here in this terrible place with these terrible people? He thinks of his parents; of sitting on the beach at Kilcoole with Agnes. He remembers her saying, 'We could just do *nothing* for the rest of our lives. Live on my allowance. I could sew samplers and make bread and you could mend houses and build shelves.'

He hears a distant scream. His heart misses a beat. Another scream. Muted shouts. He blocks his ears with his fingers, but the remembered screams are louder than the actual ones. He tries to shut out the world. He is going to die. They will never let him out.

DID HE FALL ASLEEP? He touches his eyes to make sure the darkness is on the outside not the inside. With an effort of concentration he conjures up Agnes and has her sitting next to him, holding his hand. She is wearing her dark blue dress and telling him it will be alright; she says the British know he has no information but have to be seen to be doing their duty. They're human beings with jobs. It is a difficult time for them. Some of their colleagues have been killed in France. They haven't done anything truly injurious to him. The officer throttling him is as bad as it will get. The screams outside were uttered by guards. They do that to all the prisoners. They're probably laughing about it. She says she will see him soon. They will let him out after a few hours and she will see him soon. They will celebrate. She kisses him and disappears.

Some sort of time has passed. He must have fallen asleep and now he has gone beyond the darkness and fatigue and is more awake than he's ever been. His senses are alive, as if shocked by an icy sea. He thinks he can hear the slightest creak and banging of doors on the other side of the building. He can feel a rising fear of going mad; he has to do something. He gets to his feet and touches the wall in front of him. Without knowing why, he places his forefinger on the cold plaster and draws the lines of a large square. He is creating a frame. In this he adds the rough outline of a human being—head, torso, two legs; behind him he sketches a sort of church tower, and traces lines either side to represent fields and a road. He sits down opposite his frame and stares at it and waits in the darkness. Bit by bit he can see in vivid colours the town of Bude appearing, the blue spring skies, the church, a country lane, and Jiddu standing in the foreground next to his motorbike. He can see Jiddu's calm face in the pitch black, his hair glossy, reaching to his shoulders.

Jiddu puts his hands together and bows his head in greeting. 'What is there to fear, Patrick? You have been alone before on an island, and this is no different. You have been following the way of your conscience and that they cannot take from you. You are working out your destiny at every turn. This motorbike can take me only to another part of this country. You are travelling into a realm few people have reached. Take heart, Patrick, the person of conscience is never alone.'

Jiddu bows again and it's as if a mist has crept up and obscured the picture; he knows Jiddu has gone and he lets his painting fade. He feels reassured for a while. He is not alone; not alone.

More time slips away and his alertness fades; tiredness builds again in his brain and every muscle of his body. He wants to stay awake—he somehow fears that if he falls asleep he may never wake again. He devises a routine of walking round the room clockwise touching the wall with his outstretched left hand, then doing the same anticlockwise with his right hand. He sits down on the floor and appreciates its solidity. He stares in the direction of the frame he traced with his finger on the wall. Another image begins to materialise: this time it isn't the figure of Jiddu, but a woman. It's night time and he can see she's standing under the stars, with a mountain behind her. Grace Henry, her face lit by her orange lamps. She is pointing to something—he thinks it must be the stars, but then realises she is pointing to telegraph poles. They are stretching away down the road. He knows what this means: she is saying there are voices to be heard, friendly voices talking about nothing in particular. He listens and can *hear life*, and can feel himself drifting off...

LIGHT DAZZLING; SOUND OF the door opening; two men, a soldier and a man in plain clothes walking in and speaking without formalities: 'Good morning Mr Bowley. Easter Monday in case you're wondering.'

The man has an English accent. 'Long time no see. Told you back in Limerick that if we met again I wouldn't be so kindly.'

He blinks, peers into the man's face. Same pale grey eyes. Smith. Razor Smith.

'We've been tracking your movements, informally. Since Athy, actually. The newspapers have done most of our reconnaissance for us. Our conclusion is that you are... how can I put this delicately... a worthless piece of shit. In case you're wondering, that's good news for you. It seems I'm going to be kindly yet again. We don't think you have any information worth a farthing. But we are obliged to explore every avenue. Our informers said there was to be a rebellion yesterday. A rising on Easter Sunday. Very poetic I'm sure. But I'm happy to report there wasn't. Mr Eoin MacNeill was a decent enough chap to put an advertisement in yesterday's paper telling everyone the "manoeuvres" had been cancelled.' Smith smirks at his henchman then turns back to him. 'How civilised we all are! We British allow you rebels to train openly, and you in turn have the courtesy to inform us of your movements in a national newspaper. The upshot is we can all go home and enjoy a Monday off. It's the races for me. Fairyhouse. You're free to go, Mr Bowley. I think it's Castle policy to apologise for wrongful arrests. Please accept ours. The corporal will see you out. A word of advice. Go back to Galway with your wife. I entertain no hope that you will contribute to our war effort. But do yourself a favour and get a job and settle down and shut up about the Germans not being our enemies. *They are.* Last thing: I have to say that while I abhor your sentiments, I have a grudging respect for someone who walks across half the country to preach to a few peasants, cripples and sparrows.' Smith walks out.

The soldier leads him from the room into the khaki glow of dim-lit corridors.

As free as a bird on Skellig Michael. Free but nauseous. His eyes full of the dazzle of the day, his head with the darkness of the cell. His legs are wobbly. He seems to see pale rainbow colours around everything he looks at. He leaves the Castle compound and walks to College Green; streets are quiet; a few soldiers walking arm in arm with women friends; cyclists coming and going, perhaps to mass; he's not sure what time it is; sun's quite high behind the cloud.

He'll walk to Westland Row station, the long way by the river, clear away the terror that's already diminishing; he cannot wait to see Agnes's face. He sings a song to himself on Burgh Quay; the Liffey is trying to absorb grey light from the sky and nearly succeeding; he can see a crowd moving up Sackville Street; a demonstration? The Workers? Volunteers? He thinks about seeing what's going on, but he must get back to Monkstown; then he changes his mind; he's not ready to return to sleepy Monkstown quite yet; he wants to feel more normal in himself, more calm, before he sees Agnes; he doesn't want to frighten her by looking half dead and gibbering; some fresh air and a walk will bring colour to his cheeks.

He crosses O'Connell Bridge and heads up Sackville Street to see what the fuss is about; could be the Metropole Hotel, someone important arriving. No, it's the General Post Office. He joins the back of the crowd that's gathered there. Figures in uniform addressing the crowd; British recruitment at the GPO? He can just about hear a voice. Unmistakeable. Pearse! Pádraig bloody Pearse. What's he doing there? He can't hear what he's saying. The listeners seem uninterested. But he can see that Pearse has that glow about him. That same orange aura around his head.

A boy shoves a leaflet into his hands. It says: 'The Provisional Government of the Irish Republic to the People of Ireland.' He thinks of Smith going off to Fairyhouse and bursts into laughter. He reads the leaflet. The words have meaning but he can't think what they add up to: 'We declare the right of the people of Ireland to the ownership of Ireland, and to the unfettered control of Irish destinies, to be sovereign and indefeasible...' It sounds like a declaration of independence! 'We place the cause of the Irish Republic under the protection of the Most High God, Whose blessing we invoke upon our arms, and we pray that no one who serves that cause will dishonour it by cowardice, inhumanity, or rapine.' *What is going on?* Cowardice, inhumanity, or rapine? Another rush of light-headedness. He looks at Pearse again and the hairs rise on the back of his neck: the orange aura is turning into a deep wine colour and it's flowing off him, like a dark version of Cuchullain's warrior light. *Why doesn't Pearse go home or to Fairyhouse instead of whipping up trouble?* He is too weak to heckle Pearse, but he knows he must get away from him. He can smell violence, war. He must get away, anywhere, and sit down; must sit down, rest for a moment; then on to Westland Row and the train. Agnes will be worried out of her skin. Half an hour won't make a difference. She probably went to the Castle. They'd listen to her accent. They'd tell her he was to be released. *Worthless piece of shit.*

He walks back to the Metropole, relieved to get away from the crowd; he leans against the façade and sinks gently to the pavement. He still can't believe he's not in that cell. He opens his eyes to check the world is still there. He shuts them again, half aware of people walking past, the GPO crowd dispersing. Restful just sitting there, being free; pleasant being drowsy. A clock strikes one o'clock. He keeps thinking he can hear shots in the distance. An Easter Parade? He opens his eyes and Sackville Street is almost empty; a few shouts, someone smashing a window—probably bloody suffragettes! Good for them! More shots in the distance. He must get up. The shouts are closer. Jesus Christ—horses galloping down the road! Gunfire. He leaps to his feet and sees men on horses careering away from Nelson's Pillar. Soldiers on horses and people firing at them—must be Pearse and his lot. He must get out. His legs are loaded with pins and needles but he limps then stagger-runs towards O'Connell bridge.

The river seems like the border to a safer country. He crosses it, turns into D'Olier Street and sees two soldiers; they shout at him, so he retreats and runs towards Trinity College, which is all shut up. He turns into Nassau Street—men sprinting for cover and shouting. He diverts to Grafton Street; empty thank God. St Stephen's Green. Must be safe there. But something strange has happened to Stephen's Green. A uniformed man near him is going berserk, shouting and pointing at an old man, who has shrunk down and pulled his jacket over his head. He's never heard such shouting, such rage, and wonders why the old man won't do what he's told. *Just do what he bloody says!* Perhaps he's deaf? He cannot bear it. He wants to run in the opposite direction. But he is mesmerised by the soldier, who is still shouting, as if he wants to kill the old man with his shouts. He must do something. He runs over and stands between the old man and the soldier. He thinks he'll scream or burst into laughter at the soldier's distorted face and big moustache and pointing finger—as if Lord Kitchener had jumped out of his recruiting poster. It's strange the way the soldier's finger has turned into metal, as if his hand has been amputated and replaced with steel. The soldier is yelling obscenities, face completely red, comical frowning lines on his forehead, a trace of spittle on his bottom lip. The soldier wants him to do something, but what? His shouting is disjointed. He either wants him to run away, or stay rooted to the spot. *He must decide.* Somehow he is too late—he knows this from the sudden noise, loud but distant, like a door banged shut in the wind or something crashing down; the noise thuds into him, knocks him over, shocks a sweet numbness all the way through him. It has the most unusual effect on his brain.

And then he knows what's happening.

He nearly laughs—it is just how he imagined it to be, quite beautiful in its way: now the noise has transformed itself into a key, slipping into an infinite number of locks and sliding open the remotest drawers of memory. He can feel them flowing out, precise and luminous, in order...

He can see himself in a horse and cart with his father, Joe, a bag of clothes and a bag of tools slung in behind them. They are trundling up an avenue towards Tulira Castle. The grey is peeling off the sky like plaster from a Galway warehouse, and the grass has the shimmer of lake water on a still, overcast day. They are emerging from an avenue of trees and there it is, the castle, as if caught in sunlight. Not a medieval ruin as he imagined, but a big sprawling house with towers, tongue-and-groove battlements, high rectangular windows, a grand wooden door tucked in behind a pointed stone arch—he is aware that he doesn't want this memory to continue, he wants to move away, but his thoughts are slow and laboured, and under tremendous pressure, as if he's under water and swimming upwards from a great depth to the surface of a lake, a milky light above him—he pushes down with hands and feet, propelling himself higher; lungs straining for air—nearing the surface, he hears a voice shouting, 'This one's alive, this one's still alive.'

He knows the owner of the voice is speaking about him, and knows in a strange, omniscient way that if the voice has an Irish accent he will live, because it means he will be taken to hospital. He isn't sure why this should be so, but he knows it to be true. He wants to hear the voice again, to check on the accent, but fears it.

Faces are looking down on him, faces of strangers, or is it Agnes? and Benjamin? Agnes, he is sure, is crouching down and saying, 'It's alright, you're going to be alright.' How beautiful she looks, dressed in lavender, and smelling of herbs or wild flowers, or is he just telling himself that?

She's helping him to his feet; he feels unexpectedly light; the air is bright yet misty. She's leading him somewhere, through a door, probably a hospital, or is it home? Two people standing at a respectful distance—they look like his parents. Perhaps he lost consciousness and was taken back to Galway? They're so much younger than he remembers them; they have cheerful faces and are waving at him. They're speaking but he cannot hear the words. He knows they're saying kindly things, like best of luck, or God be with you, or something similar.

They are joined by another figure who stands next to Agnes. It's Jiddu. How did he arrive in Ireland? He looks older and somehow more authoritative and radiant, his black hair shorter.

He says to Jiddu: 'You've changed—it is you, isn't it?'

'It *is* me Patrick, but you are seeing me in a different way—in what Mrs Besant calls the divine aspect.'

He fires questions at Jiddu: 'Did you leave Bude? Are you still with the theosophists? Did you get into Oxford? What's been happening?'

Jiddu says: 'I can do better than that. I can *show* you what happened to me, or what will happen, I should say! Present, past and future have no meaning in the place where the energy of life is blending with the energy of death and the outcome is still uncertain. At this moment there is only one continuous present and in certain conditions you can glimpse it. Follow me.'

Jiddu beckons to him and Agnes, and they follow him as he leads them through a mist that clears without warning. They step into brightness—it reminds him of emerging on top of Croagh Patrick, but what he sees is a level field with trees around the margins; in the near distance he can see the shapes of backs of chairs with hundreds of people sitting on them, all looking at a man who is standing up and mesmerising them with his words.

Jiddu points towards the man and says: 'We are in Ommen, in the Netherlands. And please look, that's me—I'm the speaker at the front!'

The three of them make their way to the back of the audience. Now he can see that it is, indeed, Jiddu, addressing the gathering. The latter cuts a tiny figure, with rows and rows of people staring at him. They are listening to his address:

'We are going to discuss this morning the dissolution of the Order of the Star... I maintain that Truth is a pathless land, and you cannot approach it by any path whatsoever, by any religion, by any sect... For years you have been preparing for this event, for the Coming of the World Teacher. For years you have organised, you have looked for someone who would give a new delight to your hearts and minds... Organisations cannot make you free. No man from outside can make you free; nor can organised worship, nor the immolation of yourselves for a cause, make you free; nor can forming yourselves into an organisation, nor throwing yourselves into works, make you free... For two years I have been thinking about this, slowly, carefully, patiently, and I have now decided to disband the Order, as I happen to be its Head. You can form other organisations and expect someone else. With that I am not concerned, nor with creating new cages, new decorations for those cages. My only concern is to set men absolutely, unconditionally free.'

At the back of the gathering, he and Agnes can see that Jiddu's face is like that of a child at a fairground. Jiddu turns to them: 'How stern I sound! You see, I did it. I killed the world teacher. It took me eighteen years to do it. I broke Mrs Besant's heart, and I will always feel sad about that. But they also broke mine...' He lets the sentence dangle and looks at the ground. He lifts his head quickly, with a renewed smile: 'And now it is time to go. We must leave here and cross the woods.'

They do not question his authority.

Jiddu leads them from the open field and the silent audience into the twilight of the surrounding woods, moving ahead of them between the trees; before they know it, Agnes and he are lagging far behind. Agnes holds his hand and for a moment he is taken back to their pilgrimage and walking down the lane at Kilcoole that opened up into the panorama of the beach and the sea.

At some point, before a small clearing in the woods, where the light is brighter green, Jiddu pauses, looks around and waves.

They catch him up, and Agnes says: 'We thought we'd lost you.'

Jiddu says: 'You can't get lost if you follow your two feet.'

They enter the circular clearing, hemmed in by trees and undergrowth; it's like the bottom of a giant tree-lined well, with light filtering down. The ground is soft with decomposed leaves and twigs; shadows of branches create mosaics of light.

Jiddu turns to him and says, 'Patrick—do not look so sad!'

He hasn't been aware he is looking sad. Jiddu waits for him to speak.

'Everything I did and said… useless. A rising in Dublin. Killings, reprisals no doubt; more killings. War in Europe. I've done nothing to break the cycle. Perhaps I feared too much for my safety; for our safety. I fear that I have deflected my true destiny.'

Agnes looks sorrowful and Jiddu takes her hand, then looks at him and says: 'Jesus was crucified, but the Buddha died peacefully with a smile on his face. The Maitreya pattern chooses people in different ways. You question your destiny. Have you asked whether your love for Agnes saved you from the *wrong* destiny? Mrs Besant once said to me, "How easily a man possessed with the need to save the world can turn from love to bitterness and violence—he only has to move away from the reach of humility on a wave of popular power or prideful self-sacrifice." You are fortunate, Patrick, to have Agnes, and I speak as someone who knows what it is like to be alone. My soul-mate was my brother, Nitya. You do not know this—because the time on earth has not yet arrived—but Nitya died. The theosophists *promised me* he wouldn't die. I was unable to save him from his illness and it broke my heart. It was only a matter of time before I disbanded the Order.'

Agnes puts her arm around Jiddu, and for a moment the two of them seem like one entity, like a glowing Hindu statue with many arms and legs, surrounded by a nimbus.

He can feel his thoughts changing beneath the weight of Jiddu's words. And yet… He says again: 'What have I achieved in my life? The killings have started. What did I do to prevent them? Look at the suffragettes. Their sacrifice and courage!'

His words come out more vehemently than he anticipated and Jiddu, unexpectedly, laughs: 'Patience! Who knows what you've achieved? It's too early to say. Anybody who refuses to follow someone else's path, but creates his own afresh, every day, every moment, breaks the cycle, not just for himself, but for *everyone*. What happens after that is not his concern. You do not know what your words meant to the farmer in the market place; or to the woman in Galway city hall. You cannot change countries, only yourself, and perhaps, then, inspire a few individuals to do the same. That's all. One day there will be so many changed individuals, there won't be any need to change the country. It will have happened already.'

Jiddu looks surprised by his own words. Without warning he embraces them, turns and makes his way to a partially bracken-covered footpath leading from the clearing.

He and Agnes watch him disappear and stand there alone among the trees, not knowing what to do or say. Just then, he doesn't care. Jiddu's parting words have pierced him. He feels as if he has confessed and been absolved; he is at peace, in harmony with Agnes and the half-lit world around them. He can hear, as if for the first time, the gently moving branches and birdsong. She holds his hand and looks as if she wants to tell him something he doesn't want to hear. He wonders, in a calm detached way, whether she thinks or whether she knows he is dying or is going to live. 'We'll get through this, won't we?' he says. 'The two of us will get through this.'

'Three of us,' she says and pats her stomach. He suddenly remembers her being sick on Kilcoole beach, and laughs with incredulity: 'Why didn't you tell me?'

For a reply she says, 'We cannot stay here. We have work to do. Let's go.'

They head for the footpath Jiddu took but can only see impenetrable undergrowth. They stare at where he disappeared, thinking they must have got it wrong, and walk slowly round the clearing looking for a way out. Round and round they go, and each time he becomes more sure they must find it. But any exit remains elusive.

Then Agnes stops and says, 'Don't you see? We're trying to follow the way *Jiddu* went. *His* path.'

He claps his hands as he understands what she means. Then he hears a voice shouting in his face, a voice outside, or inside, his head, '*This one's alive.*' He grips Agnes's hand, unsure what will happen next. He can sense the indecision draining him of vitality, and starts to feel weary in every atom of his being, but still in a leisurely, peaceful way, as if he could simply evaporate... 'We have to leave,' she says. 'If we don't go now, we never will.'

'I'm so tired,' he says, 'let's stay here. We could be happy together right here.'

As he says these words, he can see himself in Tulira Castle, staring at the two ballet dancers in the painting. They have turned to him, with faces of softness and warmth and welcome. He says to himself, 'We could stay here forever.' But as the word 'forever' leaves his mouth he feels a slap on his face as if he has affronted Agnes with a blasphemy: her face is in shadow but the top frizz of her hair has been lit into burnt gold; she is gripping both his hands and he can feel the life force in her, pulsing into him. He feels stronger, or is it an illusion of strength? And now he sees a darkened room, with the curtains closed and a red light glowing in the corner; he can see two female figures sitting opposite each other across a round table with a shiny polished surface; one of the women is talking with a strange voice, or with an accent, and he thinks he hears the words 'Barricades in the heart of Dublin... People scuttling around holding their heads.'

Now he is smelling fresh air and can see the sky above, and buildings, like those of Stephen's Green; there's a soldier standing over him and for a moment he fears the puce Kitchener face; but he senses the soldier is calm and smiling; the smile is strangely beautiful; he almost recognises it... the soldier takes his cap off, as if to jog his memory. Dominic. He wants to say to him, 'Is that you? Aren't you dead?' But Dominic's smile pours over him like a blessing and renders him silent. Dominic says: 'I'm getting you a taxi cab. If it takes you home, can you get yourself into your house?' He grunts a yes. Dominic hails a taxi cab chugging its way up the street, opens the passenger door and helps him in before shouting at the driver, 'This one's alive.'

He looks at the driver as he clambers inside. He has a familiar face, bearded. He knows who it is: William Stead.

Stead has sympathetic eyes and says, 'I'll take you home. Agnes will join you later, and your parents too.'

He looks out of the window and instead of a London street he sees the forest glade where he was; he has the sensation that his story is beginning for the very first time. He can see that Agnes has found a spot between two trees where the bracken is tall and forbidding but—miraculously—can be easily brushed away. Streaks of red sunlight touch the leaves; she turns and waves and mouths something at him; she does it again more slowly and he can see and hear the words, 'Our souls are love'; at first he wants to jump out of the taxi and run and hold her, but her smile disarms him, takes away his will to move. He feels peaceful, and watches as she enters the foliage, which springs back and closes the path she has entered.

James Harpur has published seven poetry collections and is a member of Aosdána, the Irish academy of arts. He has won a number of awards for his poetry, including the UK National Poetry Competition. His books include *The Oratory of Light* (2021), poems inspired by Iona and St Columba; *The Examined Life* (2021), winner of the Vincent Buckley Poetry Prize; and *The White Silhouette* (2018) an *Irish Times* Book of the Year. James regularly broadcasts his work on radio and gives readings and talks about writing, inspiration and the imagination at literary festivals and in schools and universities. *The Pathless Country* is his debut novel. *www.jamesharpur.com*

Praise for Harpur's work:

The Examined Life: 'A quite marvellous work … an Odyssey, a *Ulysses* shaken up in the snow-dome of *A Portrait of the Artist as a Young Man*.'

Stephen Fry, from the foreword

The Monk's Dream: 'Harpur's use of classical allusion is gentle, sentient, profound … "The Frame of Furnace Light" is an extraordinary piece of writing.'

Maggie O'Farrell, *Poetry Review*

The Dark Age: 'His brilliant imagery and luxuriant natural descriptions offer plenty to enjoy.'

Sarah Crown, *The Guardian*

The White Silhouette: 'A resonant, moving pilgrimage of great beauty.'

Martina Evans, *The Irish Times*